More More Time

David B. Seaburn

Savant Books and Publications
Honolulu, HI, USA
2015

Published in the USA by Savant Books and Publications
2630 Kapiolani Blvd #1601
Honolulu, HI 96826
http://www.savantbooksandpublications.com

Printed in the USA

Edited by Suzanne Langford
Cover by Daniel S. Janik

13 digit ISBN: 9780991562237

Dedication

For Gianna and Makayla

Acknowledgements

Thanks to Wendy Dunn and Jerri Lynn Sparks. Special thanks to Suzanne Langford who played a key role in bringing this project to fruition. As always, my deepest appreciation goes to my wife, Bonnie, and my whole family for their support of my scribbling.

More More Time

Chapter 1

What the hell is going on? thought Maxwell Ruth as he stretched his arms out on the cold cement floor and breathed in the musty air. Sweat trickled through the graying hair on his arms and puddled around his elbows. His head was pressed tight against the basement wall, his neck aching; his legs lay limp on the last two steps of the staircase he had climbed ten thousand times or more. He stared up at his feet. It was several minutes before he noticed the blood streaming across his forehead into his right ear and on to the floor. He tried to move and then thought better of it, his aching body convincing him to stay put.

Max reached into his pants pocket and pulled out a handkerchief to mop his bleeding brow. He folded it over time and again, trying to absorb as much blood as possible. He checked his head with his fingers and noted a gash over his right eye, but the pain did not register. Scattered all over and about him were underwear, T-shirts, knee-high black socks, white dress shirts, and gray trousers. And beside him lay *Our Nation's Heritage*, the history textbook he had planned on reading while waiting for his laundry to run its many cycles, and the wicker clothes basket, right side up, waiting to be filled again. He dropped his handkerchief to the floor and lay back, trying to get his bearings.

The clotting blood was turning into paste across his forehead and temple. Now Max's head throbbed. He drew his legs to one side and wriggled around so that his head was no longer wedged against the wall. His body stretched out flat, he mentally checked his legs and arms, hips, chest, abdomen; neck and finally his head, the trouble spot.

He took a deep breath and looked up the stairs again. Propped up on his elbows, Max rolled his neck slowly from side to side, rubbed his thighs, and moved his ankles in circles. Unsure whether to stand, he leaned back against the wall. By then the familiar ringing in his ears returned. "You have tinnitus," the doctor had told him ten years earlier. "You'll have to learn to live with it." At the time he shrugged and went on. It was one more item on a long list of things he had to live with.

Maxwell sat up, leaned over on his knees and then stood, his body wavering slightly, his head light. He held onto the railing and closed his eyes while the dizziness passed. He took one step and then another, making his way up the rickety stairs, finally tumbling into a kitchen chair, the last bite of his English muffin and a half cup of cold coffee before him. His head was bleeding again, so he reached for a dish towel and tried to pull the washday pieces together.

His Saturday ritual was simple. He carried his laundry to the basement, washed his white shirts first and let them hang dry. Then the coloreds. Finally the towels. It usually took three loads. While the washer and dryer whirred, he sat reading *Our Nation's Heritage*, planning his class lessons for the following week, and sometimes disappearing into reverie about his hero, Abraham Lincoln, and the Great Man's melancholic endurance, his deeply wounded resilience. When done, everything except his white shirts went back into the clothes basket to be folded and hung, then returned to their appointed closets or drawers. He'd been teaching for almost forty years and following the same Saturday routine for almost as long. How could this happen? He shook his head in disbelief.

He hated the idea of calling someone for help. He should be able to handle this on his own. But when the bleeding refused to subside and his aching head felt like it might burst, he called 911.

"Hello," he said and then cleared his throat.

"Hello," said the dispatcher. "Is this an emergency?"

Her question stumped him. What's an emergency? His father, his mother, those were emergencies. Was this an emergency? "I don't know if you would call this an emergency."

"Can you tell me what happened, sir?"

"Well, that's why I called."

"And so what happened?"

"I'm trying to get to that, if you'd give me a chance."

"Okay, sir."

"I woke up at the bottom of my basement stairs."

"You think you fell, sir?"

"Don't know exactly…"

"Have you broken anything, sir?"

"I don't think so. I just came back up the steps, and…"

"Are you injured, sir?"

"Well, yes, my head. It's bleeding some."

"How bad is the bleeding?"

"It's messy."

"Have you lost a lot of blood?"

"I don't know. I suppose."

"Anything else, sir?"

"I don't really know. I…"

"Is anyone with you that I could speak to?"

"No, there's no one else here. I live a…"

"What is your address, sir?"

He hated being battered with questions. In the years after his father had died, his mother badgered him constantly about every little bump, scratch, or sniffle that came along, as if she could protect them both from life's unpredictability. Little did she know.

"Someone will be there as soon as possible. Do you want me to stay on the line with you?"

"God, no," said Max.

He sat at the kitchen table, deciding whether to go back down stairs to do the laundry, but if he could do that, then why did he need an ambulance? Maybe he should call 911 back. They must have better things to do. He picked up the phone, but the numbers were all a blur. He dropped the receiver on the table and rubbed the back of his increasingly painful neck. He squinted and stretched his arm and curled his ankles and toes. He dabbed his head with a towel. Folded it and dabbed again. There was a little less blood each time. He tried to stand, but the room began to spin; and he fell back in his chair.

He closed his eyes and cradled his head in the crook of one arm. The table top felt cool. *When will they get here?* He opened his eyes and stared at the kitchen wall clock; a black cat with glaring white eyes and a Cheshire smile, its tail hung low, slinking back and forth with every tick, every tock. "Don't you just love this," his mother had said when she bought it. Max stuck an index finger in his left ear, hoping to reduce the effect of the tinnitus. When he removed his finger, he heard something else. Something faint. At first he thought it might be someone at the front door, beckoning him in a low voice.

4

Then it was gone. He sat up, listening more closely. This time he heard the ambulance pull into his driveway; red lights flashed across his kitchen walls.

Max didn't argue when the EMTs insisted he lie on the gurney as they hustled him to the ambulance. Several neighbors came out to see what was going on. He waved at them as if to say, "Move along; show's over; nothing to see here." A head wound and his age put Max at the top of the list when he reached the emergency room. They quickly rolled him into a private space and pulled the curtain around him. Then he waited and waited some more. A nurse came in every few minutes to check on him, clean his wound and encourage him not to fall asleep.

A jovial young doctor finally appeared. "So, what do we have here? Someone take a swan dive?" A CT scan and twenty-five stitches later and he was done. "You should be fine, Mr. Ruth. Just take it easy. Get some rest. Don't exert yourself much." Max wanted to ask why he was talking so loudly, enunciating so distinctly. "It might leave a slight scar, but the ladies will love it," he said, patting Max on the shoulder. The doctor also recommended that Max see his family physician before he went back to work. "That gurney could have been taking you somewhere else, you know," he said with raised eyebrows.

Sitting in the back of the taxi, Max rubbed his hands, trying to remove the blood stains. He glanced into the rearview mirror at the gauzy bandage plastered across his forehead and left temple.

"What happened to you, mister?"

"Nothing."

"Don't look like nothing to me."

Max leaned back in his seat and closed his eyes. His head was still thumping. He felt embarrassed. Embarrassed that he had fallen

5

like some old fool. Embarrassed that the whole neighborhood had gawked at him.

"Anyone at home?" said the driver as he pulled into the driveway. "Somebody there to look after you?"

"Don't need looked after," said Max as his struggled to pull out his wallet.

"No, no, no, this one's on me. Looks to me like you've had a pretty shitty day."

Max's eyes met the driver's in the mirror. "What is your name?"

"Lionel."

"Thank you very much, Lionel." Max handed him some cash. "At least I can give you a tip."

"No, really…"

"I wouldn't have it any other way."

The driver waited until Max unlocked the door and entered the house. Max tossed his jacket onto the bannister and then waited for a moment, regaining his composure, his balance, steadying his legs. He touched his fingers to the patch on his head, feeling for the stitches underneath. *Jesus.*

The cat on the kitchen wall said 7:00 p.m., but Max was so tired that he decided to turn in for the night. At the head of the stairs, he paused, looking across the hall to his mother's room. He walked over to the door and placed his hand on the knob. He held it firmly and started to turn it. Then he let go. Patting her door, he walked down the hall to his room where he crawled into bed, shoes and all, and fell asleep.

Max awakened with a start around 5:00 a.m., his head aching, his neck stiff. He could have sworn that someone was calling to him. He turned on his reading lamp and sat up in bed, listening. Nothing. He swung his legs over the side of the bed and was surprised to see his shoes still on. He tilted forward and groaned as he stood, his whole body discontented. He walked into the bathroom and flipped on the light. As he stood over the toilet, one hand against the wall, he heard it again. "Just a goddam minute," he said. It sounded like someone was talking, or repeating something, over and over. He cupped his hands over both ears, trying to muffle the background ringing so he could hear the words, but the words eluded him. He closed his eyes and concentrated.

The words were still there, coming faster, their cadence like an approaching train. He thought he could make them out, but then they slipped away again. He waited, and sure enough he heard them again, low and steady, relentless, inescapable. "What?" he said, surprised at the crackle in his voice. Then, with a pop, they were there, vivid, pressing, constant. Max fell back against the wall, his head feeling light, his arms going slack. "Enough," he said, but the words continued. Round and round, over and over, they swept through his mind. He sat on the edge of the bathtub, his heart lurching into his throat. But just as quickly as they had arrived, they began to recede, like a train rounding a distant bend, leaving behind a vibrating track and a cloud of smoke.

Max pressed his hand against his chest and breathed deep. The gauze on his head was damp, this time with perspiration. He tilted his head to one side, listening, making sure the words were gone. He stood again, not moving, waiting a moment more. Finally confident that everything was back to normal, he chuckled and shook his head. He flushed the toilet, turned off the bathroom light, and then looked out the window at the neighborhood. The morning paperboy was gunning down the street in an old Dodge Dart, swerving into each driveway, tossing a paper on the yard, then zooming off. Max looked east where shafts of light, pink against purple clouds, shown softly. It was almost morning; a new day was insinuating itself.

Max yawned and began to stretch, stopping short when a pain shot from his neck down his arm. He walked back into his room, sat on the bed, and then lay back, pulling the sheet up to his chin. He rolled over onto his left side. His head sank deep into the pillow, and he closed his eyes. The events of the day slowly receded into darkness. His breathing deepened and slowed as exhaustion took over. The room was still. A mourning dove cooed outside his bedroom window. Just as sleep was about to overtake him, Max's eyes shot open again. He sat bolt upright. This time it wasn't necessary to cup his ears. They were back, The Words, clearer than before.

Chapter 2

Beth Hazelwood stood at the kitchen sink washing her hands, a half cup of coffee beside her. She parted the lace curtains and watched the flashing gumball lights on the ambulance across the street. She dried her hands, ran her fingers through her blonde hair, and reached for the hand lotion.

"What's going on?" called Bob from the hallway.

Beth squeezed lotion into her palms, rubbing them together vigorously, and then took a sip of her coffee.

"Honey, what's going on?" asked Bob, now at her side.

"Don't know."

Bob leaned in and looked out the window.

"Jesus, something must have happened to Mr. Ruth."

"Suppose so," said Beth, turning her shoulder and stepping back from the window.

"I hope he's okay," said Bob, his brow furrowed. "I guess he *is* getting on."

"Uh huh."

"Saw him at the mailbox just the other day. He was walking slow, but he was more friendly than usual. Actually talked to me."

Beth poured her coffee into the sink.

"He sure was tough when I had him in school," mused Bob. "Everyone was scared of him."

Beth opened the door to the dishwasher and slid her cup in.

"Did I tell you that he gave me a copy of the Gettysburg Address when I graduated?" Bob let out a breathy laugh. "He said he thought I'd appreciate it."

Beth took a lunch bag from the refrigerator.

"Boy, was I surprised. Still have it around here somewhere."

Beth took a bottle of water from the pantry. Bob watched her as she moved briskly around the kitchen and entryway. "But I guess I've told you that before," said Bob.

Beth tucked her hair behind her ears and went to the closet to get her parka.

"Honey?"

"Uh huh," said Beth, pulling at her collar.

"Busy day ahead?" asked Bob.

Beth reached for the car keys that were hanging on the hook by the back door.

"I've got a couple of houses to show this afternoon," said Bob as much to himself as Beth. "Crossing my fingers. But this morning, well, I cleared the morning."

"I gotta go." Beth opened the door.

"Our appointment with the shrink is at ten. Will you make it?"

Beth glanced at Bob. "I haven't decided."

"Jesus, Beth."

"Look, I haven't decided, okay?"

"Okay." He picked up the newspaper from the kitchen table and then put it down again. "It's just…"

"It's just what?"

"I don't want things to go on like this."

"I'm sure you don't," said Beth, as she closed the door behind her.

Beth watched through her rearview mirror as they rolled Mr. Ruth to the ambulance. Bob was standing at the kitchen window. She could see Mr. Ruth's ashen face as they carefully lifted the gurney. She tapped her fingers on the steering wheel, looked at her watch, and sighed. Finally, the gaping ambulance doors closed, swallowing him whole, and the ambulance sped away, lights still flashing.

Beth felt lighter as she pulled into the tiny plaza parking lot. Sandwiched between *Antonio's Pizza* and *Carson's Insurance* was *Serenity Massage*, formerly the *Everything Old is New* consignment store. She unlocked the front door and walked through the waiting room into her office. Moving quickly about the office, she turned on the heat and the lights. Beth put a CD in the player, and soon the air was full of feathery lutes, resonant Tibetan bells, gentle chimes, and the distant hum of a chorus. To her it sounded like the beginning of time, the first dawn of the first day. She went into the massage room, turned on the lights, adjusted the dimmer, and lit a stick of incense. The smell of sandalwood slowly filling the air. Then she returned to her office.

The chimes at the front door jingled.

"I'll be with you in a minute. Please make yourself comfortable," she called out. It had been two months since Mr. Stinson's first appointment. Looking into the mirror behind the office door, she pulled her hair back into a ponytail, held by a purple elastic. She rolled her neck in a slow circle, trying to relieve the stiffness across her shoulders. Beth studied her face, the round and faintly freckled cheeks, the lines at the corners of her eyes, the dry, thin lips. She took a deep breath, forced a smile, and headed to the waiting room. Mr. Stinson sat by the door.

"Hello, Mr. Stinson. It's nice to see you again."

"Thank you." Mr. Stinson stared at the floor, his jacket folded in his arms.

"Let me take that for you." Beth reached for the jacket and hung it behind the front door.

There was a long silence. Beth struggled to maintain her smile. "Well."

"Well, here I am again," said Mr. Stinson, folding and unfolding his hands, his cheeks turning red. "I'm very sorry about last time."

"That's okay, Mr. Stinson. These things happen."

It was not unusual for some male clients to get an erection during a massage, especially in the beginning. But to have someone get up from the table and suddenly leave, barely clothed was more than unusual. To return was a surprise. She studied his expressionless face.

Mr. Stinson took a breath but said nothing. He licked his lips and looked in her direction. She ventured another smile.

"I guess it was all so new," said Mr. Stinson.

"Yes, I know."

"I've never had…"

The fluorescent ceiling light above them hummed and flickered. Beth wondered how she had never noticed it before. She wanted to look, but didn't dare take her eyes off Mr. Stinson, who didn't appear to be aware of the light at all. He sat before her, contrite, as if in a confessional. "I didn't expect…I don't know. I hope that I didn't offend you."

"Of course not," said Beth, her voice higher, more airy than she anticipated. "It's how the body responds sometimes to physical sensation, to touch." Her massage instructors had suggested to students that they memorize a line such as this, so that, when the occasion arose, they could repeat it matter-of-factly, avoiding any display of embarrassment or discomfort. Beth tried to breathe more deeply.

"Oh." Mr. Stinson unwrapped his hands and placed them on the armrests. "Then it's not a bad thing?"

"No, it's just something that happens."

"Okay, that's good." Mr. Stinson looked directly at Beth for the first time, their eyes meeting. "I wouldn't want you to think I was, well, that I was…"

"Think nothing of it, Mr. Stinson, really." Something in his grey-blue eyes, hidden under the ridge of his forehead, unsettled Beth. She had seen eyes like these before and had heard the words that went with them: "I wouldn't want you to think I was a bad person, Bethy." Her breathing quickened. Mr. Stinson's lips continued to move, but she no longer heard him. The smell of sandalwood evaporated, replaced by that of fading cologne, day old coffee, and cigarette-ash breath. She blinked and looked at Mr. Stinson who was now smiling.

"I'm sorry, what was that?" she said, gulping awkwardly.

"I was saying that maybe we just need a do-over." Mr. Stinson's once-squared jaw was jowly, his hair thin and grey; his shoulders were bent and his soft-soled shoes were angled in at the toes towards each other. He looked like nobody and everybody.

"Yes, yes, of course, a 'do-over' is what we need," said Beth, her lips stretched into a grimace. "Why don't you go into the other room? Go ahead and undress. Leave your underwear on if you'd like. Then lie on your stomach with your face in the cradle. Use the sheets to cover yourself, and I'll be in shortly."

"I remember." He hesitated as he stood, and then walked across the waiting room, opened the door, and closed it behind him.

Beth retreated to her office powder room, where she ran cold water in the sink and bathed her face repeatedly. She hit the soap dispenser twice and washed her hands, then washed them again. She dried her face and hands slowly, thoroughly.

When Beth opened her practice, she had planned on seeing only women, but because business was slow, she started accepting a few men. They were young, athletic, and self-assured, but on the table they were like clay in her ample hands. She untied their knots and relieved their stress, knowing all the while that, if she wanted, or if she needed, she could send them home with aches that would last for days. And they would never know she'd meant to hurt them. They would think it was just part of the deal. It was the kind of power that she had only dreamed of as a young girl.

Older men seldom called for an appointment, and if they did, they rarely returned after a visit or two. It wasn't that she turned them away or openly discouraged them from coming. It was more that she did little to keep them. Maybe it was a distance in her hands, a prickliness in her touch. She felt relieved when, like Mr. Stinson had done initially, they walked out the door, their names never to appear on her schedule again.

She had ignored Mr. Stinson's first phone message asking for another appointment, but when he called again a week later, she felt impelled to respond. When he said he couldn't come on Saturday mornings, she told him that was the only time she had. He said he would make the necessary arrangements.

As she turned to leave her office, Beth's phone vibrated on the table. It was a text message from Bob: *Please try*. She pressed delete and headed back to Mr. Stinson. "Mr. Stinson, are you ready for me?" she called, as she knocked on the door. When she entered, he was laying completely still, his legs together, his back stiff, his face in the cradle.

"As I said last time, I'll be using different oils and creams. Is that okay?"

He raised his head and said, "Yes."

"Okay, good. I'll uncover only the parts of you I'm working on. If you feel uncomfortable at all, just let me know, okay? We'll go slowly this time."

"Uh huh."

Mr. Stinson's body was soft. His back was dotted with age spots, and she could see tiny knots, like marbles, along his shoulder blades. Beth spread oil across his shoulders and down his lower back using broad circular motions, his skin stretching, his muscles retreating with each pass. She began pressing firmly with her finger tips and then rolled his back with her forearm. Beth could hear his thick breathing. She stopped, her hands resting on his back.

"Is that okay?"

"Yes, yes, that's good."

Beth began kneading Mr. Stinson's shoulders, rhythmically lifting, and pressing, and releasing. He groaned slightly as she added more pressure. She tapped with her finger tips; she tilted her hands on their sides and began to drum, gently at first, but then more firmly. Mr. Stinson groaned again.

"Is that too much?" she asked.

"No, really, that's fine."

She continued working on him, moving down to his mottled, sinewy legs.

"Please turn over." She lifted the sheet slightly, assisting Mr. Stinson as he struggled to roll over on his back. She was surprised to see the waistband of what appeared to be bright red, silk boxers.

"Do you want to pause for a moment?" she asked, remembering it was at this point last time that he had made his abrupt exit.

"No, I think I'm fine, thank you. I haven't felt like this…"

She pressed hard with her thumbs along the length of his arms. When she moved to his legs, she saw his chest tighten, his legs stiffen, his hands clench as she pressed his thighs.

"Am I hurting you?"

"No, no. It's just…"

"Should I stop?"

"No, it's okay…I'm sorry, I…"

"There's no reason to apologize." Beth frowned. She lightened her touch, gliding her hands over his legs without pressing. "There, is that a little better?"

"I don't know what's wrong with me," he murmured, turning his head away.

Beth pursed her lips. She lifted her hands from him, moved to the end of the table, and started working on his feet.

"I'm afraid we should probably stop," said Mr. Stinson, his voice a whisper.

Beth's arms immediately dropped to her side. She studied Mr. Stinson, his hands now covering his face. She was familiar with looks like this; looks that said, 'I'll never do this again'; so convincing, so apologetic. Looks that faded as quickly as they appeared.

"Mr. Stinson." Her words were sterner than she intended. She grabbed a towel and wiped her hands, then threw the towel into the wicker basket in the corner. "Look, Mr. Stinson, you're a little sensitive, that's all; like I said, it's not uncommon."

Mr. Stinson uncovered his face, and leaned up on both elbows.

"I think that if you decide to continue coming here, which is completely up to you, you'll get used to massage. It won't seem so out of the ordinary. I think everything will work out." Beth raised her eyebrows and drew up the corners of her mouth, but couldn't smile.

"Everything will work out," Mr. Stinson repeated slowly as if digesting each word. "That would be good."

His eyes abruptly met hers causing Beth's insides to clench. She stepped back. "You know, Mr. Stinson, if you think it would help you feel more comfortable, your wife could come with you once or twice."

"I don't think…"

"She could wait in the waiting room. Sometimes that…"

"No, really." He sat with his hands in his lap again. Then Mr. Stinson pulled the sheet up a little higher to hide his stomach. "Thank you, though. You see, my wife is not a well person."

"Oh, that's fine, then. I don't need to know…"

"She's a sheltered kind of person. I don't know what she would make of all this." Mr. Stinson clutched at his sheet.

Beth looked away.

"I'd rather come alone, if that's okay."

"Of course it's okay."

"I want to keep this for myself. Something to help me feel good every once in a while. You know what I mean?"

Beth didn't respond. She looked past Mr. Stinson at the door behind him. "Your mother doesn't understand how to make a man feel good, how to make a man feel like a man, Bethy," her father often said. "I'm sorry, but it's true. I don't want you ending up like your mother. What a waste. I love you too much for that."

Beth swallowed hard, then left while Mr. Stinson got dressed. She was in the waiting room when he came out. He took her hand in both of his, shaking it as he spoke. "Thank you so much for listening to me, for putting up with…everything, really. I feel so much better about coming here."

"Good," replied Beth, as Mr. Stinson removed his jacket from the rack and left. Beth stood for a moment in the middle of the room examining her hand, which seemed small and doughy. Then she retreated to the powder room, leaned over the sink, grabbed the soap, and ran hot water until it steamed.

When Beth opened the back door of her house, she could hear Bob at the refrigerator in the kitchen. The TV was blaring in the background. She tried to close the door quietly.

"Honey?"

Beth hung her parka in the closet; then stood in the shadows by the back door, collecting herself.

"Hope your day wasn't as shitty as mine. I showed two houses and got zero buyers. A complete waste of time."

She heard the pop of a beer can as an empty clanked into the sink.

"I called you," said Bob. "Several times."

She heard him tear open a bag of chips.

"I cancelled the therapy appointment. He asked if we wanted to reschedule. I said, 'How am I supposed to know'?" The house was quiet. "Beth? Are you there?"

Beth huddled near the door, wondering if she should leave. She reached for her parka as Bob came around the corner. "Beth?"

She opened her mouth and then closed it again.

"Where've you been? I didn't think you'd be gone all day."

Beth shrunk back from him.

"Is something wrong?" asked Bob.

Beth stepped into the dim light, raising her arms in front of her.

"Jesus, Beth, what happened?" said Bob, startled by her raw hands and bloodstained fingers.

More More Time

Chapter 3

Hargrove Stinson closed the car door, pressed the remote to lock it, and then stood for a moment in front of the pillared entrance to the high school, Max on his mind. After learning from a former student at the supermarket that Max had been taken to the hospital, Hargrove had called him multiple times. Max never picked up, which wasn't unusual. He was not a fan of the phone. He was ferociously protective of his privacy.

He was relieved to find a message on his cell: "It's me. I suppose you heard. I'm okay. Won't be in today. Have to see the damn doctor. Just a bump on the head, but wanted you to know. If possible, I'd like to see you before first period tomorrow. My best to Gwen." Hargrove couldn't remember the last time that Max had asked him for anything.

Hargrove watched the students swarm, tossing stinging barbs and jokes at one another, a moment later disappearing through the front doors. He shook his head. He had heard the rumors circulating among some students. The one that gained the most traction was that Max, dressed in women's underwear, had gotten drunk and fallen down his basement stairs where a neighbor had found him dead. What else could explain why Max, who hadn't missed a day of work in years, was a no-show for school on Monday morning? Even though the sub insisted

21

Mr. Ruth was fine and would be back on Tuesday, no one believed her. She was just part of the cover-up.

Hargrove Stinson was not shocked in the least by the students' fabrications, but he frowned at the impudence of his youthful and woefully immature colleagues. A second year teacher said, "Nothing would surprise me. The man is a goddam dinosaur."

"You should hope to be such a dinosaur one day," said Hargrove, silencing the faculty lounge. Several of his contemporaries gave him a thumbs up as he left.

Throughout the day, Hargrove was never far from his thoughts. The two men had arrived in Castlewood Central School District from their respective state teachers' colleges in the early 1970s when, as they liked to say, "history was being made." At the new teacher orientation, they gravitated to each other immediately, he with his Fu Manchu moustache and Max with his thick muttonchops, looking, even then, like a Civil War veteran.

Max's mother lived with him, so Max escaped to Hargrove's apartment every Saturday night, where they smoked pot, laughed about the good fortune of their draft lottery numbers (309 and 348), and speculated about the significance of the 1960s. Dylan was right, man, the times they were a-changin', and the two of them were there to live it and pass its meaning along to the next generation of young radicals.

Sadly, the next generation of young radicals turned out to be more interested in disco than changing the world. They were followed by a flood of Reaganites who were about as socially radical as Eisenhower-era suburbanites. The revolution never came, and each subsequent generation was more disappointing than the one before, at least for Max.

"They're just kids," suggested Hargrove with resignation.

"That's no excuse. No excuse for not caring about the world around them, not caring about all that has gone before, all that has been done so that they can live free in the best nation in all of history." He looked at Hargrove. "I'm telling you, we were never 'just kids'."

Hargrove could only shake his head and smile, for, of course, this wasn't true. In their day they had spent as much time trying to figure out when and where they could get laid as they had about the course of American history; they had skipped many faculty meetings so they could check out the varsity cheerleading squad, fantasizing what it would be like to be back in high school themselves; more than a few times they had called in sick on Monday mornings because they were too hung over to get out of bed. But he didn't say this to Max who was thoroughly committed to a revisionist view of his personal history. Hargrove, on the other hand, understood that history could not be revised, no matter how hard one tried. Time marched inexorably on, and you marched with it, whether you wanted to or not.

Hargrove watched as his friend's impassioned righteousness devolved into self-righteous indignation, sometimes bordering on judgmental cynicism. Hargrove, on the other hand, set his jaw and quietly kept on, shoulder against the headwind of time, expecting little in return.

Until massage and Beth.

Even now, after his third visit, he couldn't explain why he had gone in the first place. He had driven past the plaza many times after noticing the sign on one small storefront—*Serenity Massage*.

"Serenity?" he had asked aloud. Sometimes he went out of his way to drive past the plaza just to see the sign, each time feeling more curious about what was inside. A fount of peace and calmness?

Tranquility? Was there magic inside? He thought of his wife, Gwen. Maybe it could help her, since nothing else had. Over dinner one night, he planned on bringing it up, but Gwen seemed ever wearier, so he never did. He watched for other opportunities, but the time never seemed right. Soon he stopped thinking about it for Gwen and began to think about it for himself. But how would he justify doing something like that, something so frivolous, so impractical? How would he explain it to Gwen when he couldn't explain it to himself?

Hargrove googled *Serenity Massage* to get the number. He wrote it on a slip of paper and buried it in his wallet. From time to time, he took it out and stared at it, only to tuck it away again. He rehearsed what he would say to Gwen if he ever did call. But each rehearsal ended in confused mumblings. Gwen would not understand and just become more anxious. How dare he upset her more than she already was? Hasn't she been through enough? *Yet,* he argued in his mind, *is it so unreasonable to want something for myself? Don't I deserve something?* The thought left him feeling angry, then remorseful.

One day at the end of his last class, he was packing up his briefcase and, without thinking, took the number out of his wallet and called. The voice on the other end sounded light, airy, gentle. In a matter of seconds the deed was done. He stood alone in the classroom. *What to tell Gwen? Why tell Gwen? I won't tell Gwen. It's better for her if she doesn't know.*

Thinking of his first visit, his face reddened and his jaw locked. He had resolved never to go back. But he did. Again. And then yet again.

"Hey, Mr. S? Where's your buddy today?" asked a boy lingering after class.

"Had a fall; he's okay. Will be back tomorrow, no doubt."

"That's good," said the student, scrambling to catch a book that was about to fall from the crook of his arm.

"Yes, it is."

"Y'know I heard some things. Some not nice things about Mr. Ruth."

"I know," said Hargrove. "All lies. Remember that."

"I will, Mr. S."

"And tell your friends."

"I will." Ready to walk away, the student paused, his hand on his chin. "You know, Mr. S, Mr. Ruth is really tough. I think that's why…"

"I know," said Hargrove, a slight grin spreading across on his face.

Max gave homework over holidays. He never graded on the curve. He was unsympathetic when students complained that they didn't have time to do the work he gave them. If a student asked a question in class that Max thought was inane, rather than answering, he turned it into an assignment: "Research your question and give us a report on Friday." Many of his students thought he was mean; that he demanded too much and gave too little. "And that's a problem?" Max would say. His defenses always up, few got to know him as a person; few got to see under the gruff veneer, behind the wire-rimmed glasses and his owly disposition.

In spite of the rough edges, whenever Hargrove neared the end of his own rope and didn't know what to do with Gwen, it was Max he called. It was Max who came to the house and sat with Gwen, making her hot tea and listening to her worries, while Hargrove retreated to their bedroom. It was Max who went with Hargrove when he had Gwen admitted to a psychiatric hospital. Three times. It was Max who covered Hargrove's classes whenever Gwen called in tears, threatening to kill herself. And it was Max who stopped by Hargrove's room every morning for weeks just to say, "Hang in there, my friend; this too shall pass." He never asked how Hargrove was feeling; he didn't have to. He understood and was there.

The final bell of the day having rung, Hargrove struggled upstream against the tide of students rushing for the exits. He wanted to stop by Max's room to leave a Three Musketeers bar on his desk. They were Max's favorite. When he opened the door, he was startled by a crude cartoon drawing on the blackboard of Max with a bow tie the size of elephant ears, on his knees in front of a boy. Cartoon Max asked, "What is a 'blow job'?" and the caption underneath read, "Do the research, Ruthie, and report back at the end of the week."

Hargrove strode to the front of the class and erased the board. In its place, he wrote "Welcome back, Mr. Ruth!" He returned the chalk to the tray, placed the candy bar on Max's desk, and checked the time. He would have to hurry if he wanted to get to his massage on time.

Chapter 4

Constance Young spoke distinctly into the microphone at the Tim Horton drive through. "One large black with two Splenda and one cream, please." When the hollow electrified voice on the other end asked if she wanted anything else, she said, "I'd love some fat-free, calorie-free donuts," and smiled, enjoying her little joke.

"Please proceed to the next window," said the unemotional voice in a rush of static.

Constance half-thanked half-apologized profusely into the microphone, and when the young girl with tired eyes at the next window handed her the coffee, Constance said sheepishly, "Could you double-cup it?" Double-cupped and ready to go, she checked her watch. She was running behind. The clinic opened at 8:30 a.m., but she was supposed to be there no later than 8:15 a.m. so she could get her computer up and running. Why they hadn't bought a newer system, she couldn't say. Constance never complained. She was happy to have a full-time job doing anything, the economy being so bad. Her heart broke for many of their patients who didn't have health insurance. You could see the desperation in their eyes, having waited too long, hoping their illness would pass on its own, and now having to make difficult decisions about whether to go to the doctor and pay for medication, or for that day's food.

"I'm so sorry," she often whispered from the cashier's window. "I just think it's way too much. Please take care of yourself. I'll be thinking about you." She stored them in her heart, hoping she the voiced compassion might make some small difference, no matter how little it might be; perhaps if she kept them coming back long enough, their lives would actually change for the better. Patients often thanked her and lingered at her window just to visit. Some of the nurses joked that Constance should have her own exam room, so that she could do a proper job of caring for all the patients who depended on her cheery, hopeful spirit.

At the end of the day, Constance usually stopped at the local Wegman's grocery store to buy a Six Dollar Meal and then headed home in time to catch the end of Ellen, followed by the local news. Before relaxing into Brian Williams and the evening news, she liked to pour herself a glass of Riesling and curl up in the corner of her sofa with a pillow on her stomach where she rested her wine. Then she sat back and enjoyed the view, caring little about what Brian had to say, instead loving his boyishness, his perfect hair, his wry humor. He reminded her a little of Gerry in his younger days, although, admittedly, Gerry wasn't quite as handsome. But there was a comparable innocence. Sometimes she turned the volume off and tried to imagine her husband's voice coming from Brian Williams' mouth. Sometimes she just watched Brian and didn't think about Gerry at all.

She often poured a second glass of wine before watching the Kardashians. She didn't understand how they got so rich and famous, but she loved the fact that all the women looked like women, for God's sake, which is to say, they had hips and breasts and weren't little

Popsicle stick figures with fabric hanging off them. She had looked like them once upon a time herself. In fact, the first time Gerry laid eyes on her he mumbled, "Oh, my God." Her friend Lucille had fixed them up on a blind date. She told Constance that Gerry was a real nice guy—tall, average to good looks, decent job, all the usual things people say about blind dates. And Constance figured, *What the heck?* They made it a double date. When Constance and Lucille went to the powder room before dessert, Lucille said she was appalled that all Gerry did was stare at Constance's, well, "lady parts." "Did he ever once look at your eyes or your hair or anything above your neckline?" she asked, angrily, and apologized for fixing Constance up with such a low-down character. Constance told Lucille that it wasn't her fault. You could never tell about men, and anyway, it was only for this one night, so they should go ahead and have fun.

She didn't dare say that she didn't mind Gerry's ogling one little bit. It wasn't his fault that she was put together the way she was. Was it really so rude to show appreciation for what a woman looked like? She didn't think it made her any less liberated to enjoy a man's eyes when they fell upon her body. What was the harm in that?

At least once a week, Constance took her second glass of wine into the bedroom and stood in front of the mirror for what she called the Grand Inspection. She took off her blouse and her skirt. She stood straight and tall, always proud that she was five feet seven inches. She held her chin high and took a long look at herself from head to toe and back again. Her heavy breasts, supported by a firm bra, stood up more than they hung down. She turned sideways to look at her hips and derriere, accepting that a few new suburbs had been added to the metropolis of her behind. She was thicker in the waist as well, but not flabby. And when she looked for that hour-glass figure she so admired, it was still there. Everything was in proportion, especially if she held her stomach in just slightly. She was proud she had succeeded in avoiding the pear shape that time forced on so many women her age.

When she looked at her face, though, she became more concerned. It was aging at what seemed like warp speed. There were wrinkles at the corners of her mouth that multiplied with each grin— wrinkles that matched the ones at the corners of her eyes. And the creases in her forehead no longer disappeared from view. Her skin was always dry, and there was hair in the most unlikely places. Her once thick red hair had thinned and looked weary no matter what she did with it. She wore stylish glasses with blue-green frames that brightened her face, while hiding some of the crinkles. Her natural expression had always been a smile. People often commented on that fact. But in recent years, maybe since Gregory, and definitely since Gerry, she had to work to keep that smile in place. In fact, when she let her face relax, everything looked like it might slide right off onto her chest.

It was 8:10 a.m. when Constance arrived at the clinic parking lot. She juggled her keys, purse, lunch sack, and coffee, pulling the door open with her one free finger and walked into the clinic. One patient was already sitting in the waiting area. His back was to her as he read the morning paper, but the edge of his red bow tie was visible.

"Good morning, Mr. Ruth."

Maxwell Ruth folded his paper and turned slightly, looking over his shoulder, his face dour.

"Good morning, Mrs. Young."

Constance had known Mr. Ruth for a few years. He always called her missus; he was formal that way; she took it as a show of respect.

"And how are you this bright Monday morning?"

"I'm here, so I'd say I'm not as good as I'd like."

Constance studied Mr. Ruth more closely, noticing the ugly stapling across his forehead and temple. "Oh my, what happened?" she asked, putting her coffee on the counter and her keys in her purse.

"Nothing really."

Mr. Ruth was a curious sort. Most of the nurses knew him as their old history teacher who famously recited the Gettysburg Address each year in full Lincoln regalia. Sometimes when he arrived for an appointment, one of the nurses would whisper, "Mr. Lincoln is here," and everyone would snicker. It didn't help that he was gruff and sometimes uncooperative. He declined being weighed, saying his weight was no one's business. He didn't like the "newfangled" way they took his temperature, rolling the instrument across his forehead to his ear; he insisted they do it the "time-tested way," meaning a mercury thermometer. He seemed to bristle at anything different, anything new.

But to Constance, Mr. Ruth was a just a sad sack, and she suspected his crusty exterior was just that, an exterior coating that hid a softer inside. She tried to bring out this other, more vulnerable, side of Mr. Ruth whenever she could, making it her goal to put a smile on his face before he left the office after each visit. When he came to the counter after his appointment, she might say, "Did you straighten them all out today?" Or "I hope you didn't let them do anything to you that was unnecessary." Or "Okay, I want a full report on what the nurses forced you to do this time." He would look at her straight-faced and then a grin would twitch awake at the corners of his mouth. While Constance checked his insurance, she would ask about the weather and what he was planning to do over the weekend, almost anything to get him to talk. If he voluntarily asked any question or made any

31

comment, she felt she had more than succeeded in bringing the socially awkward Mr. Ruth out of his hardened shell.

Once he said, "That's a very nice dress you're wearing today, Mrs. Young," which almost knocked her off her chair. "Why, thank you," she'd said, blushing. When he left, Constance's office mates had a field day. "Constance has a new admirer!" one said. "I don't know, Constance, he's awfully sweet on you!" said another. They joked that she might have to wear a bow tie with her wedding gown while he wore a stovepipe hat. She laughed and waved them off, hoping that Mr. Ruth was out of earshot. She feared overhearing them would hurt his feelings, even if no one else did.

"Looks like more than a little fall," said Constance. She walked over to where Mr. Ruth sat and knelt to take a closer look. "My goodness, that looks pretty awful. Does your head hurt?"

"Only when I roll down the cellar steps and hit it against the wall," he said without expression, staring at the floor.

Constance was taken aback and stood straight up. "Oh my, I'm so sorry." Without thinking, she patted his shoulder.

"The people who sewed me up said I should see my doctor before going back to work."

"And you are doing what they told you to do, Mr. Ruth."

He chuckled. "Yes, though against my better judgment."

"Well, whatever the reason, Mr. Ruth, I'm happy to see you again. Why don't I sneak into the back and see if I can get you some coffee," she whispered. Constance went into the office, put her purse on her desk, booted her computer, and sighed as she waited for it to come to life. She then headed to the staff room, where Angela, one of the LPNs, was leaning against the wall with a salacious grin on her face.

"Ohhhh, Mr. Ruth," she said in her best Marilyn Monroe voice, "would you like me to get you some coffee or would you like me to get you something with a little more, well, pickup to it. Oooooo."

"Stop it! He'll hear you."

"I don't know," said Angela. "I think the two of you are adorable together."

"I'm just being nice to the man, Angela. Look at him. He's a lost soul."

"Well, he didn't look all that lost when you were talking together. He looked like a man who liked what he saw."

"Jesus, Angela, keep your voice down and get your mind out of the gutter."

"Okay, I'm just sayin'." Angela sashayed away.

Constance poured a cup of coffee for Mr. Ruth and returned to the waiting area.

"Here you go."

"Oh, thank you. Very kind of you."

She turned, smiling, and breathed a sigh of relief that Angela wasn't listening at the office window. She went back to her desk and was pleased to see her computer up and running. She got her pens and forms in order, filled her stapler, and generally readied herself for the deluge of patients that would be coming through the office soon. Constance checked in three patients, then retreated to the staff lounge, looking for sweets. Happily enough, there was a box of Dunkin' Donut holes for the taking. She picked two cinnamon then, throwing caution to the wind, added a chocolate-covered. When she got back to her desk, the waiting area was already three-quarters full. She could smell them all, their fevers and strep throat, they're perspiration and urine.

Despite this, she smiled to think of them as *her* people, as the people she served.

There was a knock at her window. Mrs. Turgelson, wiry and eighty, smiled through yellowed teeth. Constance slid the window open.

"I'm so sorry to bother you, dear," said Mrs. Turgelson.

"Don't think anything of it, Mrs. Turgelson."

"Well, there's a man out here who seems to be in some distress. I thought someone should know."

Constance stood on her tiptoes to see over Mrs. Turgelson. The patients in the waiting room were standing, each as still as a mannequin in a department store window. No one spoke. And there, in the midst of it all, sat Mr. Ruth, hands cupped over his ears, face taut, eyes closed, head swaying back and forth.

Constance's smile evaporated.

Chapter 5

Max looked at his watch. It was 6:00 a.m. He had pulled into the faculty lot at 5:45 a.m., parked in his usual spot, and walked quietly to the back entrance where he could determine whether the hall was empty. He opened the metal door slowly, hoping not to make a sound. Once inside, he nodded to the night janitor, then headed to the faculty lounge, opened the door to the men's lavatory, and went to the stall in the farthest corner. Thankfully, first period was not until 7:35 a.m.

His briefcase was open on his lap. He stared at *Our Nation's Heritage* but chose, instead, his thermos of coffee. He untwisted the cup on top, the wafting aroma of French roast battling valiantly against competing smells, then tipped the thermos and filled the cup to the brim. He balanced the cup while he cleaned the toilet paper dispenser with a sanitary wipe, and then delicately set his coffee on the curved surface. He reached into his briefcase for the bear-claw he had bought at the Tops grocery store on his way to work. He took a bite and wiped the flaky sugar from his lips. A sip of coffee to wash it down. Another bite. Another wipe. Another sip. He wrapped the remainder of the bear-claw back up in wax paper and put it in his briefcase beside his copy of *Our Nation's Heritage*. He would save it for the end of the day.

For now, he reveled the feeling that, at this very moment, no one in the world knew where he was. He sighed. He stretched his legs and ran a finger along the seam on his head. He sipped the last of his cup of coffee and then refilled the cup. He leaned back against the water pipe behind him and listened for The Words, but could hear nothing but the usual tinnitus noise. He sighed again. Still nothing. In the relative silence, he recalled his visit to the doctor's office. He had been quite a sensation.

"Mr. Ruth! Are you all right?" Mrs. Young had asked. She stood over him, her eyes so blue with concern that at first he couldn't speak, which only worried her more.

"Mr. Ruth?" Constance touched his arm with her hand so gently that he felt it down to his toes. Several people craned their necks to see what was going on, no doubt hoping for something dramatic, something they could tell their family or their colleagues at work.

"I'm sorry; I didn't mean to…" Mr. Ruth replied as if awakening from a trance.

"Are you okay?" Constance knelt at his side.

Max took a deep breath, the smell of her perfume filling him. He looked at Mrs. Young's left hand, as he did almost every time he stood at her window. She wasn't wearing a wedding band. She had a dimple on her left cheek when she smiled, and her eyelashes were the longest he'd ever seen.

Once he told Mrs. Young that her dress was pretty. If someone had told him one minute before he complimented her that he was going to say it, he would have called the person a fool. It just came out without warning. She smiled and blushed at the same time, not embarrassed like she wished he hadn't said anything, but embarrassed like she was surprised at what he had said and appreciated him saying it. "Thank you so much, Mr. Ruth!" He, on the other hand, felt embarrassed, as in wishing he had never opened his mouth. She was little more than a stranger, really, or an acquaintance, but not someone he should be flattering.

"Mr. Ruth?" she asked again. Her face was the only thing he could see. She was so close he could have kissed her if he were another kind of man. "Please, are you all right?"

"What's that?"

"Are you in pain? You're holding your head." She pointed discreetly to his hands cupped over his ears. He was swaying his upper body slowly back and forth.

"Oh, no, no, I'm fine. Well, not really fine. But, no, I'm not having a problem." The creases in Constance's forehead deepened. "Really, there's nothing for you to worry about," he affirmed.

She rubbed his arm. "Whew! There better not be. You scared me, Mr. Ruth."

"I'm so sorry."

She smiled and stood. He listened to her steps as she walked back to the office. He didn't dare look.

The sound of teachers coming and going in the lavatory shook Max from his revelry, but no one bothered him. He could hear them swapping football scores and commiserations about students and advice about the upcoming state tests and complaints about "this asshole" and "that asshole" and all the various "State Ed assholes" who made teaching harder than it should be. He understood the complaints and was often chief among those deriding The Assholes of the World. It didn't take much to get on his list. You could cut him off in traffic, or have a viewpoint he didn't like, or decide you needed another grocery item just as you reached the check-out. You could question him about teaching or his knowledge of American history or, God forbid, Lincoln ("Oh my God, have you read this idiot who thinks that Lincoln was homosexual!"), or you could treat him like he was incidental, unimportant, or invisible.

As he got older, more and more people made it onto The List for this final reason. After breaking through the age-sixty barrier, he felt that people acted like he was merely background scenery on the larger stage of life. "You'd think that anyone with a receding hairline or a bulging gut or a slower gait, anyone over the age of sixty, was just a lawn ornament or an artificial plant, just some prop in the lives of the Really Important People who had Really Important Things To Do."

Max looked at his watch. Hargrove should be here soon. He was the kind of person Max wished he would be when he grew up. Hargrove and his wife, Gwen, had gone through so much, yet his friend remained dignified in demeanor, reserved, private about his life and his opinions, steady, dependable, and respected by his students and colleagues. Once upon a time, he and Hargrove were going to change the world, but, instead, they had settled for tenure and a long teaching career in one place.

Despite their long friendship, Max hesitated to ask much of Hargrove. In the years since Sally, his daughter, died, Hargrove seemed to retreat from life, burying himself in a very personal cocoon. He emerged only reluctantly, the demands of work and day-to-day life impinging grievously on his self-imposed emotional exile. Hargrove rarely talked about Sally. He carried a picture of her in his wallet, and for the longest time, when asked, he would reply only, "Yes, I have a daughter." Always in the present tense.

Through it all, Hargrove maintained an implacability that was difficult to understand. "It's life. What else can I say?" he would answer when, on rare occasions, Max would ask how he was doing. In time, he stopped asking and Hargrove stopped offering.

Setting down his coffee cup, Max leaned against the stall and listened hard. The Words were there, somewhere in his head, even when he couldn't hear them. He closed his eyes and they came. He shook his head hard, hoping to dislodge them, hoping to be free of the worrisome annoyance, but only managed to make his head ache.

"What in the world happened to you?" were the first words out of Dr. Davenport's mouth when he entered the exam room the day before.

Max shrugged.

"I got the emergency room report, but I want to hear it from the horse's...mouth."

Max gave a shorthand version of events—how he'd found himself at the bottom of his basement stairs, all of his laundry on top of him. "That's it in a nutshell," he said, sitting in a chair across from Dr. Davenport, who stood at a computer typing and listening.

"Did you feel anything unusual before this happened? Any tingling or lightheadedness? Anything different or unusual?"

"No." Should he dare say he didn't remember anything about what happened?

"Did you trip on anything or did you just collapse?"

"I don't know exactly."

Dr. Davenport's fingers explored Max's neck and shoulders. He looked closely at the stitches on Max's head. "They did a pretty good job, but by the looks of it, you're still going to have a scar." Dr. Davenport sat back on his rolly chair. "So, as far as you can remember, you went to the stairs carrying your basket and all of a sudden you were at the bottom. Is that right?"

Max nodded his head.

"Nothing at all out of the ordinary before falling?"

He shook his head.

"Did you lose consciousness at any time?"

"I don't know if I lost consciousness. Who can say?"

Dr. Davenport glared. "Did hitting the wall knock you out, Mr. Ruth?"

Max nodded his head in the affirmative, then stated he didn't know how long he had been out.

Dr. Davenport studied him for a moment. "You're sure you're telling me everything?"

Max concurred.

"How have things been since?"

Max talked about the headaches and not going to work that day and feeling some residual aches and pains almost everywhere. He joked that he was "hearing voices."

Dr. Davenport stopped typing when he heard this. "Voices?"

"Kidding, really," said Max, gazing at the floor, fiddling with his hands.

"Max?"

Max explained that in the hours after the fall he had started hearing something, but it was getting better. Max never mentioned The Words, that he had broken out in a sweat the first time he heard them, or that they kept him awake at night. He didn't want Dr. Davenport to think he was crazy, something that also concerned Max. "It's getting better, really," he said, still studying the floor.

Dr. Davenport leaned back in his chair. "Are you hearing anything specific, a song or tune?"

"No," said Max, clearing his throat and looking out the window at his car in the parking lot.

"Hmm." Dr. Davenport rubbed his chin and watched him closely. "Are they words or a voice or anything of that sort?"

"I know what you're thinking. I'm nuts."

"No, no, not at all."

"Well, I'm not. I'm not any crazier than you."

"Then we may actually have something to be concerned about," said Davenport, leaning forward and grinned.

Max forced a smile.

"What do you think it is?" Dr. Davenport asked.

"Jesus, Doc, I'm not the one with the medical degree."

Dr. Davenport laughed. "Okay, Max. There's something called Musical Ear Syndrome that can occur after a head injury. Patients report hearing songs, sometimes even hearing the words of the song. And, no, they're not crazy."

"What can you do for it?"

"I think we should watch and wait. Let's give it some time. My hunch is that it will fade on its own."

When Max left the exam room and walked to Mrs. Young's window, she greeted him with a broad smile.

"So, is everything okay, Mr. Ruth?"

"Yes, I think it is."

"I'm so glad." She handed him a receipt.

"You know," said Max, "I want to thank you."

"For what?"

"For being concerned. For being kind," he said haltingly.

"Well, Mr. Ruth…"

"You know, you can call me Max if you'd like. I mean, I don't know if you're allowed to, but it's okay."

Mrs. Young leaned forward in her chair and looked up at Mr. Ruth. "Well, then, that's what I'll call you—Max. And, if you like, you can call me Constance."

"Well, thank you. Constance," he said. Now at a loss for words, he nodded his head and backed away from the window. He was glad he hadn't told Dr. Davenport about what he was hearing. If Constance found out, who knows what she'd think of him.

Still settled in his lavatory stall, Max looked at his watch. It was exactly 7:00 a.m. but he figured, given the events of the past few days, he deserved to take a little more time. He poured more coffee from his thermos. There were footsteps coming across the lavatory floor, footsteps that stopped in front of his stall. He looked under the door at a pair of black wingtips. There was a gentle knock.

"Hello. Anyone home?" It was Hargrove.

"Go away," said Max. "This one's taken."

"Come out Max and tell me what the hell is going on."

Chapter 6

"It's not as bad as it looks," said Max, as Hargrove closed the classroom door.

"My God, Max, it looks awful. What did the doctor say?" Hargrove was not only startled by Max's stitched head but by the grayness of his face and his disheveled appearance—wrinkled shirt and pants wrinkled, cockeyed bow tie. He didn't look at all like the Max he had spoken to in the parking lot on Friday afternoon. He looked downright old and worn out.

"What do the doctors ever say? Give it time," said Max with a harrumphing sigh.

"Max, are you okay?" Frown lines collected at the corners of Hargrove's mouth as he studied his friend's ghostly demeanor.

"Of course, I'm okay!"

"Don't get upset. It's just that you look like, I don't know, you look like you've been through the wringer."

Someone pushed a boy through the classroom door; he laughed and hooted at Hargrove and Max.

"Please leave this room immediately," said Hargrove calmly, his precisely enunciated words belying the flash of anger in his eyes.

The boy exited the room, wide-eyed.

"Little bastards," said Max

"Max, what are you doing here today?"

Max's hands trembled as he slid them into his pockets. "What do you mean, what am I doing here? Where the hell else would I go?" He paced the front of the room.

"Max. Sit down. Please." Hargrove pulled the chair out from behind Max's desk but Max declined. Hargrove leaned against the desk. "Tell me what's going on."

Max walked to the window. Hargrove joined him. They looked out across the parking lot at the busses belching students onto the pavement.

"Why are we still here?"

"Max," said Hargrove with a sigh of impatience.

"I mean it. We've been in this building for damn near our whole lives. And what do we have to show for it? Nothing."

Hargrove patted his friend's back. "Come on now."

"Look at them out there. They could care less what we chose to do forty years ago." Max shook his head and then looked at his friend. "We taught their parents."

"Yes, we did. The good news is that we probably won't teach their children." Max looked out the window again, this time at nothing at all. "Max?"

Max looked back at his friend, then walked to the whiteboard and picked up an erasable marker, looking like he was about to write something, but leaned against the board instead.

"Are you really okay?"

"I don't know."

"What do you mean? Are you hurt worse than you're saying?"

"No."

"Well, that's good."

"But something's wrong." Max grimaced, his eyes widening.

"Something's wrong? What are you talking about?"

"Not long after I fell, I started hearing things."

"What things?" Hargrove thought of Gwen. "Did you hear that?" she'd often say with fear in her eyes. His heart skipped a beat.

"I don't know. It's hard to explain. I don't want you to think I'm…"

"What are you hearing, Max?" Hargrove's words were more clipped than he had intended.

"It's like, these Words."

"Someone talking?"

"No, nothing like that. It's just this repetitive…" Max's voice trailed off.

"A repetitive what?"

"Look, Hargrove, you've been through enough of this…"

"Max, tell me what's going on." Hargrove's eyes didn't move.

Max looked out the window from where he was standing.

"Words. I'm hearing Words with a capital 'W'. They woke me up after I got home from the hospital. Words slung together over and over again." Max shrugged, his jaw went slack. "They go away. They come back. I don't know what the hell's going on."

"Words?" Hargrove's back stiffened. The hair on his neck prickled. "Listen. I hear her," Gwen would say. "It's Sally, I'm sure of it. She's calling. She needs me!" He scrutinized Max's face, looking for the terror, for the cold panic so familiar to Hargrove, but it wasn't there.

"What did your doctor say? Did you tell him you're hearing voices?"

45

"Jesus Christ, I'm not hearing voices!" Max threw the marker on the floor and walked to the window again. He wiped his face with his hand.

Hargrove went to him and reached for his shoulder but withdrew his hand just before making contact. "Okay, okay, you're not hearing voices. You're hearing words."

"Yes, but not just words. I'm hearing Words." Max turned around to face his friend.

"What Words?"

"One is 'ending' and the other is 'time'." Max shrugged his shoulders.

"Time ending?" asked Hargrove, his voice a monotone.

"When I hear it, it's 'ending time'. And the Words run together when I'm hearing them, like they are a single word playing on a continuous loop: endingtimeendingtimeendingtime." Max frowned and nodded his head to one side as he said this.

"That's it?" Max shook his head in the affirmative. The corner of Hargrove's mouth twitched slightly. "What did the doctor say?"

"Well," said Max, looking at the floor. "I didn't exactly tell him."

"Jesus, Max."

"Look, that'd be all I need: A doctor thinking I've gone off the deep end." Max paused. "I don't need a friend thinking I've gone off the deep end, either."

"Of course not." Hargrove cleared his throat.

Max put his hand on his briefcase as if he were preparing to leave.

"But, Jesus, Max, you should have told your doctor about this. I mean, maybe something can be done. Maybe if you had a CT or an MRI, they could find the cause. It has to be something."

"Had those. Nothing's wrong."

Hargrove was quiet.

"You think I'm crazy, don't you?" asked Max.

Hargrove studied Max's face. The man's full cheeks and wide eyes seemed almost childlike. "No, Max, I don't think you're crazy," said Hargrove, haltingly, hoping he was right. His friend met his eyes. "But something's going on, Max, and you owe it to yourself to find out what it is."

"Well, the doctor said, 'Let's wait and see'." Max waved his arms in mock alarm. "Who knows?"

"It's your call. You know what my vote is."

Max picked up the briefcase and started to walk away. Hargrove sat on the desk. "So what do *you* think it means, Max?"

Max turned and put his briefcase back down. "What does it mean? I haven't the foggiest notion."

"'Ending time'. 'Ending time'. It always sounds like that?"

"I've only heard it about a half-dozen times, but, yes, it always sounds like that," said Max. "Why?"

"I don't know. It's just…odd."

"Well, Jesus Christ, of course it's odd!"

"Max, I didn't mean anything. It's just that, 'ending time', 'time ending', no matter how you say it, it's an odd thing to start hearing. It has to mean something, don't you think?" Hargrove's voice was low and halting.

"I don't know. If it means the world is coming to an end, then good riddance."

"You don't mean that."

"Why shouldn't I mean it? Look around you. Look at your own life, Hargrove." Max took a deep breath. "I'm sorry. I shouldn't have…

47

but, really, if you look at everything that's happened, don't you wonder what the point is? Why it's turned out the way it has?" Max squinted at his friend.

Hargrove bowed his head. "We don't get to choose what comes," said Hargrove, his voice distant.

"Why the hell don't we? If we're here anyway, why the hell don't we get to choose?"

"We get to choose some things, sometimes, I suppose. It's just that…"

"It's just that what? Just that we don't get to choose about the really important things? The really important things just happen to us? And then it's all over? Endingtimeendingtime?"

Hargrove folded his arms. "Max, you make of life what you can make of it. I'll bet you've told me a thousand times that one of the things that made Lincoln a great president was that he didn't question what came his way; he didn't shrink from all that happened in his personal life, or the catastrophes that gripped the country. Instead, he picked it up and carried it on his shoulders, because he didn't have any other choice in the matter."

"Yes, he was a great man. He was." Max continued looking out the window as if searching the distant horizon. "When I was in my twenties—you remember those days—when I was a young man and all my life was ahead of me, I wasn't arrogant enough to think that I would *be* great, but I thought there would be plenty of time for me to *do* something great."

"Didn't we all?"

"Yes, we did. But I *believed* it. I did." Max's eyes were moist and glowing. "But it didn't happen." Max gestured to the door where the sound of teenagers seemed to rattle its hinges. "This happened instead."

"Max, you've been a good teacher all these years. You've been true to your profession. You can't ask for much more."

Max didn't answer. He seemed lost in his thoughts. "The road ahead seems so short now."

Students began leaning into the room. "Can we come in now, Mr. Stinson?"

"Give us one more minute," he replied and then turned to his friend. "Max. The road has always been short. It has just taken us a long time to realize it."

Max pursed his lips, disagreement in his eyes. "Thanks for listening, my friend." He picked up his briefcase and headed to the door.

"Hey, Max."

Max turned.

"Ending time, ending time—any idea when it's going to happen?" Hargrove said, half-smiling.

"No idea whatsoever."

More More Time

Chapter 7

Gwen Stinson sat in the rocking chair by the living room window, her robe wrapped tightly around her. She peered through the lace curtains as a car passed by, the late afternoon sun casting horizontal streaks through the tall maples that gave the street its character. A neighbor pulled mercilessly on a lawnmower cord, but the machine would not start. His wife called out to him, and he waved at her as if to say, "Shut up!" Another car passed, then another. The UPS truck cruised slowly by, looking for an address. The grandfather clock in the far corner struck five times.

He was late. School let out at 3:10 p.m. and even when he stayed to grade tests or to work on lessons, he was always home by 4:30 p.m. Gwen looked at the pair of boxers resting in her lap. They had sailing ships on them and were trimmed in blue. In their thirty-eight years of marriage, she had never known Hargrove to wear boxer shorts.

"Honey, why don't you get dressed today? When I come home this afternoon, we can take a nice walk. It will do you good," he had said that morning.

She had smiled. "That sounds lovely."

Hargrove had stood over her. He put his hands on her shoulder. She reached for one and squeezed it tightly. Just as quickly, he pulled it away and stepped back.

"No, really," he said. "Why don't you get dressed today?"

She had every intention of dressing for the day, or at least dressing before Hargrove got home from work. The day had started off well. By 10:00 a.m. she was at the sink doing the dishes from the night before.

"Instead of using the dishwasher, why don't you wash them by hand? It will give you something to do," Hargrove had urged. He was always making suggestions designed to get her up and going. "It will give you energy. You'll feel better." It might be mail that had to be taken to the post office, laundry to the dry cleaner, a bill to be paid, a book to be bought, or 2% milk to be purchased from the grocery store. It was never much, but always enough to make Gwen anxious about the day, knowing that she had a test to take, a hurdle to clear.

"Thank you," she always said.

By 2:00 p.m., she was ready to dress. She went to the clothes basket and searched through the dirty laundry to find a bra and underwear. That's when she noticed them. The boxers. They were so foreign that she didn't know what to think. She almost threw them in with the dust rags, until she noticed that they were brand new, the elastic waist taut, the blue trim bright, the sailing vessels adventurous. It was ten minutes, maybe more, before she accepted that they were Hargrove's. She looked through his dresser and found piles of whites, the kind he'd been wearing all his life. Then, in the back of the bottom drawer where long forgotten socks typically lay crinkled, she found two more pairs of dazzling boxers. One was fire engine red with orange and yellow flowers; the other, black with gold stripes. She stared at them. How could she not have noticed? Had it been that long since she had washed the laundry or seen her husband get dressed? Or undressed?

Gwen dropped her bra and underwear on the bed and went back to the kitchen, boxers in hand. While waiting for the water to boil, she played solitaire. She poured the water into a scallop-edged china cup and saucer that was once her mother's. She dipped the bag into the water and then let it steep for several minutes until it was strong and bitter. She finished her hand, leaving the cards arrayed on the table like so many flights of stairs. She returned to her rocking chair by the front window in time to see the first school bus stop down the street. Three middle school girls got off, one turning to give the finger to someone on the bus.

More buses came and went, and then some mothers and fathers returning from long days at work, and then no one else. The clock struck again, this time 5:15 p.m. A cold cup of tea sat on the table beside the rocker. A colorful pair of boxer shorts sat in her lap. The late afternoon light began to fade behind the rooftops, and Gwen started to wonder whether this time he would come home at all. "Why do you think such things?" Hargrove would say. "I don't know," she would reply. "I just do." The next time she looked up from her lap, Hargrove's car came around the corner, down the street, and into their driveway. She listened for the rumbling sound of the garage door opening. She put the boxers in the pocket of her robe.

"Gwen, I'm home!"

Gwen got up from the rocker and went toward the kitchen, stopping suddenly when she realized she hadn't gotten dressed. Her heart pounded.

"There you are," said Hargrove, his smile vanishing when he saw her robe. He kissed her on the forehead. "You're a little clammy, honey. Are you not feeling well?"

"Just a headache."

"I'm sorry to hear that," said Hargrove, turning from her.

"A bad one, actually. I've had to stay out of the light today."

Hargrove turned again to her. "I'm sure it must be awful."

"That's why I'm not..."

"Don't say another word." Hargrove smiled at her.

Gwen had heard that some couples kiss when they see each other at the end of the day. Instead, she and Hargrove, Hargrove mostly, assessed her emotional state. Hargrove seemed relieved, almost buoyant, on those rare days when Gwen reported feeling "okay." He would then go about his evening routine, watching the news, catching up on school work, reading, and making the next day's lunch. It made her feel good to see him so happy, although she felt even more alone. When she didn't feel well, though, he dropped everything to sit with her, wait on her, do almost anything for her. Since most days it was impossible to tell how she felt, Gwen found it expedient to say, more often than not, that she felt "poorly" or that it had been a "hard day" or that she wished she could give him "good news." The nagging guilt she felt about this mendacity was relieved only slightly by the constant, if grudging, attention he gave her, trying as best he could to feel "poorly" with her. On those evenings, they sat together on the couch hardly saying a word, except for the occasional inquiry from Hargrove. Could he get something for her, another cup of tea, a pillow for her neck, a hot water bottle for her stomach? She was to be cared for, like a sickly garden on a forgotten patch of ground where the sun seldom shone.

At 9:00 p.m., he would accompany her to bed, tuck her in, turn out the light, then go back downstairs for reasons she never understood. Rarely did he join her. Rarely did the care he gave her in the evening continue into the night. She lay awake feeling dry as an August creek bed, hoping he would come, hoping he would lay with her. But by the time she felt him beside her, it was morning, the alarm having gone off, the same day having started once again.

She felt for the boxers in the pocket of her robe.

"How was school today?"

"The usual."

"Must have had a lot of work to do."

"Why do you say that?" he said, clearing the table for dinner. They always ate at the kitchen table, never in front of the TV, something Gwen appreciated, even when the dinners were eaten in silence.

"It's so late."

Hargrove looked at the wall-clock. "I suppose I lost track of time."

"You're so busy," she said, reaching for the knives and forks. "I never lose track of time. Not a minute goes by that I don't know it." She could see the back of her husband's neck tighten. "It's a kind of curse. Never to be so swept up in something that time disappears."

Hargrove held the plates in his hands for a moment, then placed them on the table and reached for some napkins. "I saw Max today."

"Of course. How is he?"

"Fell down his basement steps, the old fool."

"Oh my," she said, stopping mid-motion, fork in the air.

"Damn near killed himself."

"Is he okay?"

"Stitches all across his forehead. Looked awful, but he'll be okay."

"That's terrible. Poor man." She always liked Max, despite his gloomy outlook on almost everything. He was there for them when they most needed it, and, as far as she could tell, Max was the only true friend Hargrove had, truer in some ways than her.

Gwen laid the flatware beside the plates and added salad bowls and glasses to the table. Hargrove whisked eggs into a bowl for omelets and sautéed mushrooms and red peppers on the stove. Gwen filled the glasses with ice and then water. She put two slices of Texas toast in the toaster and jams on the table. They often ate breakfast for dinner; it was fast and easy. Gwen used to cook, but not in recent years. She couldn't remember the last time she made dinner on a regular basis. It just slipped away like so many other things. She opened the refrigerator door and reached for a bag of lettuce, emptying some into the bowls and then placing several bottles of salad dressing on the table. Salad made it seem more like a real dinner.

She watched Hargrove gently folding the omelet, biting his lower lip in concentration. She reached into her pocket, removed the boxer shorts, and placed them on his chair. Then she sat and waited until he was done.

"Here you go," he said, sliding half the omelet onto her plate.

"Thank you, honey." Gwen reached for the balsamic vinaigrette and drizzled it onto her salad. Hargrove placed the remaining omelet onto his plate, returned the skillet to the burner, and sat down, only then noticing what was on his seat.

"What's this?" he said, pulling the boxers out from under him. He held them over his plate, his eyes narrowing, as if he were examining an intricate puzzle for the first time.

"Found them today in the clothes basket."

"Uh huh."

"At first, I didn't know what they were." She took a bite of her omelet. "Delicious."

"Well, they're obviously a pair of my underwear." Hargrove dropped them on the floor beside him. He looked at Gwen again, a curt smile. He reached for his fork and was about to cut his omelet.

"They must be new."

"What's that?" he asked, his voice flat.

"They must be new, I said. At least, I've never seen them." Gwen pushed some of the omelet across her plate with the fork.

"Thought you had."

"No, I haven't. Not in all our years of marriage."

Hargrove took a bite of his omelet. "These peppers really make the omelet, don't they?"

"Yes, they're so fresh." But she wasn't eating now. Hargrove spread raspberry preserves on his toast and took a bite. He sipped his glass of water and cut into his omelet again.

"Are there more?" she asked.

"More what?"

"More of them." She pointed to the crumpled boxers on the floor.

"What does it matter?"

"It doesn't matter, I suppose." Gwen's voice was thin with anxiety. She watched her husband eat. *He's a good man, isn't he?* she asked herself. Anyone would be happy to have such a husband. *This is foolish.* And yet, there were times when he seemed like a stranger. He was always reserved, polite, a little distant in a way that made him attractive to her in those early, fast-paced days of courtship. Circumstances dictated that they marry sooner than they had planned.

Once married, Gwen thought she would discover what treasure lay beneath his surface, but she never did. There was something about him that remained closed to her; something she couldn't reach. He always told her that it was her imagination. "What you see is what you get, unfortunately," he'd reply with a laugh.

"I found two other pairs in the back of your sock drawer."

"My sock drawer." Hargrove laid his fork carefully down beside his plate. He picked up the napkin and wiped his mouth slowly, then wadded the napkin and dropped it on the table. "Dear, please. Do we have to discuss my choice of underwear over dinner?"

A flash of doubt made Gwen flinch. Her hands fell to her side. Hargrove leaned back in his chair, measuring her. She noticed a hole in the table cloth near the blue and white fringe. Perhaps if she crawled through it, she would come out somewhere entirely different, in another time, far away, where you laughed about your husband's new underwear, and you dressed in bright flowered blouses and fitted skirts to meet each new day, and you forgot that once upon a time you had a daughter and a life.

"I didn't mean to upset you," Gwen offered.

"Upset me?" asked Hargrove, a laugh spilling from the corners of his mouth. "Dear, you could never upset me. I just don't understand why my underwear is suddenly so important to you. Perhaps you need something more to do during the day, something more constructive or rewarding than looking through my sock drawer for my underwear." He paused, his words circling the room. "If you like, I'll throw them away."

"No, of course not. I just didn't..." Gwen wiped her mouth with her napkin, then held it in place.

"Didn't what?" There was a chilling calm in his voice.

Gwen stood, placed her utensils on her plate, and carried them to the sink.

"Didn't what?"

She leaned against the sink staring at the pale yellow cupboard, trying to remember when they had painted it last, trying to remember why they had chosen that shade, so dull it made her feel numb.

"Dear? Didn't what?"

"I didn't know why you chose them. They're so…" The words clogged her throat.

"They're so, what?"

"They're so…*not like you.*"

"Not like me in what way?" asked Hargrove, standing and taking his plate to the sink. "It's true they aren't my usual underwear, my usual 'tighty whities'. I hadn't though it was a crime to buy different underwear." He picked up the boxers and came to her side.

Gwen stood still, her arms across her chest, her hands clutched under her chin. "I'm sorry I brought it up." She looked at Hargrove as if seeing him for the first time, a complete stranger.

"Not at all. You know you can always talk to me." He put his arm around her, hugged her to his side, and then let go. "If it's okay with you, I'm going upstairs now to take a bath. I'll take the offending boxers with me and return them to my drawer. Are you okay for me to leave you?"

"Yes," she said, her voice a hush. "Yes, I'm fine. Go. Do whatever you need to do. I'll finish cleaning up."

"Are you sure? You don't sound well."

"I sound the way I sound, Hargrove. Go."

Hargrove patted her back and then turned to leave the kitchen.

"Don't put them back."

"What's that? Don't put what back?"

"Don't put the boxers back in the drawer." Her back was to him as she wiped the counter with a damp dish cloth.

"Gwen, please." She could see the crimped corners of his mouth, the disappointed tilt of his head, even without looking at him.

"They look dirty to me," she said, wringing the dish cloth and then folding it over the lip of the sink.

Chapter 8

Bob Hazelwood held the cooler door open and stared vacantly at the stacks of diet entrees while an icy mist surrounded him. A woman reached awkwardly past him for several boxes of pasta primavera.

"Excuse me," she said, balancing on one foot.

Bob tried to focus. He studied the endless variety of weight loss meals: angel hair marinara, broccoli and cheddar roasted potatoes, chicken enchiladas suiza, creamy rigatoni with broccoli, and on and on. He reached for the Santa Fe rice and beans and then put it back, unsure. He stepped back, one hand on his chin.

"First time?" said the woman with the airy confidence of a seasoned pro encouraging a rookie.

"Well..."

"Can be overwhelming for the uninitiated."

"That's for sure."

"Your wife sent you on this mission?"

Bob looked at the fifty-something woman, dressed in a light gray sweat suit with "PINK" stretched across her bottom. Her shopping cart was piled high, her balding, semi-comatose husband was standing a few feet away.

"Uh..."

"Consider it a vote of confidence. I'd never send Alvin out on his own," she said, looking over her shoulder at her husband. "Who knows what would happen." The woman backed her cart up and started down the aisle again, calling to her husband, "Let's go!" Alvin made beckoning eye contact with Bob and then continued on his forced march.

Bob looked at his watch, then realized it didn't matter what time it was. He looked down the empty aisle. He was alone in the frozen food section of the grocery store trying to figure out what dinners to buy for his wife, who, for all he knew, wouldn't want any of them. What was going on with her, anyway? Since she came home with her hands a mess, he didn't have a clue, and she wasn't talking. Was she having an affair? Was she planning to leave him? Would she ever go back to the therapist? Would she ever forgive him? He was afraid to ask. Instead, he waited and watched, trying to read tea leaves that, as of yet, he couldn't decipher.

These thoughts only added weight to the burden he carried since this morning's meeting with his boss, Gabe Swenson. "Come on in," Gabe had said. Bob stepped onto the thick-pile, burgundy carpet and looked around the room. On the wall behind Gabe's desk, there were ten Million-Dollar-Seller plaques, eight Year-End-Sales Leader framed certificates, and a Sales-Office-of-the-Year trophy. On the wall behind his desk was a sign that said, "Let Me Put You in a Place Called Home." Gabe had managed Happy Homes Realty for twenty years, ever since his father, Gabe, Sr., had died. A Rolex hung from his wrist, a gold ring with raised onyx commanded his fat pinky.

"Have a seat, Bob," said Gabe gesturing to the wing-backed leather chair in front of his desk. Gabe leaned back and put his feet up on his mahogany desk, his Italian loafers gleaming.

Bob sat gingerly. He cleared his throat. He thought of crossing his legs, but didn't want to make any move that might draw unwanted attention.

Gabe had hired Bob as a friendly gesture after a chance meeting at a local fitness club. Bob was selling life insurance at the time.

Beth was confused when Bob came home that day with his news. "Real estate? Why are you making a change so soon? You've only been at insurance a few months." Years ago when Beth was laid off from her job at a resort spa in Maine, Bob convinced her that opportunities were greater for both of them back home. But since their return, Bob had moved from job to job. He tried his hand at retail, managing a Foot Locker at the mall for a short while, working at Penny's, and then at a discount jewelry store, which was where he got into all the trouble. Insurance came next.

The day he started his job with Met Life was also the day that Beth found out everything. For months afterwards, he was barely functional. When he met Gabe Swenson, he thought it might be time for a fresh start. Shortly thereafter, he approached Beth about marriage therapy. He felt himself turning a corner. But he hadn't seen the wall waiting for him around the bend.

"I know I've gotten off to a slow start," said Bob, unable to look Gabe in the eyes.

"Slow start hardly captures it." Gabe wasn't smiling. "You haven't sold a thing. A blind man without a cane could find leads faster than you, Bob." Gabe offered Bob a cigar from the humidor on his desk.

"No thanks."

Gabe clipped the end of the cigar, moistened it in his mouth, then held a lighter to the other end, drawing repeatedly until the tip was burning, gold.

"As I said, Bob, Gabe likes you. But he's never had anyone stall out like this. He's never had anyone get so stuck at the start line."

"Look, I know my performance has been awful so far, but I've got a lot of troubles at home that have…"

"Whoa, wait a minute there. If you and Gabe were just a couple of guys shooting the shit at some bar, I'd be interested in your troubles at home. As it stands, all I care about is you moving some real estate. And that just hasn't happened." Gabe held his cigar with three fingers, lifting it to his nose and breathing deep. "It isn't working out, Bob."

Bob stepped back from the grocery store freezer and stared at its contents. The thought of making a choice among all these options, a choice that would satisfy Beth, was daunting. She had started Weight Watchers again. He didn't understand why. When he said this to her, she glared at him, as if he were insulting her.

"I think you look great," he had said as she disappeared into the bathroom. "No reason to change anything!"

Bob was all thumbs and left feet around her. If he was breathing in, he wondered if he should be breathing out. If he was going this way, would she prefer him to go that way? Was he suddenly too short, or too tall? Nothing came easy. She didn't seem to want anything from him, and yet she stayed. He thought of asking her, "Why?" but was afraid of the answer.

Bob walked down the aisle, deciding to take a break from the diet entrees. He went to the attached cafe and ordered coffee and a cherry Danish. He took a seat near the window. The only other person in the café was a sixty-ish looking woman sitting several tables away. She was leaning forward on the Formica top holding a cup of coffee with both hands. She stared absently at the floor. He took a bite of his

Danish and put it down on the wax paper bag. He was not a Danish lover.

He glanced again at his café companion. She had not moved a muscle in five minutes. She sat, statue-like, while shoppers rolled by, their kids' legs dangling from their carts. Her face was devoid of detail, hidden behind a gray aspect. Her hair was short and thin. Her fingers were long. She wore a brown cloth coat, one season too early. He watched her for several minutes, curious at how motionless she was. The woman blinked. She moved a finger. He cleared his throat, but she did not look.

Bob got up to leave when a guy in an orange "Go 'Cuse" T-shirt walked by, bumping the woman's table inadvertently. She reached for her cup of coffee, but it slid from her hand, spilling across the table and onto the floor. By then, the T-shirt man was an aisle away. She took the cup in both hands and sat it up again.

"Excuse me," called Bob, but she didn't hear him. He walked over to the woman. "Here, let me help you."

She looked up at him with searching eyes. "I'm so clumsy."

Bob went to the nearby salad bar and pulled some napkins from the dispenser. When he turned, the woman was still seated, coffee now dripping onto her coat.

"Let me." Bob carefully wiped her coat.

"Thank you. I don't know what I would have done if you hadn't come by." She said this as if he had found her on a deserted road, her tire flat, a blizzard engulfing her.

"No problem whatsoever." Bob threw the first sopping pile of napkins away and returned with the dispenser in hand. As he cleaned the table, he studied the woman, who couldn't stop thanking him. Her eyes had dark pillows under them; her mouth was dry at the corners, her chin narrow, her hands wrinkled, her nails short and ragged. But when she smiled, her face changed, her eyes brightened, the pillows deflated, her skin took on color.

"How can I ever thank you?"

"No need to thank me. I'm just glad I was here to help you out. Never can tell when something like this might happen, you know, and when it does, it's sure not much fun cleaning up the mess all by yourself." Bob smiled, then laughed, saying "We're all in this together, after all, aren't we?" his optimism somehow buoyed. "Did you get burned?"

"No, no."

"You know they make coffee so hot nowadays, you can never be too careful."

"I can't remember the last time someone has been so kind to me. I mean a complete stranger." She shook her head and laughed, then put her hand over her mouth as if surprised at being able to laugh.

"It's nothing, really," Bob offered.

"Oh, but you're wrong," replied the woman, reaching into her purse. "Let me at least repay you in some way."

"Oh my, absolutely not. It's my pleasure. I'm glad I was here."

"Well, at least could you give me your name?"

"My name?"

"Yes. I would like to send you a note, a thank you card or something. Please."

Bob hesitated at first, but her face had such longing that he could not resist.

"It's Bob."

"Bob what?"

"Bob Hazelwood."

"Bob Hazelwood," she said as she rifled through her purse, searching unsuccessfully for a pen and paper. "My name is Gwen Stinson." She extended her hand.

"Very nice to meet you." He bowed slightly as he took her hand. "Here, I might have something." He took a receipt from his wallet and a pen from his shirt. "This should do," he said, as he wrote down his name and address and handed the receipt to her.

"Thank you so much." Gwen took the paper from his hand and slid it into her purse. Then she squeezed his hand. "I mean it. You know, I really can't remember the last time someone did something so thoughtful for me."

"Well, I'm glad I had a chance to meet you, despite all this," he said, waving his hand over the repaired spill site. Quickly they realized there was nothing more to say. "You may want to…" He pointed at some coffee on her ankles.

"Oh my, yes. I must go to the lady's room or everyone will wonder." She leaned her head back slightly, so she could look at him directly and smiled broadly. "Thank you so much."

Bob headed back to the frozen food section, standing just a little taller. He selected an assortment of diet entrees and diet desserts, juggling them as he walked to the checkout. He joked with the young checkout girl, explaining that while he should be the one eating all this diet food, it was actually for his wife. Then feeling that he had somehow betrayed her, he said, "But, believe me, she doesn't need it." The girl blinked and asked if he had a Shoppers Club card or any coupons.

"Have a nice day," she said, handing him the receipt as she started scanning groceries for the next customer.

Bob grabbed his bags and headed for the exit. He stopped at the newspaper rack. He put the bags on the floor and pulled a *Democrat and Chronicle* from the display. He turned to the employment section and stared at the ample listings. Tucking the paper under his arm, he walked back to the service desk to pay.

"Thank you very much," he said as the teenage girl attendant gave him his change.

Once outside, he stood for a moment scanning the parking lot for his car. Until then, he hadn't noticed what a beautiful day it was. Billowy white clouds slid away in the distance; the sun was warm on his neck, the air cool on his cheeks. He closed his eyes, a smile crossing his face. Maybe his conversation with Gabe wasn't a bad thing after all. He had gone into real estate because he was desperate to do something, anything. Is that really the way to decide your future? To go from thing to thing, afraid to stop, even though you don't know what you're doing, just running scared all the time?

Standing in the Wegman's parking lot while people all around him went about their business, it didn't seem like there was anything to worry about at all; and no need to hurry. If he had been in a hurry, would he have noticed that woman? Or would he have just kept going, caught up in his own worries, unable to see anything else, unavailable to anyone including himself. And if he hadn't seen that woman, would he be feeling as good, as hopeful, as he felt right now? Of course, not. Time isn't always of the essence; sometimes it's best to go slow and stop along the way, even if stopping doesn't make much sense at first.

He would go home, but instead of scouring every ad in the paper under his arm then devouring every listing online, he would take his time and think about what he really wanted to do. He would figure things out and soon enough, he'd be on his way. Things always have a way of working out. He and Beth had enough money to get by for a while if they were careful. Who knows, maybe this would bring them closer together. Working side by side, shoulder to shoulder, it might take some time, but their marriage might be better for it. Bob looked up into the blue, full of hope. He took the paper from under his arm, refolded it, and dropped it into the nearest garbage can.

Bob strode to his car, nodding and joking with each person he passed, complimenting the cart-boy who was pushing a line of thirty shopping carts back into the store. "Wow, that's amazing."

The boy smiled back. "Have a nice day, sir."

It was that simple. If you give something, you get something back. If you help a woman with her spilt coffee, you get a thank-you. If you try to do something thoughtful for your wife, it matters. Things didn't have to be a struggle. It could be easy. If he'd let it.

Bob tossed the bags on the passenger seat. He walked around to the driver's side and looked back at the store. The café was almost full now. He was about to get into the car when he noticed her. Gwen Stinson. Still sitting at the same table, with a cup in front of her. She sat with her head down again, arms outstretched, hands around the cup. He stood by his car and watched her for a moment, his smile dissipating.

"Move," he whispered. "Just move."

More More Time

Chapter 9

"Yo, Mr. Ruth," called the boy wearing the gray hoody, fourth row, sixth seat. Max looked up from his desk, surprised that the classroom was full. He breathed in the smell of teenagers, scanned their baggy jeans and pastel hair, and thought briefly about their reckless attitudes and thoughtless confidence.

"Yes," said Max, pushing back from his desk, standing, and taking his place in front of the class.

"What happened to your melon, Mr. Ruth?" This was so hilarious to some that they bent over their desks overcome by gales of laughter, while others sat idly doing their makeup, or watching the squirrel on the tree limb outside the window. Two students asked if he was okay, since they had heard he was dead.

"I don't think that is a topic for discussion today," stated Max.

"Oooooo," sounded several students.

"Just sayin'. You look a little Frankensteinish today, you know what I mean?" The boy with the shoulder length hair, fifth row, last seat, stood up and walked stiff-legged down the aisle making growling sounds. Max watched, expressionless.

The mousy girl, fourth row, second seat, shook her head at her peers and said, "Assholes," and laid her head on her desk.

Max had brought a portable TV into his classroom in the early 1970s so his students could study the Watergate hearings. They sat together in a semi-circle on the floor so everyone could see the proceedings. "You are watching history being made, people." They watched with rapt attention, asking questions about Sen. Sam Ervin and John Dean and Deep Throat and the rag-tag cast of break-in characters. "You may never see anything like this again in your lifetime." He felt exhilarated to be a part of it, even driving with Hargrove to D.C. so they could witness Nixon's resignation.

Once Nixon was gone and the war over, everything changed. No one cared anymore. His students seemed oblivious to anything that happened beyond their noses.

The giraffe-faced girl, last-row, last-seat called, "Hey Mr. R, don't listen to those idiots. I like what you done to your head. You look like an old time rapper, Mr. R, looking good."

The boy with a muscle shirt, second row, last seat: "Hey, I gotta pee so bad my eyes are turning yellow; can I have a piss-pass?"

His friend, a boy with spiky hair, sitting next to him, added that he was also suffering with the, "I gotta pees."

The idea that this great nation would be turned over to the girls and boys in his classroom made Max want to weep.

The pencil thin boy with large horn-rimmed glasses, first row, first seat raised his hand and asked, "Since you weren't here yesterday, do we have to do the research thingy for this Friday. I mean, like, it leaves us with only, like, three days to do it, and I have two nights out for play practice and…"

The boy with the scraggly goatee, second row, second-seat shook his head. "What a pussy."

"Hey, you wanna see some pussy..." said the boy with the giant pimple on his nose, third row, second seat, pointing to the girl smacking her chewing gum, third row, first seat, who smiled and said, "Get in line."

Why couldn't the world end today? thought Max. *Why must it be delayed?*

Max pointed to the boys with the bladder problems. "You two, go to the lav, and don't come back today or tomorrow or for the rest of the week. As for the research 'thingy'," he said to the curious boy with his hand still up. "Since you asked, yes, of course it is due on Friday, and I, for one, don't give a hoot about play practice."

"Hoot! Hoot! Hoot!" chanted several boys from the back of the room.

"And, as for your crude reference to your classmate's private parts, you should be ashamed," he said to the pussy boys. Then he turned to the get-in-line girl: "Just as you should be ashamed for not being outraged by what these two oafs insinuated."

"Hang tough, Mr. R," called the boy wearing a do-rag, fourth row, fifth seat.

Max sighed deeply and putting his hands in his sport jacket pockets, then removing them to straighten his blue and white polka-dotted bow tie, and push his glasses back up the bridge of his nose.

"And to you, young lady with your head still on your desk. You made a general reference to the population of anal sphincters inhabiting this classroom, and while I deplore the use of such language, I can only say that I understand and share the sentiment."

"You go!" cried a half-dozen or more students, while the others laughed.

"Now, let's get on to Mr. Lincoln." He opened his text and held it before him in the palm of his hand. "He is the single most important person in all of American history. Can anyone tell me why this statement is true?"

"Because you said so?" ventured the girl with a pleasant smile, first row, fourth seat.

The bell rang.

"And there you have it," said Max. "A perfect ending to a perfect class." Above the din of departing students, he called, "People! Read chapter 14 and be ready to work when you come to class next time. Dismissed."

When the bell rang for the final period of the day, Max gathered up his things and headed to his car, bypassing the faculty lounge and the latest school gossip. He ran his finger across the scar, feeling for the prickly edges of dissolving sutures and listening for The Words.

"Max!" came the call from across the lot. He turned and smiled as Hargrove approached, his shoulders more rounded than usual, his gait favoring his left leg slightly, something Max had noticed of late. Even after all these years, Hargrove remained an appealing, even commanding figure, angular and trim, if not exactly fit, taller by several inches than his squattier friend, formal and steady, removed in a way that drew people to him.

"How did it go today?" Hargrove asked.

Max chuckled. "As usual."

"Sorry to hear that," said Hargrove, patting Max's shoulder once. The sun broke through the clouds, and Hargrove covered his eyes with his hand. "What about the other, what should I call it, situation?" He pointed to Max's ears.

"The same," said Max, turning his head and closing one eye against the glaring sun.

"Seen the doctor again?" Max didn't answer. "Look. Let's go for a beer. On me," offered Hargrove."

Max turned back to his friend, tilting his head up to study Hargrove's eyes, which seldom belied much. "Can you do that?"

"I can do anything I want; I am the freest of free agents; I can come and go as I please; no questions asked, no answers given." Hargrove jutted his chin with confidence. They both laughed.

"Yes, of course you are. How is Gwen anyway? I haven't seen her in months."

"Count yourself lucky." Hargrove frowned at himself. "I'm sorry. I didn't mean it to come out that way."

"No need to apologize," said Max, trying to recall if Hargrove had ever even hinted publicly at what life was like with Gwen. Always understated, Hargrove had called finding Gwen lost in the woods wearing nothing but her bra and underwear an "unfortunate mishap." He had sat calmly stone-faced in the emergency room as she screamed at him not to "put me away." Ever since Sally had died, it seemed to Max that Hargrove had become the granite shore upon which Gwen's waves of despair crashed. Max admired his friend's Stoic resolve; though he puzzled over the invisible toll it must be taking.

"Things worse?" he ventured.

"Things are the way they are, Max."

"Do you think you should call her first?"

Hargrove removed a cell phone from his shirt pocket, looked at it, and then put it back. "It should be fine."

Time Travelers was a neighborhood sports bar on the city line that attracted education-types in the late afternoon before the prowling twenty-somethings took over for the night. Booths surrounded high tables and stools, the floor covered with peanut shells; over the bar was a frayed "Go Bills!" banner that had been hoisted during the team's Super Bowl losing streak. On the walls were pictures of fan favorites, including an autographed photo of Jim Kelly donating a game jersey to the Time Travelers Wall of Fame. Hargrove and Max had first come here as two young bucks starting their teaching career. In those days, they had left Time Travelers with their share of young women on their arms, most of whose names had long been forgotten. The frequency of their visits had dwindled in recent years, as the general tiredness that comes with aging set in.

Hargrove waved to the waitress—a perky brunette with a short black skirt, button down white shirt open at the neck, black stockings, flats, and hair tied back with a bandana, who looked little more than nineteen.

"Hello, gentleman. What can I get you?" she said, laying down napkins while looking at a gaggle of guys coming through the door. She smiled and waved to them heartily. "Good to see ya, fellas!" Max gazed at her long fingernails, painted with daisies, as she turned back to the two of them. "So, beers?"

"I'll have a white wine; Reisling, if you have it," said Hargrove. "And my friend will have a beer, I'm sure."

"Sam Adams," said Max, looking up at the girl's bronzed tan and perfect skin, as she ogled a young professional invading the middle of the bar.

"Got it," she said, hurrying away.

"Jesus, do you think she'll remember where to bring our order? She didn't even look at us."

Hargrove gazed at Max with the seriousness of a news anchor. "Gee whiz, Max, would you look at us if you could avoid it?"

Max's bleak mood was not to be broken. "People don't look at other people anymore." Max's hands curled into soft fists.

"You mean *women* don't look at *you* anymore." Hargrove slipped a youthful grin onto his face, and shook his head.

"Yes, I guess that's exactly what I mean, if you have to put a fine point on it," said Max, feeling disgruntled and foolish. "I know, at my age, it shouldn't matter, but it does, for Christ's sake. When we were that girl's age," he said, nodding discretely at their distant waitress, "sex was a young man's preoccupation. Wild oats galore, all that sort of thing. And by the time life started to grey out, we weren't supposed to be preoccupied with, well, with the kind of thoughts that used to bother the hell out of us when we were like them." He nodded towards the bar. He looked around to see if anyone was listening. "But, goddammit I still think about it. A lot."

The waitress approached with their drinks, her tray above her shoulders, her trim legs tooling along briskly.

"One Riesling and one Sam. And here're some pretzels and peanuts for your enjoyment, gentlemen," she said with a broad smile directed at no one in particular. Max clutched his beer and lifted it to his mouth, resisting the impulse to watch her walk away.

"Is there something wrong with me?"

"You're hearing voices talking about the end of time, and can't keep your eyes off a girl who's probably a third your age. You tell me." Hargrove held up his glass in a toast, then took a sip.

Waves of testosterone lapped the middle of the bar, the men and women so young they didn't even know there was a tomorrow.

"You know how long it's been since I've been with a woman?" asked Max, looking at his friend with defeat in his eyes.

"Please don't tell…"

"Five years. No wait. Six years."

"Okay, you're going to tell me."

Max took a long gulp of beer and clunked the glass back onto the table. "Six years. Can you imagine?"

His last had been a substitute teacher for Hargrove. In her early fifties, tall and thin, long legged, but not shapely in the least—flat in front and back—her face was appealing, though offset by her wide-set eyes and pale complexion. She tilted her head to one side when she listened, causing her hair to flow off the other shoulder. She was friendly and laughed nervously at everything Max said. He helped her plan her lessons for the day. What was her name? She was widowed, as he recalled. Recently so. She cried at the end of the day, fearing she would never get a full-time teaching job, that she was already over the hill. She had stayed home to raise her two boys who were on their own now, one married. She talked and talked like a dam had broken inside her. Had she driven to school that day, nothing would have happened between them, but her car was in the shop, and she had come by cab. Max offered to drive her home, and at the front door, she had said, "Please come in." Max replied, "Are you sure?" She took his hand and guided him through the doorway. They barely made it to the living room couch; still partially dressed and in a jumble of awkward half-caresses they made love, or at least, had sex. She had substituted one more time. They waved to each other across the hall. What was her name?

"You know what I'm going to say."

"Don't even bring it up," said Max, staring vacantly into his beer.

"Gail."

"History. Long gone."

"Should have married her when you had the chance. She was bright, pretty, loved you—God only knows why—and more importantly, would have gladly been your wife."

Their waitress tripped up to the table again.

"Can I get you gents another?"

"No thank you," said Hargrove.

"Yes, absolutely," said Max. This time, he watched her walk away. "Hargrove, we've been over this ten-thousand times. It would never have worked. My mother would have slit her own throat if I had married Gail."

"Because?"

"Because, because, because." Max shrugged his shoulders. He resented Hargrove maneuvering him into bringing up his mother, and yet never prevented him from doing so. It felt like penance. He tried not to think about his mother often, although her room sat untouched now for almost fifteen years, her bed made, ruffled bed skirts, and the good, warm quilt she loved so much in winter lying across a pale yellow spread.

"Come on Max; you know as well as I do."

"Then tell me, Professor Know-It-All."

"Vell," said Hargrove, one eyebrow raised. "It iss dat she loved you, Maxvell, more dan life eetself; so much zat she could not bear sharing you viss anozzer voman. She vould razzer die, or better yet, she vould razzer that dee uzzer voman die." With that, Hargrove raised his clenched fist in mock victory.

Max looked at his friend, his face blank. "You know, you try and you try and you try, and yet, you cannot do a German accent to save your life."

They both forced a laugh, and then fell into silence. Max looked at his beer and then across the bar at their waitress, who was talking and laughing with another customer. He hated that his friend was right, that his adult life, his choices in women, had been controlled by someone he barely loved. And yet he had served his mother unquestioningly until her gruesome ending, the circumstances of which seemed to bind him to her even more in death than in life.

Hargrove opened his mouth and then closed it. He smiled apologetically at Max, balancing his empty wine glass between his thumb and forefinger. "Look, Max. I'm sorry. That was uncalled for. I didn't mean anything."

Max waved to the waitress, signaling that he wanted another. "I know," he said, not believing his own words.

The brunette—and her bandana—arrived with beer in hand. Max gazed up at her face, so smooth, not a visible pore, her eyes carefree.

"Thank you."

"You're very welcome." She turned on her heels and started to leave.

"Excuse me, miss." She pivoted, her eyebrows raised expectantly.

"Can I get you something else?"

"No, it's just…May I ask what your name is?"

"Sure. It's Cassie," she said, pointing to the tag on her shirt.

"Thank you, Cassie, for your service. You are a very attractive young woman and a fine waitress."

Cassie laughed. "Thank you! You just made my day!"

Max smiled at her as she walked away. Hargrove cleared his throat and shifted in his seat. "Look, Max." Hargrove glanced at his watch. "I've got to get going. I've got a thing—an appointment."

"An appointment?"

"Yeah."

"What's that?" Max asked, raising his glass to his mouth as he watched their waitress cross the room to another table.

Hargrove's eyes locked. He licked his lips, looked at his glass and then at his friend.

"I'm, it's…it's not an appointment. Really, it's more of meeting. I have to…it's some parents. Curriculum questions, that's all." Hargrove's face blanched.

"Are you okay?" asked Max. "You don't look so good."

"Just tired, that's all. Wine, empty stomach, you know."

Max squinted at his friend, as if trying to see through a shuttered window.

"Okay then."

Hargrove stood. "Ready to go?"

Max paused, looked around the room and tilted his head to one side. "No. I think I'll finish my beer. You go ahead."

Hargrove opened his wallet.

"No need, my friend," said Max, with a limp wave of his hand.

Hargrove dropped a twenty on the table. "My pleasure," he said. "The answer is yes, by the way."

Max stared up at his friend, puzzled.

"You asked me if I could imagine not having sex for six years. The answer is yes." Hargrove put two fingers to his forehead, and saluted Max as he retreated from the bar.

More More Time

Chapter 10

Max stared at the bottom of his empty beer glass and then at the fingers holding it. He slid them up and down the glass, noting the wrinkles across his knuckles, the hair, the pores so prominent, the squared nails. His father's hands. At sixty-two, he was older by fifteen years than his father was at the time of his death. *How senseless,* he thought.

"My God! Maxy, come here! Something's happened!" his mother had yelled.

"What is it?" As Max ran out the front door, he saw the answer to his question as the words left his mouth. "No, Mom! Move it forward! Move it *forward*!" he yelled at his mother. In her panic, she backed up. He ran to the car, opened the driver's side door, and pushed his mother into the passenger seat, her face in shock. He took the wheel and eased the car forward as if navigating an especially large speed bump.

"Are you okay?" asked Cassie.

Max looked up into her brown eyes as if waking from a dream. She looked sympathetic, as she might if her grandfather had momentarily choked on a bone at Thanksgiving dinner. "Yes, yes, I'm fine." He smiled at her. She bent over to take his glass. She was so close that he felt his heart skip a beat then pound like an explosion—

ka-whoomp—and his breath catch. It wasn't just that her neck was so long and tan, but that she seemed so fresh and new. She was at the sinewy beginning of her life and, like him at that age, didn't even know it.

There were long years in his twenties when he felt like he was walking on an endless beach, the distant horizon never approaching and never receding. Timeless. Although he was a worrier even then, there wasn't any reason to worry in the larger sense: Life was big, fat, and juicy. There was so much of it that you didn't have to worry about wasting a little. That's why it was there. Try a little weed, get a little drunk, have a little sex here and there with whomever and whenever you wanted, listen to some Janis and some Doors and some Jimi, hop in the van and go. What the hell; spend a little time. You've got more than you know what to do with, for chrissakes, so go ahead.

"Can I ask you something?"

"Sure," said Cassie, leaning comfortably on one hip.

"Can I ask how old you are?"

Cassie threw her head back and laughed. She shifted her weight and put one finger on her lower lip, striking a thoughtful pose.

"I'm sorry, I shouldn't have…"

"No, no, no, that's fine," she said, with a wave of her hand. "I get this all the time, though usually the men are a little younger than you." She laughed again, covering her mouth in embarrassment. "Now, I'm the one who shouldn't have said something!"

Max was beguiled. He smiled and hoped she would go on like this, saying whatever came to her mind, laughing however she wanted, just so he could watch.

"Why do you want to know?" she asked, her forehead furrowed slightly, though she continued to grin.

"I don't actually know." He couldn't very well say, "Because I'm trying to save my life."

"Okay. So, how old am I?" She asked, giving him a mysterious, playful sideways look. "How old do you think I am?"

Could this just go on forever? thought Max; it felt so delicious.

"I don't know if I should say." Max hoped he sounded flirtatious, but feared he sounded lecherous.

"No, no, really, go ahead. I wanna know." Her face was broad as the ocean at dawn and just as welcoming.

For a moment, Max couldn't speak. He swallowed. "Well, I would say maybe…nineteen." With that, she broke into snorting laughter, bending over in delight.

"Now you have made my whole freakin' week!" She patted his shoulder. "If I were nineteen, I wouldn't be able to work here." She looked down at Max, a glint in her eye. "You were bullshittin' me, weren't you?"

"No, no, really, I wouldn't do that." Max wondered if he had offended her, if he had come off, after all, as a sad little man trying to coax an innocent young girl into his pathetic lair.

It was quiet. She was still smiling and looking at him, her hands resting on her hips. "Twenty-six. But don't tell anyone, okay? Just let them think I'm nineteen or twenty or whatever. Keeps the tips coming!" She patted his shoulder again and that was it. Max fell suddenly and foolishly in love with her.

"That's not possible."

"Well, it is. I got a birth certificate somewhere to prove it." She raised her eyebrows conspiratorially.

"Well, you look much younger, if that is possible."

"Thank you so much. That's very sweet of you." She waved to another customer at the bar. "Now, turnabout is fair play. How old are you?" she said with a gotcha look on her face.

Max blushed and stammered, not sure he wanted to answer. Couldn't they just continue the illusion that they were just a young man and a young woman talking, rather than a girl being polite to a dinosaur?

"Well," said Max with a chuckle, more guttural than he had hoped. "How old do you think I am?"

"Oh my, you're going to do this to me now, aren't you? I'm terrible at this game." She squinted apologetically at Max and said, "Sixty-two?"

Max felt his insides collapse. There was no pretending, no disguise. Sixty-two was the awful truth.

"Oh no, was I wrong, as in wrong in the wrong direction? I'm so…"

"No, no, no," said Max. "You weren't wrong at all. In fact, you were exactly right." He put his thumb and forefinger together and poked the air as if adding punctuation.

"No. Really? I never get people's ages right." A silence followed, announcing the end of their conversation. "Well, that's okay, you don't look it," she said, patting his shoulder one last time and then darting away like a hummingbird.

Max watched her disappear into the undulating crowd, laughing with patrons she knew well, smiling crookedly at some, as if they shared some fleeting intimacy. He looked at his hands again and slowly closed them, the pain in his arthritic thumbs now so familiar. He leaned back against the booth, feeling the ache in his lower back and right hip. He smiled disapprovingly at himself.

When he stood, the room spun and his legs wobbled a bit, the third beer having done the trick. He bobbed his way through the eager drinkers, seeking solace in the men's room, which smelled like the second floor boys' lav at school. He gazed at his creases in the mirror, turned on the spigot and filled his hands with cold water, then tried to splash some sense back into his face. His eyes, shocked into awakening, looked suddenly alert. He pulled for a paper towel, and finding none, waved his hand in front of the dispenser, hoping that by some magic of technology, the paper would appear. It didn't. "Shit." The water dripped onto his shirt collar as he wiped his face with his hands; he pulled his shirt-tail out to finish the job. "Jesus."

As he leaned into the door, it opened from the other side and a young man with wire rims, a gold stud earring, and an indefinable tattoo splashed across his left forearm, stood before him. The young man stepped back gallantly to let Max pass.

"Go ahead, old timer," he said with a broad grin.

Max flinched and then exited the door. "Thanks." He took another step and then turned to his youthful aide. "By the way, fuck you."

Once outside, Max, disoriented by the late afternoon sunlight glinting off several dozen windshields, tried to locate his car. He shielded his eyes and looked left, then right, noticing only a woman nearby who was also searching the lot. At first he didn't recognize her, but once his eyes adjusted to the glare, he could tell by the shock of red hair that it could only be one person. He looked anxiously for his car, aware of his embarrassing state. As he saw the familiar hood a few rows over, a voice called out.

"Is that you?"

He turned and, with false surprise in his voice, answered, "My goodness, Mrs. Young."

"Mr. Ruth, it is you!" she said with genuine surprise. "Son of a gun."

"Yes, I suppose it is." Max rustled in his pocket for his keys. While it pleased him to run into Mrs. Young, seeing her outside her natural habitat away from the desk and no longer framed by the sliding glass window, he felt unsure of himself and wanted to nod, grin, and slink off to his car.

"Do you come here often?" She crossed the lot to his side. "Oh my, isn't that just about the worst line you've ever heard?" With this, Max stopped his retreat to his car. She gazed at him, her bold, blue eyes shining through her glasses. When he looked at them, he found it hard to speak. He shifted his gaze to her mouth—full, cherry red lips—but, nevertheless, safer than her eyes.

"Well, sometimes, yes, I don't know…"

She went on smiling and talking. Thankfully, she didn't seem to notice his crumpled awkwardness. "I'm waiting for some of the girls from the office. We all left together, but somehow…" She stood on tiptoes looking at the oncoming traffic. "Maybe that's Veronica now." The car passed. "Or not," she said, laughing. She turned from the road to face Max squarely. Her breathless laughter stopped. "How are you doing, Max? When I saw you the other day, I was worried. You didn't look…well, you didn't look like yourself."

Listing precariously to the right, Max righted himself. He narrowed his gaze on Mrs. Young, hoping that whatever came out of his mouth would be coherent. "It is so nice to see you, Mrs. Young. So very nice to see you, I should say. That is what I really meant. It is so very nice of you to be here. Not here in the parking lot. But, here, in general. Where I can see you. Mrs. Young. Constance, actually."

Constance stared at Max, cocked her head, and then poked his arm. "You either conked your head worse than I thought, or someone's been sitting at the bar for a while." With that, she squeezed his arm and smiled.

"Guilty on both counts," said Max, appalled at what kept coming out of his mouth. "I have been here since a while."

"Uh huh." Mrs. Young shook her head knowingly. "I can see that you have."

"Not alone at the bar, though," said Max, in defense of himself. "With a friend."

"A lady friend?"

"Oh, no, no." Max was surprised at how rubbery his mouth had gotten. "Just an old friend. A teacher friend. And colleajjj. I mean colleague."

"That's good. I wouldn't want to think of you sitting there all by yourself. That just wouldn't be right." A powder-blue VW bug pulled into the lot. Constance waved and her friends circled for an empty space.

"Maybe you could come sit with me sometime." Max was surprised by his own words, wondering for a moment if he had spoken them at all.

Constance spun to face him, her mouth half open. "What did you say?"

"Nothing. Really."

"There they are." Constance waved to her friends again, catching their attention.

Max gulped, a half-smile on his face. Was this happening? "Well, I said, maybe you could come sit with me sometime."

Constance's face was a pleasant question mark. She blinked her extraordinary eyes. "Are you asking me out on a date?"

"No, no, of course not. I just thought if you wanted to come here sometime by yourself…and I came by myself…maybe we could sit together by ourselves." He shrugged his sagging shoulders.

Constance didn't speak at first. "Well, that would be…actually that sounds like a lot of fun," she said, her voice rising as she spoke. "I would be glad to sit alone with you. Together." She stuck out her hand. "It's a date."

Max took her hand in his. It was as soft and warm as he had imagined. He had never expected to touch her this way, or any way, for that matter. She shook his hand heartily and said, "Call me," and then turned to meet her friends. She looked over her shoulder at Max, fluttering her fingers at him. She had already looked away by the time he raised his hand.

Chapter 11

Beth closed the door after Mrs. Steiner left and returned to her office. She didn't look at her appointment book. She knew who the next client was. She went into her powder room and sat for a moment before standing in front of the mirror. Her face was slack. There was alarm in her eyes. She turned on the water and cooled a washcloth, then held it gently to her face. Her eyes closed, she breathed slowly, and held the cloth in place until it was warm.

She had seen Mr. Stinson a half dozen times now and each time he had had the same problem. She never mentioned it. After the fourth visit, he had stopped apologizing. He seemed to have accepted Beth's explanation—"It's just something that happens"—even though Beth hadn't. She thought it was unusual. Beth had rescheduled Mr. Stinson's sixth appointment. He left three messages to say he hoped she was feeling better. And when he arrived for his next appointment, he had a brought a potted plant. "Devil's ivy," he said. "It helps keep the air clean. At least that's what they told me." She tried to explain that she didn't accept gifts, but he looked so hurt that she made an exception. "Thank you." She put the plant on the table nearest the front door.

Beth laid the washcloth on the edge of the sink. She pulled the elastic out of her hair and held it between her teeth. She shook her head once; then pulled her hair back again as tight as possible. She took the elastic from her mouth and swiftly wound it around her ponytail several times until not a single hair moved. "You have such pretty hair, Bethy, why do you pull it back," her father often said.

Mr. Stinson's thin, graying hair was brushed briskly back, curling slightly at the nape of his neck. He had narrow eyes, barely visible under bushy brows. He was probably a handsome young man in his day, the residue of his good looks still evident. When he smiled, one crooked tooth gave him a look of youthfulness. He was always polite. He talked about teaching, about his students, his love of American history. He had not mentioned his wife since his second visit and she hadn't asked.

There was nothing out of the ordinary about Mr. Stinson, but, nevertheless, Beth felt uneasy around him. It wasn't anything he said. It was more the way he looked at her, like there was something that he wanted.

Beth heard the door open. "Go ahead on in Mr. Stinson; I'll be there in a minute."

He didn't respond but obeyed. He was always eager to please her, to do anything that might bring a smile to her face or endear him to her in some way. He offered to roll up the linens and towels after each massage or put her oils and lotions in order. She always thanked him, but declined any offer that would encourage him to think there was anything more to their relationship. His pleasantness made her feel guilty.

"Good morning, Beth."

"Good morning, Mr. Stinson."

"Pretty day, isn't it?"

"Uh huh."

"How have you been? Well—I hope."

"Yes, I have been well."

"That's good."

Her father had owned a shoe store. As a young girl she would go with him on Saturday mornings to help organize the stacks of shoe boxes. When customers entered the store, a broad smile would cross his face and he would greet them as if they were the most important people in the world. "It's so good to see you again, Mrs. Nelson." He would ruffle the hair of any child. "And how is Jackson doing today? Have you lost that tooth yet?" She would watch him spin his magic, always making the sale, every customer leaving with a laugh and a smile. "Always remember, Bethy, if you satisfy others, you will be rewarded. It doesn't take much to be nice."

"Can I ask you a question?" asked Mr. Stinson.

"Sure."

"How long have you been doing massage?"

"About five years now."

"You are very good. Your hands work magic, I must say." Mr. Stinson chuckled and then was silent as if waiting for Beth's response.

Beth was nine when she stood at her parents' bedroom door watching her father lying on the bed, grimacing as if in unbearable pain, his fist clenched and moving rapidly up and down under the sheet, his eyes closed, his breathing anguished. At first she was afraid for him and turned away, wondering if she should call her mother; but then she looked through the cracked door again. This time his eyes were open. He looked at her and then closed them again. She watched until his groaning ended with a gasp. He lay silent afterwards as if unable to move. She couldn't understand why he would put himself through such agony. Later he would teach her.

It wasn't until after her mother had separated from her father that Beth, eleven at the time, had said anything. Her mother stared at her blankly. "I'm sorry that happened to you, honey," she said, as if Beth had told her she had fallen on the playground during recess. "But you have to remember one thing." She took a long draw from her cigarette and released a blue cloud into the air above her. "Don't make too big a deal about it. Men want it. And we better give it to them. It's just the way it is. It's not the end of the world. It's not." With that, her mother got up from the kitchen table, put the dinner dishes in the sink, and began washing them. Beth got a towel, dried the dishes, and put them in the pantry.

Beth finished working on Mr. Stinson's calves. "You can roll over on your back."

Beth had her first boyfriend when she was thirteen. Ted was a gawky neighbor boy who had mooned over her since they were in grade school. When he asked her to the eighth grade dance, Beth said, "Okay," not so much because she wanted to go, but because he had invited her.

"Well, I guess it had to happen sometime," said her mother. "Might as well be now." She looked Beth up and down. "For God's sake, you are a woman." She took Beth to the mall the same day. She found a pink, low-cut, chiffon, cocktail dress with spaghetti straps. "Try it on, Bethy." When Beth stood in front of the mirror in her glittering, high heels, her mother said, "Jesus, girl, I never had a body like that."

"How old's your daughter?" said the lady at the checkout.

"Old enough," said Beth's mom. The lady looked at Beth disapprovingly and shook her head.

At home she tried the dress on again and stood in front of the mirror, her mother watching.

"You're gonna be a big hit with all the boys." Her mother shook her head in jealous approval. "They won't be able to get their fill of you. Just you wait and see."

"Mom, stop."

"You stop. Listen to me, because I know what I'm talking about. That Ted of yours? May look like one big, pimple-faced, innocent dope, but trust me, when he gets you alone in that dress, you'll find out he's not so innocent after all. He'll want something from you. And you know exactly what I mean. If you're smart, make him work for it, but in the end, give him what he wants. As long as you've got what he can't live without, you'll have him eatin' out of the palm of your hand. And that's the way you want it." She walked up behind Beth and placed her hands on Beth's shoulders. "They're all like your daddy, honey. You might as well get used to it."

Beth had frowned, her insides twisting. Her mother's face was leathery, her eyes slightly swollen, her hair colorless. "Don't look at me like that, Miss High and Mighty," said her mother. "Just trying to get you ready for what's coming."

She was right about Ted. He practically begged. He smelled like her father. He smelled like Mr. Stinson.

Beth glanced down at Mr. Stinson's face and was startled that he was staring at her, his eyes moist.

"I don't know if I should say this." Mr. Stinson cleared his throat. "My daughter. You remind me so much of my daughter." Beth stepped back from the table, her hands trembling at her side.

95

More More Time

Chapter 12

Beth took the groceries that had been thawing on the kitchen counter and threw them into the freezer. "What do you mean, he said, 'it's not working out'? What the hell are you talking about?" She slammed the freezer door shut. "Seriously, have you managed to lose another job?"

Bob swerved to his right, as if trying to avoid a skidding automobile.

"Well?" she asked.

Bob looked wide-eyed, as if the teacher had called on him, and he not only didn't have the answer, he didn't even know what page they were on. He ran his fingers through his hair and shrugged. "Look Beth, it wasn't the right thing for me."

"Jesus Christ! How many times are you going to tell me that?" Beth ripped the elastic from her hair. "Nothing changes with you, Bob. Nothing."

When Beth had first met Bob, she had been working at the Sea Chambers Inn Day Spa full-time as a massage therapist for almost two years. To celebrate her second anniversary, she stopped at the lobster pound in York Beach to buy some fresh lobster. Behind the counter was a guy she hadn't seen before; he greeted her with a broad and easy-going smile. "I'm Bob, can I help you?" Bob had come to Ogunquit, Maine, on vacation and had never gone back to his home in western New York. He told her that he enjoyed the simple routine of his work, the friendly customers always talking about the weather, the complete lack of pressure. Beth became a regular. After a few months, Bob asked if she'd like to go out for dinner.

He was different than any of the men Beth had known. When asked, he said he didn't know what he wanted to do with his life. But when he said it, he seemed so relaxed and unworried that she thought it was a sign of confidence, rather than bewilderment, uncalculated cool, rather than thinly veiled fear. "There'll be time for that," he said. Unlike Beth, who was always racing towards some finish line, Bob was comfortable stopping to smell the lobsters, at ease with the notion that whatever he was doing now may not be what he would be doing tomorrow.

They dated for three months before he ever touched her. And when he did, he asked if it was "okay." She laughed at this endearing innocence, thinking to herself, *This is new*. She only hinted to him about her past, which he interpreted as her being more experienced than him. Which, of course, was true in every way.

Some men weighed on you and held you down, or held you so close that you couldn't breathe. Bob was light; he didn't impose; he didn't demand; he didn't press or push or grab. He didn't play games, manipulate, worry or obsess. Bob seemed comfortable not having all the answers to all the questions. She loved him for it. She could breathe around him. She could be herself.

In time, though, she found that his lightness of being wasn't because he was a free spirit, at ease with where he was going no matter where it led him. He was light, instead, because he had no direction whatsoever. Bob was like a feather blowing in the wind, turning this way and then that, unable to set its own course. It left her breathless and, at times, lost, and feeling lost, scared.

Standing in the middle of the kitchen, Bob avoided her angry glare. "I don't know what to tell you. I don't know what you want from me. I'm trying my best."

Beth's mouth fell open, words faltering on her lips. They were having this conversation again, the same conversation they had had when he left the insurance job, the mall job, the jewelry store job, all the jobs that weren't the right thing, that weren't the perfect match, that didn't feel right, all the jobs where his best wasn't good enough, and with a shrug of his shoulders, he left for one reason or another. Of course, the jewelry job was a little different. Had he not fucked his boss's daughter, he might be the assistant manager by now. "Jesus Christ, Bob, please tell me that this is not your best." She leaned against the refrigerator and folded her arms, daring him to answer. "Please tell me that you can do better."

Bob took a couple of steps toward her, his arms outstretched. "Look, Honey…"

"Don't 'Look, Honey' me!" She pushed him back against the sink, her jaws clenched, her eyes burning with tears now, not because she was sad or remorseful, but because it was the only way she knew how to respond. And she hated it. She wiped her face roughly.

Beth stepped away from Bob.

Bob looked at her, his face sorrowful, his arms still out, as if he might hold her if only she came near. As always, they moved in synchrony, him approaching and her retreating. Sometimes she let him catch her; sometimes she melted into him, not wanting to face the prospect of being alone. But each time, as she felt them becoming one, the fear of being swallowed up took over, and she vaulted away into her own desperate separateness where she felt safe, if only briefly.

Bob had proposed to her on Ogunquit Beach. She had just started back to work after an emergency appendectomy, Bob having been by her side throughout the ordeal, making soup, folding clothes. To celebrate her being back on her feet, Bob had suggested dinner at the Whistling Oyster on Perkin's Cove and then a walk on the beach.

It was early evening, the light so clear and the air so pure that everything seemed awash with promise. Ogunquit Beach stretched far to the north, disappearing into the rocks some three miles away. To the south, the river, empty now at low tide, was full of vacationers exploring, like astronauts on a moonscape. Bob and Beth stood at the Norseman Hotel watching a man in rolled-up khakis scour the soft sand with his metal detector. They took off their shoes and headed out to the retreating tide. The water was green, the surf white; each wave left behind a crackle of foam.

When they stopped walking, Bob took Beth by the shoulders and turned her to face him. The corner of his mouth was twitching slightly and his forehead was moist.

"Look, Beth, we've known each other for a long while now and, well, I was thinking that, you know I love you very much; in fact I think I'm going to love you forever." He took her in his arms and then whispered in her ear. "I would like to be with you always. Would you, do you think you would...I mean, will you marry me?"

Beth had held him close, saying nothing at first. He was thoughtful, considerate, accepting, gentle. In those ways, he was much like her father, who had loved her more than anyone; more, certainly, than her mother. Her father smiled at her and soothed her and was interested in what she thought and what she did in school. He would do anything for her. Beth gravitated to him, learning to accept the cost, learning to "give back," as her father called it, his hand convincing; his smile compelling.

Bob had stood by her at every turn. Although he hadn't quite found his path yet, he was the kind of man any woman would want. He listened and was considerate. Though he was not great looking, he had a sweet smile. And he was funny. He wasn't controlling; quite the opposite; he let her take the lead in most things. She liked him and thought she could love him one day, as well.

"Yes," she said. It was the best way she could give back.

A fly attacked the light that hung from the kitchen ceiling. Bob took a napkin from the holder and wiped his forehead slowly and then the inside corners of his eyes. He swatted helplessly at the fly. "We need time," he said.

"For what?" Beth was surprised that her voice quavered.

"I'm not sure," said Bob. The fly buzzed furiously against the kitchen window. "I just believe that the more time we have..." His voice trailed off.

"What? The more time we have, what?" Beth sat down at the kitchen table, folded her arms again, and narrowed her gaze.

Bob spoke again, his voice thin as paper. "I keep hoping that with more time, things will work themselves out. That we'll make it through."

Beth pointed at the clock above the kitchen sink. "So, you think the hands on that clock are going to make a difference? Then let's sit here and watch them go round and round until everything is better. Maybe that will do the trick. Why didn't I think of that?"

The veins on Bob's neck flared. "Don't do that."

"Don't do what? Don't be upset?"

"You know the whole thing with Becky was just a big mistake. She didn't mean anything to me. You know that. I would never hurt you on purpose." Bob leaned forward on the back of a kitchen chair, his jaw squared as if trying to sell his closing argument to a skeptical jury. "I never stopped loving you."

Beth opened her hands and stretched her fingers. Her arms limp at her side. "Are you okay?" her father would ask, brushing the hair from her face and taking her chin in his hand. "I didn't hurt you, did I?" he would say gently. Her eyes still closed, she hoped she had been dreaming, Beth would shake her head. He would kiss her cheek. "Remember, this is just between you and Daddy."

Beth's face tightened as she glared at Bob. "That's so sweet," she said. "When you leaned her back on the desk, were you thinking, 'Oh my, I love Beth'? Huh?"

"Goddammit, Beth, why are you doing this? I'm sorry!"

"Don't apologize anymore." Beth's voice was dry, raspy.

Beth looked at the floor in front of Bob and waved listlessly at the fly that was now tormenting her ear. When her father would finish, she would go into the bathroom and wash. She would throw the washcloth and towel down the clothes' chute. Then she would go next door to play with a friend.

"Sometimes you act like you hate me." The skin below Bob's eyes were puffy now.

Once, her friend, Sarah, had said, "You're bleeding," and Beth had called her a liar. When Sarah persisted, Beth hit her and then ran home where she stayed in her bedroom until Sarah's accusation was no longer true.

"But I can't let myself believe it." Bob breathed deeply, slowly as a tight rope walker. "And I won't accept it."

Beth looked up at his face, her expression blank. It had been a long time since she had examined the lines, the contours, the creases, the geography of Bob's face—the face she had always admired for its lack of guile. She felt heaviness behind her eyes.

"You know why I can't believe it?" he asked, as if to no one in particular. "I can't believe it, because I love you. And I can't believe that I would love someone who hated me." The fly circled the room slowly now. The refrigerator motor began to hum, and the sunlight, which had been crossing the floor, was resting on the counter top.

"So, do I hate you?" asked Beth plaintively, but Bob had left the room.

In the drawn, yellow light of late afternoon, Beth could feel the walls closing in. Perspiration ran down the middle of her back and her hair stuck to her forehead. Her heart drummed, and her fingers tingled no matter how hard she shook them. She was breathing rapidly as a newborn. Her legs went soft as she melted to the floor, stretching out on the tile, its cool surface like fresh water. The room began to spin, and she closed her eyes, holding on to nothing, desperate for it to end.

More More Time

Chapter 13

Max stood in the hall outside his mother's room, trying to remember the last time he had gone in. He lay his hand gently on the door, much as he had when she was alive and he was about to awaken her in the morning. He would call to her, and upon hearing her moving and sighing, he would push the door open slowly and peek in to see if she were all right. The door creaked as he opened it today, his shoulders tensing out of habit, though she was no longer there to startle. After his father died, she was an open nerve ending, reacting to anything and everything that seemed out of the ordinary—heavy rain at night, an errant bird hitting the window, the grinding noise of a garbage truck on Monday mornings or the prolonged silence of her son.

His father had worked long days as a copy editor and occasional columnist at the local paper. She volunteered at the nursing home down the street and played bridge with friends. Dinner was always ready at 5:00 p.m. Max's father read the sports page while she busied herself; he never seemed to sit and eat with them. As an only child, Max was an observant boy. By the age of ten, he could count the number of times he had seen his parents touch, their subtle choreography giving the illusion of closeness while maintaining the most exacting distance. They smiled while not looking at each other. They puckered but did not kiss. They reached but did not embrace.

From time to time, his mother took to her bed for days on end, his father explaining that she was "worn out" or "not feeling well" or "just under the weather." His father worked longer hours during these periods, leaving Maxwell to wait on his mother, making her tea and toast, sitting with her while she watched soap operas, adjusting the pillows when her back ached, and accompanying her to the bathroom, waiting outside the door until she was done.

Max was sixteen on the day of his mother's frantic cry: "My God! Maxy, come here! Something's happened!" She sat behind the wheel of the family car, which rested on her husband's chest. He was dead. From that moment on, her love and devotion to her husband, so absent before, grew exponentially as the date of his demise slipped slowly into the past.

Max slid open the closet door, looking for the suit he had worn to his mother's funeral. He took the jacket in his hands and held it to his nose, wondering if the smell of flowers might still be lingering there. "Well, Mother, wherever you are, I hope you are well," he said, laying his hand on the pillow. Max closed his eyes and shook his head slowly as he thought of her tragic end, so bizarre that it made his father's death seem pedestrian. He could still see her lying in the shallow water, crimson billows surrounding her body.

"Jesus. I'm so sorry." Endingtimeendingtimeendingtime.

"That's okay" he could imagine her saying in that breathless, high-pitched whisper that made him clench his jaw.

Years later, when his mother died, he had taken several days off. There were funeral plans and banking concerns and social security issues to address. There were subscriptions to cancel and his mother's oldest friends to notify. There were endless phone calls from stunned friends and distant relatives who needed to hear the story first hand; it seemed so unbelievable. The headstone was already in place, her name having been included when his father died. Only the dates needed to be added. He walked ponderously through these details of an ended life, knowing that her death had not only been freakish, but easily avoidable, and, ultimately, his fault.

Despite the many years since her death, nothing much had changed in Max's life. Time had both passed and stood still, as his days repeated themselves, and the deep ruts of routine became a way of life.

This began to change, though, when he started hearing The Words. They were announcing something, but what? "Shut up!" he would say, sitting on the toilet in the middle of the night when there was nothing to distract him.

"Where are you going, Maxy, that you need your suit?" he could remember his mother asking in his mind.

"Out."

"Out where?"

"Just out."

"Have you met someone, Maxy?"

He hadn't worn a long tie since the funeral, preferring what he believed was the more professorial look of a bow tie. He tied his own for years until arthritis reduced his dexterity, making clip-ons more practical, although less satisfying. He reached into his suit jacket pocket and pulled out a rumpled tie, yellow paisley on navy. He had slipped it off and tucked it into his pocket on the way home from the cemetery, hoping never to need it again. But he was glad to have it today.

"It's not that Gail person, is it? You're not seeing her again? You know I don't like her. Don't trust her one bit. Always around; moving things in my kitchen; touching things that didn't belong to her; wanting you to go places all the time. Keeping you out till dawn, for God's sake. What kind of woman is that? I never slept a wink."

He had met Gail at a school district Christmas party. She was a secretary at one of the elementary schools. Plump was the word that first came to mind when he introduced himself to her over the punch bowl. She was painfully shy, had short brown hair, in a style that defied description. Gail had a gleaming, broad smile, though, and green eyes that completely captivated Max. They stood together by the punch bowl for the rest of the evening. She was going to school at night, hoping to complete a degree in accounting. She lived in an apartment with her Cheshire cat, Archibald, and two goldfish, Thing 1 and Thing 2. She liked her secretarial job mostly because of the kids she saw every day, especially the kindergarteners with their eager yet worried little faces. She cocked her head and listened earnestly when Max talked about teaching and his love of Lincoln. He called her the next day and they went out on their first date the following week. After that, they were together constantly.

"My God, what's wrong with you?" Max's mother had asked.

Max didn't dare tell anyone how much he cared for Gail, least of all, Gail. Yet it must have been obvious even to her. She beamed when he came into her building at the end of each day. They sat in his car kissing like the teenagers he berated for necking in the high school parking lot.

"You carry your weight so well, dear" and "Those cheeks of yours!" were among the kinder comments Max's mother made when finally he dared invite Gail for dinner. "Would you like seconds?"

"God damn you, Mother!" Max had said once Gail was safely on her way home. He went to bed that night fiercely committed to Gail, not recognizing that the high-water mark of their relationship had been reached and that the tide would now begin to slowly recede, so strong was the pull of his mother. In four months, Max's fierceness was gone.

"But don't you love me?" asked Gail, her green eyes moist.

"Yes, of course," Max replied, meaning it as best he could. "It's just that…"

"It's just that what, Max? It's just that your mother can't stand me no matter what I do? Is that it?"

"What my mother thinks isn't important." He turned his head away, unable to face her.

"Then what is it?"

Max let her hands slip from his. "I'm so busy right now, what with the new curriculum and all the mandates coming down from the state. I barely have time to sleep." He looked at Gail; her eyes were searching his. He held her hands again. "Gail, I just think we should take some time." He smiled and squeezed them. "It won't be long, I'm sure."

She stared back, expressionless.

"Biggest mistake of your life, Max," Hargrove had said.

Max lifted his mother's pillow to his nose. The lilac was long gone. The late afternoon sun was warm on his hand. He replaced the pillow and stood, looking at the aging man with the graying goatee in the mirror over his mother's dresser. He was old enough now to be a contemporary of his mother at the time of her death, and yet he felt like a child.

"No, Mother, it's not Gail. It's Constance."

109

More More Time

At least, I hope it's Constance, he should have added. When Max woke up the day after seeing Constance Young in the parking lot of Time Travelers, he wondered if the whole thing had been a dream. He lay in bed reconstructing the scene and trying to remember exactly what he had said and how she had responded. He closed his eyes. He could see himself walking to his car, the heat beating down, when suddenly she appeared, as if from nowhere. She stood so close that he felt himself falling towards her, as if he had lost all sense of balance and yet it didn't matter. He would simply fall into her and disappear, and his life would end with a smile. She spoke. Then words tumbled from his mouth like nuts and bolts from a toolbox. He was horrified until she smiled, and then he realized it didn't matter what he did or said; nothing mattered, because he had entered a paradise called Constance Young.

He squinted, trying to remember what he had said just before she said, "That's a date!" When were they supposed to get together? And where? *My God, is there a chance I missed the whole damn thing?*

Max had a follow-up appointment with his doctor and hoped that seeing her would jog his memory, but when he went to the window to check in, she was at the copier. When the nurse called him, Constance was back at the window, but her head was down.

Max had sat on the red Naugahyde examining table, a long sheet of white paper beneath him, his legs dangling over the side. The nurse came in and took his vitals and then disappeared into the hall. He waited another fifteen minutes wondering what to say to Constance if he saw her when he left. "Hi. I was so drunk at Time Travelers that I don't remember much of anything." He shook his head and took a deep breath, letting his shoulders sag with the exhale.

Dr. Davenport was in a hurry. They didn't talk much. Max assured him there was nothing out of the ordinary going on. Max didn't tell Dr. Davenport about The Words that circled his mind in a continuous loop, awakening him at night, interrupting him while he read the paper, startling him as he stood in front of his class. He also didn't tell Dr. Davenport about the other words, newer words—*that's a date; that's a date; that's a date*—that now preoccupied him, and that competed for his attention with The Words that so often disturbed him. These new words did not result from a fall down the basement stairs. They came from his heart toppling over again and again.

When he walked out of the exam room to the cashier's window, Constance was there, her broad smile awaiting him, her face pink. She was polite and proper. When he handed her his charge sheet, she handed him a small piece of paper in return. "There you go!" she said, leaning forward and looking him directly in the eyes.

He tried to smile, but feared he grimaced instead.

He opened the note when he got into his car. It was her phone number and street address. "I knew I forgot something! Silly me!" it said and was signed, "Constance," in a flowing hand. Max sat in his car for the longest time, reading it over and over again.

Sitting on his mother's bed, he took the rumpled note from his pocket and examined it more closely. He noticed it smelled of roses when he first entered his car. The smell made him sneeze. He held it to his nose and smelled it again. The scent was faint but true. He ran his finger across the signature. *My God, Mother would have hated Constance*, he thought.

"Why would you say such a thing?"

"Because, Mother, Constance is...well, she is vivacious and spontaneous and forward and, I think, a little too scandalous for your taste." He chuckled at this.

It was on a Wednesday afternoon when he finally called her. He remembered that she got home around 4:30 p.m. Max sat at the kitchen table, cell phone in hand, trying to figure out what to say. How should he address her? Constance? Mrs. Young? Should he be formal? Should he be casual? Should he be friendly and familiar? After all, she had already told him she wanted to go out. It wasn't as if he were calling her out of the blue: "Hi, this is Maxwell Ruth, the guy who comes to the doctor's office all the time—thinning hair, glasses, goatee. You are such a friendly person that I thought I'd call you and...Yes, the guy with the zipper scar on his head...uh huh..." There was no way he could make a cold call. But she had invited him to phone her, for God's sake. It wasn't like he was intruding on her privacy. She was probably waiting for his call. It had been a week since she gave him the note. A week! Strap on a pair and do it! She's probably wondering what the heck is wrong with you!

"Hello, uh, hello missus, hello, is this Constance, Constance Young?"

"Max, is that you?"

"Yes, well, I suppose it is."

"How nice to hear from you!"

Max had said everything he had rehearsed and now sat at the kitchen table relaxed as a statue, staring at the floor, and breathing into the phone.

"Max? Are you still there?"

"Uh huh."

"Well, how are you feeling?"

David B. Seaburn

"Okay, I guess."

"That's good."

Max noticed mucous backing up in his throat. He coughed into the phone and stood up from the table. He rubbed his forehead and pulled on his shirt collar.

"Max, are you sure you're..."

Max cleared his throat a second time. He swallowed hard. "Mrs. Young...Constance...I think we're supposed to get together, I mean we're supposed to go out, maybe, if I remember our conversation in the parking lot correctly, although if I'm mistaken, please tell me, because I wouldn't want to make the wrong assumption, I wouldn't want to presume anything, I just thought maybe that was the case after we talked; of course, I could be wrong, it wouldn't be the first time, or the last time for that fact..." Where was Lincoln's eloquence when he needed it? "And if you're too busy or don't want to go out, that's okay, I understand; sometimes we say things, you know, and later we may not even remember what we said..."

"Max?"

"Uh huh."

"I'd be more than happy to go out with you."

And now the day had come. Max stood up from his mother's bed. He held the suit out at eye level. Max brushed the sleeve with his hand, smoothing out a fold. He lay the suit down again and took off his trousers. He pulled the suit pants on, hoisting the waist band up over his hips. He zipped the pants as far as he could, then took a deep breath while trying to join the clasp across his ample midsection. He held his breath a little longer and pulled the zipper the rest of the way. He let his stomach relax slowly, a few inches of which hung like thick meringue over the crusty edge of a pie. He exhaled and smiled at

113

himself in the mirror, feeling as successful as a carnival illusionist. He then took the jacket from the hanger and slipped his right arm into the sleeve, then his left. He knew better than to straighten his back too dramatically. Max took another deep breath and pulled his lapels as close together as possible, hoping to stretch the coat enough to accommodate the single button assigned to the awaiting hole. He struggled breathlessly for a moment until the button slipped reluctantly into the eyelet.

Max allowed his body to settle into semi-relaxation. He looked in the mirror. His lapels bowed like sails filling with a mounting breeze. The sleeves were a little short because of some bunching at the shoulders. He pulled them down to a more acceptable length. He stepped back to get the full picture. Nothing you would see on a Penny's mannequin, but, overall, good enough. He breathed a deep sigh of relief, launching his suit coat button toward the mirror like a rocket bound for the moon.

Jesus.

Chapter 14

The plan for the day was simple: After Hargrove left for work, she would dress, drive to the post office to mail the bills, stop at Wegman's grocery store, and then go on from there to her final destination. As she had anticipated, Hargrove asked her what was on her agenda for the day, but she had equivocated, not wanting to bear the burden of his judgment or his encouragement. She had said, "I'm not sure." After placing a fleeting kiss on her forehead, he left with a frown on his face. And so the day began.

It had been months since she had made plans to go anywhere. Six months to be exact. And those plans had not turned out as she had intended. It had been a Saturday. Hargrove had taken a late afternoon nap. While he slept, Gwen quietly left the house, hoping not to disturb him. She stood in the garage, not knowing why she was there, not knowing where to go. After a short time, she heard Hargrove stomping through the house, the pace of his footsteps rapid and determined. She got in the car and sat behind the wheel. She heard him slide the patio door open and call to her, like she was a lost dog: "Gwen, Gwen!" Then she couldn't hear him. She imagined that he was standing in the kitchen, one hand on his chin, deciding what to do next. She knew that soon he would come to the garage, keys in hand, to begin his search of the neighborhood. And when he did come, she was still there behind the wheel, clutching it, holding on for dear life, tears streaming down her face, not a word of explanation. He said little. He asked her to move over to the passenger side and slid in behind the steering wheel. It was then that she noticed she still had her nightgown on. He was quiet as he pushed the garage door opener, put the gearshift into reverse and backed out of the garage, his eyes glued to the side mirror, ever the cautious driver. Hargrove had never had an accident. Hargrove had never gotten a ticket. For anything.

He pulled to the curb, his foot firmly on the brake, his eyes on the street, and said matter-of-factly, "Gwen, I think you know where we're going." She didn't answer. He said, "To the hospital. We're going to the hospital." She remembered glancing at him. His skin looked like it was sliding off his face. He pulled on one ear and sighed. "I think you would agree that this warrants going to the hospital, wouldn't you?" Gwen looked at her lap and then noticed the slippers on her feet. "I mean, I don't know what else to do at this point."

Gwen looked at the dashboard, noticing a fine layer of uninterrupted dust. Hargrove spoke again. "Do you have an explanation for this?" Gwen reached for the dashboard and ran her fingers across its surface. "Do you at least understand why we have to do this again? Believe me, it's not my first choice, but I don't know what else to do." His voice cracked and he swallowed. He placed his hand on her arm and tried to smile, but failed. She looked at his hand and then at his face, noticing his lower lids and how they pulled away from his eyes. "Gwen, please, do you understand why we have to do this?"

"Yes," she had said, her voice rising in a question mark, hoping she had answered correctly.

Earlier today at the post office, the man at the counter had asked her if she needed any stamps. She thought for a moment and said, "No." Then he said, "You have a nice day now, okay?" as he nodded for the next customer to come forward. His voice was so pleasant that she didn't want to step aside. She wanted him to ask her again if she needed stamps. Maybe this time she would answer, "Yes," and maybe he'd say, "Well, I'm the man to see!" and she might laugh or say something clever, like, "I guess this is my lucky day." The thought of this made Gwen feel more at ease as she left the post office. "There you go," she said, as she held the door open for an elderly man. She felt a surge of confidence for having done something so normal, so simple, so matter-of-fact.

When she got to Wegman's, though, and stood in front of the flower display, orchids in delicate pose, mums, roses, gladiolas, long stemmed daisies, it wasn't just the smell that took her breath away. All the aisles, all the people, all the movement felt overwhelming, as if she stood in the center lane of a bustling highway.

"Can I help you?" asked a woman angle cutting some stems.

Gwen breathed a syllable, but then stepped away. She circled the store aisles trying to look purposeful; canyons of cereal and soup and detergent and potato chips loomed; young mothers with carts full of children navigated corners like seasoned truckers; pleasant grandmothers wearing paper hats and aprons offered samples of cheese and soup and cake. At the café, Gwen caught her breath, ordered coffee and settled into a seat attached to a tabletop, shoppers with their clanging carts rushing to and fro around her.

How her coffee ended up on the floor was a mystery to her. Why a complete stranger came forward to help was an even deeper mystery. Bob was his name. He was solicitous and kind and even gentle in the way he spoke and the way he moved around her and how he made sure that every drop was accounted for, even the few that had landed on her ankles.

She had watched him leave, then sat still as a portrait for more moments than she could recall, as appreciation filled her chest, its intoxicating lightness making her almost giddy with hope. Surely Bob had been sent to her on purpose with a message from the far reaches of the universe: Everything will be okay. Swept up in the high tide of this feeling, she returned to the flower display and bought a mixed bouquet that she carried eagerly to her car. She laid it on the passenger seat and breathed in deeply its radiant sweetness.

Gwen turned on the ignition, put the car in gear, cracked the window for fresh air and pulled out of the parking lot, heading across town to the Willows Cemetery where she and Hargrove had laid Sally to rest so long ago. Sally had always adored flowers. As a toddler, she would bring fists full of dandelions to the back door, awaiting her mother's exuberant praise, a broad smile on her freckled face. "My favorite!" Gwen would cry, pressing the flower heads to her nose and pulling her daughter into her arms.

Even in those years of innocence, Sally was an anxious child, finding it hard to sleep, having difficulty staying for an overnight at a friend's house, uncertain of branching out on her own without the protective arm of her mother around her shoulder.

"I don't know why she worries," Hargrove would bemoan. "She does everything perfectly!"

And it was true. Sally was captain of her field hockey team in high school, president of her class, valedictorian. She was the yardstick by which other parents measured their own children. She was the one that teachers held up as the best of the best, despite her discomfort with the attention.

Yet many were the mornings that Gwen had to cajole, even threaten Sally to get her out of bed for school, so frightened was she of the day and what might lie ahead. Would she give the wrong answer to a simple question? Would she inadvertently sleight a classmate who spoke to her in the hall? Would she miss a note on her violin solo? Would her face break out during the day and the proper makeup be missing from her backpack?

"She's such an amazing kid," her pediatrician, Dr. Allison, would say. "Yes, she can get anxious at times, but look how well she does. At everything! Trust me, most parents I see would love to have a daughter as special as Sally. Even with the anxiety."

Gwen felt embarrassed for even asking Dr. Allison if she thought there was anything wrong with Sally.

"My goodness, Gwen, think about the kids I have in class," said Hargrove. "Even the best of them are slugs compared to Sally. And I don't think I'm being biased. I hear it all the time in the faculty room. Teachers love her. Students love her."

Gwen pulled up to the stoplight, a car gliding to a halt beside her. The driver blew his horn, but she didn't think anything of it. The driver sounded his horn again, this time a little longer. Gwen glanced over and was surprised to see Maxwell Ruth waving at her. He rolled down his window.

"We must stop meeting like this, Gwen," said Max, laughing. "People will talk."

Gwen waved, embarrassed, and laughed. "I guess I have my reputation to consider."

"Good to see you." Max waved goodbye as the light turned green. He turned left. She sat for a brief moment, wondering if this was what it was like to be out in the world each day. Helpful strangers at the grocery store cleaning up your mess. Old friends joking at traffic lights.

Another horn blew. This time a driver behind her leaned hard again and again. Her foot hit the gas and the bundle of flowers rolled off the passenger seat onto the floor. She lurched through the intersection, pulled to the side of the road and reached for the flowers, noticing a broken daisy stem. She re-laid the bouquet gently on the seat and tried to repair the damaged flower.

Gwen recalled a fond memory of her daughter looking out her bedroom window at the yard below. Sally's blonde hair was pulled back in a ponytail, wisps playing at her temples. Her cheeks were round and full, much as they had been since earliest childhood. She sat on one hip, her legs under her and to the side, bare feet resting on the comforter. Her room was piled high with boxes and the dresser was clean and clear for the first time since fifth grade. Her shoes were still scattered about the floor.

Gwen could feel a lump rising in her throat as she stood at the open door. "May I come in?"

Sally turned and smiled. "Hi Mom. Of course. Come in if you can find a path."

"How's it coming?"

"It's coming, I guess."

"Your father put your computer and DVD player in the car and has your bike ready for the rack."

Sally looked at her mother appreciatively, but didn't speak. Gwen sat down beside her on the bed, lifting Sally's legs and laying them across her lap. She stroked Sally's hair.

"What is it, honey?"

"Nothing really, Mom."

Gwen took Sally's chin and gently turned her head. "Honey, this is me, remember? You can tell me."

"I know. It's just that…"

"What? It's just that what?"

"I'm sitting here on my bed looking out the window, and I don't have any idea what I'm doing or why I'm doing it!"

Gwen laughed knowingly.

"It's not funny."

"Oh honey," said Gwen, pulling her daughter to her. "I know it's not funny. This is a big step. I know there's so much that's unknown. And I also know how well you'll do. Things have a way of working out over time. You'll see." She kissed Sally on the top of her head. "I know it absolutely." With that, she hugged her daughter tightly and sighed.

Sally leaned against her mother. "I'm just so tired. Sometimes it's so hard."

Gwen stroked her daughter's arm. A crease of worry settled across her forehead. She tried to remember her own departure for college, but her memory of it was hazy at best. All she could recall was that she had been excited to go and hadn't cared at all about what might lie ahead. She pressed her cheek against Sally's head. She couldn't remember ever being tired when she was eighteen. And yet her daughter's breathing, so deep, so labored, felt old, worn, weary.

"Tell you what. Why don't I make some pancakes? With blueberries, no less." She squeezed her daughter playfully. "How would that be?"

Sally smiled. "That would be great, Mom."

"I'll get started while you finish here," called Gwen from the hallway, but Sally didn't answer. Gwen peeked into her room again. Sally was quiet, sitting, staring out the window once again.

Gwen looked over her left shoulder at the traffic, waiting for an opening. She pulled back onto the road, her hands perspiring as she clenched the steering wheel. The lunchtime traffic was moving at a glacial pace. Her cell phone buzzed and Hargrove's name appeared on the screen. Hargrove would have called home first, before trying her cell. Actually he would have called home three or four times in a row. By then he would have gotten anxious and frustrated because she didn't answer. He would have waited a short while, standing at the window of his classroom, thinking Gwen had returned home and was in the bathroom or had gone out for the mail, telling himself to calm down. Then he would have called again, and when the call had gone to voice mail—"Hi, this is Hargrove and Gwen..."—he would have hung up and slammed the phone on his desk, no longer trying to remain calm. Only then would he have considered calling her cell phone, which, admittedly, she rarely turned on. Gwen reached for the phone on the dashboard and then let it go.

She didn't need to answer because she knew what the conversation would be.

"Gwen? Where are you?"

"I'm out."

"Out where?"

"Running errands."

"You didn't say anything to me about going out today."

Silence.

"Gwen? Are you okay? Is there anything wrong?"

Of course, Hargrove would be suspicious, and for good reason. Any independent move that Gwen made, anything out of the ordinary, might end with a trip to the hospital. This always saddened Gwen, made her hate herself for being such a bother, such a jagged stone in her husband's shoe, such an unrelenting burden. And yet, she also hated him for not trusting her, for always questioning her every move, her every silence, her every unannounced, unscheduled, and unscripted act. She knew Hargrove loved her, feared for her, wanted to keep her alive, and yet sometimes his love made her feel dead.

She was glad when the phone stopped vibrating. If he knew where she was going, what she was doing, he would lecture her about the "risk" she was taking or the "questionable judgment" she was showing or the "bad outcome" that might result from her visiting her daughter's grave, something that any mother should be free to do any time she wanted to do it.

In the years since her death, it was Hargrove who took Sally's clothes to the Salvation Army; it was Hargrove who insisted they remodel her room, replacing her queen-size bed with twin beds for company that never came; it was Hargrove who put the photo albums on shelves in the basement where he insisted they would be more accessible than in their bedroom closet; it was Hargrove who still carried Sally's picture in his wallet yet rarely spoke of her. Gwen accepted that these were "necessary steps in the grief process," as he often quoted from whatever book he was reading on the subject. If Sally was being erased from the world of daily life, Gwen resolved that Sally would never be erased from Gwen's inner world where her sadness enwrapped her like a cocoon, terrifyingly warm and desperately comfortable.

"But she's not there," Hargrove would say anytime Gwen suggested they go to the cemetery. Gwen wanted to answer, "Don't you think I know that? I'm her mother. Don't you think I know that my daughter isn't in that hole, isn't inside the box that strangers lowered into the earth?" But she stayed silent instead. She resolved not to ask and not to tell. She would go whenever her strength allowed for it. He would never have to know.

Over the entrance to the Willows Cemetery was an ornate wrought iron archway with angels and decorative flourishes that said, "Peace To All Who Enter Here." Each time she drove under it, Gwen felt for a moment that she was being cleansed, that every soiled part of her was being washed clean. Willows was a sanctuary within the city. No bustle, no congestion, no vertical lines, just a horizontal plane, dotted with manicured trees, green lawns, and row upon row of granite reminders, silent yet wiser than any visitor.

Gwen drove down Gabriel Way and turned left on Eternity Place. She got out of the car, bouquet against her breast, and walked across the grass to the stone that lay between Higgonbluth and Cruz. Sally Stinson, it read simply. When Gwen and Hargrove couldn't settle on a middle name, they had decided it wasn't necessary. Perhaps Sally could choose one if she pleased. It became a running joke throughout her short life. At one point, Hargrove had convinced Sally that her middle name was Matilda, but because he and her mother worried Sally might hate the name, they kept it a secret. Sally even told her fifth grade teacher. "Isn't that a horrible name?" she asked with a stiff upper lip. She thought for a time that Stephanie might work, but the notion of three s's seemed a bit much. Pookie, Missy, Doodlebug were all early family jokes. In her teens, Petal, Yoga, and Gravel took their turns, though, in the end, Sally stood alone.

Gwen stepped forward. She leaned over and picked up the long-dead bouquet at the base of the stone, and replaced it with the fresh mix of daisies, black-eyed Susans, glads, and baby's breath. She stepped back, staring at her daughter's name. Gwen understood that she was visiting her daughter's dust, the faint remains of a life. And yet she came as often as she could bear. She came because it was the last place.

The wind rose quickly. Gwen folded her arms. After Sally was buried, she often laid awake at night worrying that Sally might be cold, still concerned about her daughter's well-being long after it mattered.

Gwen looked around her. No one else was near. She knelt on the damp ground.

"Hello, honey," she whispered. "It's me."

Hargrove had felt confident that their only child would do well at college. "Best thing for her. She'll blossom. I'm sure of it." Gwen had felt guilty that she hadn't been quite as certain. She didn't want to convey a lack of confidence in Sally. She thought the world of her daughter. She was smart and outgoing and pretty. But she was also afraid. She never used the word out loud, but it was the only one that fit. Sally was afraid of the world, afraid that it might be welcoming, and that she might fail once she entered it; that there was something sinister in the uncertainty that surrounded it.

"That's understandable," Gwen had said. "It's all so new. But look at you. You always succeed." Even now, standing on the green cemetery grass, she wondered if that word—"succeed"—had only added more weight to her daughter's invisible load.

The wind settled and Gwen's shoulders relaxed. She tried to smile as she looked at the stone before her, as if she didn't want her daughter to be worried by her mother's sadness.

Gwen had spoken to Sally one week before they were to pick her up for Christmas break, one day before her first final exam. It was a happy conversation. "Your father and I are so eager to see you. We'll wait to make Christmas cookies until you get home. I'll be at the mall this week. Do you want me to pick anything up for your father? Okay. You think you'll have some time to shop when you get home?"

Afterwards, when she played the conversation over and over again in her mind, Gwen realized that she had been the one who was excited. She had been the one who talked and talked. Sally listened, even laughed a little, but mostly just answered questions when asked. The only time her voice seemed animated was when she spoke of her upcoming exams. What exactly had she said? Gwen couldn't remember. She had been so excited her daughter would be home soon, that the house would be full of her laughter and energy, that Gwen had barely listened to Sally at all.

A man cleared his throat behind her. Gwen turned as he knelt at another grave, swiping dirt from the top of the stone, pulling tall grass from around its base. He looked up and nodded. Gwen nodded in return. She waited stiffly and soon the man stood and walked away.

"There has been a terrible accident," Hargrove had said when he called her that day. The college's Dean of Students had contacted him at work.

"A what?" Gwen had said.

"There has been a terrible accident with Sally, at her school."

An accident? Gwen waited thirty long minutes for Hargrove to pick her up. She wondered what kind of accident it could be. A fire, perhaps. Maybe her dorm had to be evacuated. Maybe she was would have to return to school a week early. God forbid that she was in an automobile accident. Sally had always understood not to go in cars with irresponsible people. She'd promised. But had she meant it? An accident? It was the word "terrible" that made Gwen shudder. It was not the kind of word that Hargrove would use. Accidents could be "a nuisance" or "regrettable," but not "terrible."

When she saw the headlights of his car as he turned into the driveway, something inside her collapsed. And when she saw him step from the car, his head down, she knew what kind of accident it was. His face was torn and twisted as he stood helplessly before her in the kitchen, his large hands hanging motionless at his sides. He looked at her, his mouth half open. He shook his head slowly from side to side. "She's gone."

Peggy was a freshman with glasses and curly brown hair. Gwen and Hargrove had met her when the girls moved into their dorm room in August. Peggy sat in the study room on the fourth floor of Warren Hall. She was bent over the table, her head between her arms, her mother and father comforting her. When Gwen and Hargrove entered the room, Peggy stood up, holding her hands in front of her as if she were about to give a report.

"I'm so sorry," was all she said before her legs gave out and her father caught her.

Gwen sat now on the grass by her daughter's grave, patting the ground with her hand. Low dark clouds rolled slowly in from the west. The late afternoon light turned dusk. She could still hear Peggy's cry as if it were her own.

Peggy told campus police that Sally had been asleep when Peggy left the dorm room for an 8:00 a.m. test. She said they had talked until

2:00 a.m. the night before and that Sally had been worried about her finals, though not necessarily more than usual. "You know, she kind of worried all the time about things; so I didn't think anything of it." She had given Peggy her favorite cardigan to wear for good luck the next day, adding that she could keep it if she liked. When Peggy came back from her test the next morning, a note on the door said, "Please don't come in. Call someone." Peggy assumed it was some kind of joke and unlocked the door. Sally was hanging from the light fixture in the middle of the room. The police said she had used three belts buckled together.

There was a pen and an open tablet on Sally's desk but not a word on the either.

Three belts. Gwen had thought about that for months after her daughter's death. Sally was always a detail person. She never tried anything without knowing exactly how it was going to turn out. She'd go over a pie recipe a dozen times, measuring all the ingredients at least twice before putting anything in the bowl. She had planned this. She had wanted to be sure that it would work, that she would not fail.

When they had talked together earlier that week, was she in the middle of planning? When Gwen was so excited and eager to see her daughter, eager to have her home where she could look at her, eager to see the changes one semester of college can bring, at that moment, had Sally known she would not be coming home? Why hadn't she said something? "Mommy, help!"

A few months later, after they had completed their investigation, the police met with Gwen and Hargrove. They had spoken at length again with Peggy, with other friends who had seen Sally the night before, with a friend who had passed her in the hall that morning after she had showered, and with another friend who had spoken with Sally in the lobby; the two of them had been leaving for class when Sally said she had forgotten something in her room. "No, go ahead," Sally had said. "I'll catch up to you."

"No one noticed anything out of the ordinary," said the officer, thinking that might be a relief. "There weren't any drugs or alcohol in her system. It looks like an impulsive act. Around finals it happens."

Should she argue with the officer? "My daughter wasn't 'impulsive'. She never did anything without a plan; that's who she was; that's what made her successful in everything she did. She never did something on a whim." Three belts.

Hargrove had stepped out of the study room and gotten physically ill. He threw up his emotions before he had the chance to feel them. As a consequence, Gwen had been left to feel everything on her own. And he had been left to look after her, as one might look after a stranger in need. He became her Good Samaritan, but barely her husband.

Gwen closed her eyes and imagined a smiling Sally, her gleaming white teeth and dimpled left cheek, her manicured brows and Roman nose, her shiny blonde hair tucked behind both ears, her head tipped to one side as if to say, "C'mon, Mom."

How could you?

Gwen never asked this question aloud, but it was always there. How could she leave? How could she decide life was not worth living after so few years? Didn't she know there was always light just beyond the dark? Had she not taught her daughter how to hope? The troubles of a single day can't outweigh the treasure of years. Time, my dear child, give it time. But she couldn't. Something inside her had stopped. She believed she had run out of time. And no one was there to argue with her, to stall her, cajole her, trick her into waiting even one more moment; in that moment's time, things might have changed, if only slightly, but enough to make a difference, enough for everything to look more tolerable—gray, at least, rather than black. *Why couldn't you have given it a little more time? Why couldn't you have called me?*

Gwen felt the chill wind crossing the back of her neck again, but she didn't move; she didn't curl her shoulders for warmth or protection. She looked at the old sneakers on her feet, the brown slacks pressed against her legs. She looked at the grass around her daughter's headstone, green, alive. She listened to the distant horns of the rush hour traffic beyond the walls and gates of the cemetery. She held her hands out, palms up, and looked at her bleached white skin, the lines like chicken scratches, the bones visible below the surface. These hands—so useless now. She breathed deep and let her hands fall, an empty calm settling upon her, a calm so empty she could as easily have been dead as alive. She closed her eyes and lifted her head to the sky, listening, hoping.

"Gwen!"

She turned and noticed Hargrove standing by his car, parked behind hers. He didn't wave. He didn't call a second time. He didn't come to her. Gwen turned to Sally and smiled faintly, then stood and walked back across the grass to where her husband waited.

Chapter 15

"Why does it matter?"

"Because it does, Gwen," said Hargrove, hanging his gray herringbone topcoat in the front closet and walking into the kitchen. Cramps tore the muscles of his left calf and thigh. He stood still, watching Gwen, who sat at the table, her coat still on, hair disheveled from the wind. He wanted to reach out and straighten it for her, to make her look proper, to stem the tide of indifference about her appearance that often announced the beginning of a crisis, the signpost at the edge of the cliff. He relaxed his feet and toes and the cramps subsided.

He worried about Gwen every moment of every day. He called her between class periods to see how she was doing, each time hearing the same litany of small fears and miniscule worries that had come to define her life. Someone rang the doorbell but when she went to the door, no one was there. The mailman was late. She didn't know whether to dress and, if so, what to wear. Some days he laid a skirt, blouse, bra, and underwear on the chair beside the bed, hoping to make it easier, hoping she would get started like everyone else in the world, that she would stop this foolish retreat from life, that she would be normal again.

"I'm fine," she insisted. How often had he heard this? "I've never felt better," were her exact words the day he found the empty bottles. He held them in his hands, turning them over and over, wondering what they were, never thinking that she had swallowed them all. When it dawned on him to ask her, he hadn't wanted to offend her by implying she would do something so cowardly, for that is what it was, a cowardly way out. Sally had been a child, really, too young to understand the finality of her decision. But Gwen understood; she was a grown woman who had seen what death by one's own hand could do to those who were left behind. Whatever squeamishness Hargrove had felt about asking Gwen such questions passed in time; questions about living and dying became as commonplace as inquiring about the weather forecast for the weekend. Each moment in time became a yardstick for whether or not there would be yet another.

"There's no reason I shouldn't go there if I want."

"If you want what?" asked Hargrove, his voice crackly.

Gwen raised her head.

"If I want to be with her."

Hargrove stood behind Gwen's chair, placing his hands on the shoulders of her coat, helping her off with it, and as he did so, smoothing the back of her hair. He had loved her long, shiny hair when they had first met, she a nursing student, he a freshly minted teacher, but she had cut it years ago never to let it grow again, a disappointment to him, a practical matter to her as a young mother.

"She's a little timid, don't you think?" said Max upon meeting Gwen for the first time.

"I don't know why you'd say that?" bristled Hargrove. "Anyone would be a little shy around you, for God's sake." Hargrove considered Max's comment further, saying finally, "No, she's not timid at all; she

132

may seem that way when you first meet her, but that's not her; she's actually quite confident once you get to know her."

Max had raised both palms in surrender. "I didn't mean anything. I think she's great."

But Max had been right. Gwen finished nursing school and got a job on the pediatric floor at Strong Hospital. Within six months, she left that position to work in a private pediatric office in the community, saying the atmosphere at the hospital was too "demanding." A year later, she left the pediatrician's office, saying it wasn't for her—too many patients, too little time. Hargrove suspected it was difficult for her to fit in at both places, places that required her to push herself, to be part of a team, things that were foreign to her personality. Weeks turned into months and Gwen's "time off" began to worry Hargrove. She didn't seem bothered at all by not using her education, not being productive. He felt she was languishing, but before he could muster the courage to tell her so, Gwen became pregnant, which quickly became her full-time job and, with Sally's birth, her career.

Hargrove pulled a chair out from the kitchen table and sat down. He swiped a crumb off the placemat and righted the lid on the sugar bowl. He watched Gwen looking out the window.

"I understand that you want to go, to be with…that you want to go to the cemetery. I do. But what I don't understand is why you couldn't have told me this morning that's what you were going to do today. I asked you specifically if you had any plans and you said, 'No'."

"I'm sorry," said Gwen, her lower lip hanging, her hands motionless on the table. "I'm sorry; I'm sorry; I'm sorry. I know that I'm the biggest problem in your life, Hargrove…"

"Don't say that!" Hargrove's voice exploded as he slammed the arm of his chair with his fist. Both were silent after the sonic boom had passed. When he finally spoke it was in a raspy whisper. "You're not a problem. I only ask that you let me know what you're doing. That's all."

Gwen stood, slid her chair under the table, went to the refrigerator, reached for a Diet Coke, lifted the tab, and sipped at it as if it were scalding coffee. "I'm glad I went," she said as if speaking to no one in particular. "I would go every day, if I could."

Hargrove watched Gwen, looking for the odd expression, the out of the ordinary movement, the sudden laugh followed by the sudden tear. Gwen walked back to the table, pulled her chair out, and sat. She took another sip of Coke then placed the can on the table in front of her at arm's length.

"Why, after all these years, do you do this to yourself?"

"Do what, Hargrove? Remember? Why do I remember? Is that what you mean?"

Hargrove caught Gwen's eyes, dark, moist, unblinking, afraid. He leaned forward on his elbows, opened his mouth to speak, then looked down at his hands.

"I didn't tell you this morning, because I didn't know for sure myself. I went to the Post Office, just like you asked me, then I went to the grocery store. I almost didn't make it any further. But I met a stranger there, a young man, who was kind to me."

Hargrove raised his head as he chewed softly on the inner corner of his lower lip. "Kind how?"

Gwen pursed her lips. "It was nothing really. I spilled my coffee, and he helped me clean it up."

Hargrove looked at Gwen quizzically.

David B. Seaburn

Taking a deep breath, she let it out slowly. "I guess it wasn't what he did; it was more the way he did it. He looked at me like I was just a person who had spilled her coffee."

"Of course he did, dear; that's what you were," said Hargrove, accusation in his voice.

Gwen took the Coke in her left hand and sipped again and again. She ran her finger along the side of the can, leaving a trail on the dewy aluminum surface. After setting the can down, she leaned her elbows on the table and rested her head into her hands.

"I mean, you are just a person. Like everyone else." Even as he spoke, Hargrove could hear the awkwardness in his words, words he wanted to believe or at least have Gwen believe.

"Dad, why do you always put Mommy down?" Sally had asked the week before she left for college. She looked at her father gravely, yet tentatively, not wanting to hurt him, but wanting to know. Worse, perhaps, she said it as if it were understood, as if it were something that had been a part of the vows her parents had exchanged on their wedding day: "You will be less and I will be more."

"Whatever gave you that idea?" he had answered. "Tell me one time that I have put your mother down, that I have been anything but kind to her." He looked at Sally, a dare in his eyes, as he reached for her hand. "Look, Sally, don't worry about your mom and me; we're fine. Ask her, if you don't believe me." He pulled his daughter into his arms; she laid her head on his chest. He could almost feel her thinking.

"I guess you are kind to Mom. I don't know."

"Look, sweetheart, maybe you've got too many things on your mind. Going off to college is a big step. That should be your focus. Your mother and I are fine."

Gwen lifted the can of Coke to her lips, but this time didn't drink. She placed it back on the table. Her cheeks tightened. "Let's not tell lies, Hargrove. We both know that I am not like everyone else." She paused as if she were leaving room for him to disagree.

He took a breath but it lapsed into a sigh.

"Today, at least, I felt like I was," she said.

Hargrove pulled the placemat closer, curling one corner, and stretching his leg again to see if the threat of cramping had disappeared. He looked at Gwen, so small sitting across the table with a faint smile, her hands folded.

"I'm glad that you met someone who was kind to you."

"He reminded me of you. When you were a younger man."

The corner of Hargrove's left eye flinched.

"I didn't mean it the way it sounded," said Gwen, glancing at Hargrove, her smile gone. She stood and walked to the counter, rinsed out her Coke can, and placed it in the sink where later Hargrove would remove it to the recycling bin in the garage. "I'm sorry." Gwen crossed the room and stood behind him, placing her hands on his shoulders and pressing gently. He reached up and took her hands in his even as she pulled them away.

"You don't have to apologize." Hargrove felt exhausted, like he was circling the drain.

"I know. I don't know what else to say."

Hargrove felt a ball forming in his throat, a choking feeling that left his insides gasping. He closed his eyes, remembering Gwen as she was when he first courted her, when she was his sparrow, light as air, and he was her nest, her safe place in the world.

Gwen crossed to the other side of the room and stood where the kitchen light shaded her face, giving her a ghostly cast. She leaned back against the counter and cleared her throat. "I only meant that he was kind, like you."

"That's good," said Hargrove, as if he might have been praising a student who had completed a class presentation.

"His name was Bob."

"Uh huh." Hargrove's attention had turned to the evening paper.

Gwen went to the table and opened a pocket in the side of her purse. From it she pulled a card, which she held with both hands, as if it were a gift. "I want to thank him, send him a note." She laid the card on the table and began to leave the room. She stopped, turned, and took a few steps back into the center of the kitchen. "I will try my best to let you know what I am doing, where I am going."

"Thank you," he said without looking up.

"Will you do the same?"

Hargrove dropped the paper to the table. "What do you mean? You always know where I am."

Gwen, stone-faced now, studied her husband. "Do I?" Gwen left the room, heading for the front staircase.

Hargrove sat in the airless kitchen trying to catch his breath. He loosened his shirt collar and wiped his forehead with the palm of his hand. His leg pumped nervously as he labored to understand what was going on with Gwen. He didn't know if he could make it through another episode, another fall into her pit. He could barely keep from falling into his own despair. Did Gwen have any idea how often he drove past the cemetery unable to turn in? How often he sat in his car in the faculty parking lot trying to remember Sally's voice? How often he wanted to share his sadness? How often he wanted to confess his loneliness, his need to be touched, to be cared for? *Is it so bad, what I'm doing? Is it so bad to long for a woman's touch? Is it so bad to want to feel something, anything?* When he looked at Gwen, he knew the truth would destroy her. He knew that some burdens and some lies must be kept deep inside so that no one else would be hurt by them, no one but him.

Hargrove was glad she had gone upstairs. She would stay there the rest of the evening, and he would have some quiet, if not peace. Hargrove picked up the card and stared at the name scrawled in black ink. It was Bob, for sure, but the last name was merely a scribble. He looked at each letter trying to decipher the code, until in a moment of recognition, he could read it.

Hazelwood.

Chapter 16

Constance Young ran her fingers through her red hair, creating the perfect windblown effect. She held the hairspray above her head, a billowing haze filling the bathroom. She stepped back into the mist and waited a moment before touching her hair lightly with her fingertips. She looked into the bathroom mirror, turning her head slowly from side to side and smiled with satisfaction.

She went to the full-length mirror in her bedroom for a more formal viewing, hoping her appearance was neither too-eager-to-impress nor too-casual-to-notice. She crouched to stretch her new jeans slightly, trying to avoid the painted on appearance that would have been desirable twenty years ago, but now might draw stares of concern. The red pumps with tiny bows peeked out from under the hem of her jeans, matching her red silk blouse with its parachute sleeves and tight wrists. She worried that her neckline was too revealing, so she added a single stitch to reassure there was no chance of being overexposed. Modesty about such things was usually not high on her list. Constance, nevertheless, preferred to keep invisible anything that makeup could not hide, unless, of course, revealing oneself was desired; then all bets were off.

There were four tubes of lipstick sitting on the counter in front of her, sleek missiles of explosive color designed not only to accent her full lips but to make a final statement. What would it be? "Keep up the Flame?" "Endless Ruby?" "All Day Cherry?" Or, perhaps, "Reliable Raspberry?" Gerry had always preferred "All Day Cherry," saying it made his mouth water just to look at her. Of course, Gerry loved anything and everything about Constance. Her face flushed, thinking of his appetites. Maybe "All Day Cherry" wasn't the right choice for a date with Maxwell Ruth, who looked like he may have lost his "appetite" long ago. She wasn't sure why he appealed to her, but ever since they first met, she had kept an eye on him. Perhaps it was a curmudgeonly teddy bear quality, so different from her husband, that drew her to Max and freed her from comparisons to Gerry.

The doorbell rang, startling her. She looked at the clock on the back of the toilet. He was ten minutes early.

"Just a minute!" she called out, but it didn't matter. He rang again and again, like a child on Halloween.

Her lips still awaiting a final decision, she ran to the front door.

There stood Max in a suit jacket and open-necked shirt, a pair of trousers that almost matched, a sheepish smile, a bouquet of flowers in his arms. "Hello, I wondered if you would be interested in buying some Girl Scout Cookies?" asked Max, his eyebrows raised in mock seriousness.

Surprised by his wit, Constance burst into laughter. "Well, little boy, if you have Thin Mints, I'll buy ten boxes! Come in, come in, please." She stepped back from the doorway and waved her arm in a welcoming gesture.

Max stepped into the apartment and handed Constance the flowers.

"Thank you!" said Constance, as she drew the bouquet to her face. "Delicious."

"I'm glad you like them."

She looked at him and grinned broadly.

He looked at his shoes. He shuffled a little and looked around the living room.

"Oh my, how rude of me to make you stand here. Please, please come in. I will be ready in a few minutes. Have a seat. Can I turn on the TV for you?"

"No, that's okay. I don't watch much TV."

"Oh dear, me and TV are great friends. If we didn't talk to each other every day, I don't know what I'd do." Max didn't respond and Constance swallowed hard, wondering for the first time if this was a good idea. Having him in her apartment, far from the doctor's office, seemed more than a little odd. There weren't any forms to fill out, no post-visit comments to exchange, no sliding glass window to make their banter easier and briefer. "Well, I'll be right back."

Constance took a long look at herself in the bathroom mirror. "C'mon, girl, focus." She perused the tubes of lipstick again and decided "Reliable Raspberry" would be best. She delicately painted her lips, pressed them together, then kissed a tissue. She sprayed her hair again and stepped in front of the full-length mirror for a final inspection. Though her jeans were a little too tight by her estimation, she wasn't sure it mattered. Her hair looked lush, the lines of her body formed an almost-perfect hourglass, and her heels gave her legs that little extra lift that accented her behind perfectly. "Damn good," she said with satisfaction. On her way out the bathroom, she blew a kiss to the mirror.

In Max's car and on their way, Max gripped the steering wheel like he was trying to choke the life out it. Constance glanced at him, noting his steely gaze at the traffic ahead.

"Crazy, isn't it?" she volunteered.

"Friday rush." He pressed the gas and made it through on yellow, only to brake quickly to avoid the slowing traffic ahead of him. Constance slid forward against her seat belt, placing her hands on the dashboard. "Jesus," said Max. "I'm so sorry."

"That's okay; it *is* a little wild out there." Constance was happy she wasn't kissing the windshield.

"I'll slow down. Don't know what I was thinking. We don't really have to be in any hurry." Max tried on a smile, looking over at Constance for the first time.

When the traffic ground to a halt, so did their conversation. Constance cracked the window to clear the fog that was creeping slowly across the windshield. Max responded by pushing the defrost button. Constance closed her window again, an expression of support for Max's initiative. She looked out the passenger window, and when she turned back, he was trying to kill the steering wheel again.

It had never been this awkward with Gerry. Around him, Constance had felt the kind of emotional safety a woman might only experience once in a lifetime. She could tell him anything and, even if she wasn't always sure what he thought, she knew he was listening and that he cared. "I've been doing all the talking," she'd say. "What do you think?" Gerry would pull her close and whisper in her ear. "I think you are the most gorgeous creature I've ever seen."

"So, are you from around here originally?" asked Max.

"I guess you could say so. I was born in Spencerport, but didn't stay there long. We moved to Ohio, then back again, this time to

Henrietta, Brockport after that, and finally Greece, before my dad got a job in Los Angeles where we really settled in. Got married there, had a son, made some roots. You know the story." She looked at Max, who looked back and forth intently between her and the road ahead.

"Been to the west coast once in my life. San Francisco, but not L.A. A long time ago." Max smiled at Constance. "It was 1967."

"Hmm, the summer of love," said Constance. "I was twelve going on twenty."

"I was a little older than twelve at the time. But not old enough to be out on my own, as my mother explained in no uncertain terms when I got back." Max eased his grip on the steering wheel and leaned a little toward Constance. "It was a great time, though."

"Haight Ashbury? The whole thing?"

"Yep."

"So, tell me, what was it like? I mean, the whole hippie thing," asked Constance, seeing for the first time some dimensionality to her date.

Max's head went back as he guffawed loudly.

"What?" she asked.

"Well, due to smoking a certain something day in and day out, I don't recall much of that summer at all."

"My God, Maxwell Ruth, you mean to tell me you were stoned the whole time?"

"I refuse to answer on the grounds that it may incriminate me. I do, however, remember feeling good."

They were both laughing now. Constance reached over and laid her hand on his arm.

"Wait till I tell the girls back at the office. They will have a whole new respect for you. So, you grew up in the Rochester area?"

"All my life. After college I came back to teach American history. Abraham Lincoln—his life, the war—is my area of special interest."

"So I've heard."

"I'm sure you have."

"The Gettysburg Address, right?"

"Yep." They both laughed. There was a grin on Constance's face. She was happy that there was more to Max than a wound on his head. He was more than a patient who came regularly to the practice. He was a person, real in every way.

"Did you like L.A.?" asked Max, his voice confident now.

"Not so much, really. It was pretty anonymous even then. Nobody seemed to know anybody. Everything about L.A. was scattered. But I have some fond memories. People mostly. I managed to make a few close friends."

"You said that's where you met your husband."

Constance looked away from Max, measuring how much she wanted to say. "Yes, that's where I met Gerry."

Max was quiet for a moment. Constance looked at him, trying to gauge what he was thinking, realizing finally there was no way to know; he was still an acquaintance after all.

"Are you still…"

"Oh, no, no, no. Not in fifteen years," said Constance.

"I'm sorry. I've never been married. I know lots of people who've gone through divorce; it must be very hard."

Constance leaned away, sizing Max up, assessing whether he was someone who would be comfortable with the truth, or whether he would prefer a half-truth or even a lie. She could easily not respond at all, letting the silence be interpreted any way he wanted; or she could thank him for what he said, and in so doing, never divulge whether it applied to her or not. Or, she could tell him.

"We never divorced."

Max looked at her but didn't speak.

"Gerry died," said Constance, the words feeling awkward again, even after so many years.

Max pulled through a light and turned cautiously into the parking lot of an abandoned strip mall. Constance's eyes widened with confusion. He brought the car to a stop, put it in park, and turned on one hip to face her. "I'm so sorry. I don't know what got into me, asking you personal questions that I have no right to ask. I had no idea. Please accept my apology."

"There's no need for you to apologize," said Constance, feeling a tender wave of warmth and curiosity at Max's sensitivity, so unexpected. Max's face looked tattered, weather beaten, vulnerable in ways that his gruff manner masked only partially. "Of course, it was not a happy time."

"Please, you don't have to say more. It's none of my business. I was just surprised…"

"No, that's okay," said Constance. She filled the ensuing silence with a deep breath, then looked at Max, who had not moved a muscle, his eyes resting on her. A half-smile crossed her lips. She studied the dashboard. "Gerry was an account executive with MetLife, and he traveled a lot. I mean a lot; he was often gone all week. But he called me constantly and somehow made me feel like he was there even when he wasn't, if you know what I mean." Constance paused, gathering her thoughts, realizing this was a story she hadn't retold in almost fifteen years. "Well, he was in Chicago, which always made me nervous because O'Hare is so crazy. I was tracking his flight online;

his departure time came and went. I didn't think anything of it, because the airlines are slow as molasses posting new information, but after about an hour, I started to worry." Constance felt heat on the back of her neck. She swallowed and smiled. "So, even though I knew it was silly, I turned on CNN to see if there had been any problems, figuring if there's nothing on the news, then there's nothing to worry about. But, instead, there was a reporter standing in a corn field in Indiana talking about a plane that had gone down."

"Oh, my God," said Max. "I'm so..."

"It was all smoke and just the tail section was visible. On the crawler at the bottom of the screen was the airline and flight number. It was Gerry's plane." Constance looked out the windshield at the boarded storefronts. "It was the strangest thing. I didn't really react. It was like I had gone numb, like I was outside my body watching the TV and feeling terrible for all the families that were getting bad news."

Max gave Constance his handkerchief. She held it in a ball in her hand, not lifting it to her face. Looking at Max, she declared, "This is very embarrassing. It's been so long."

"To lose someone that way..."

"No. Listen. I sat there for the longest time in a daze, wondering why I didn't feel a thing. Then my phone rang and I just stared at it. I didn't want to answer it, because I knew what was on the other end. It stopped ringing and then started again two minutes later. This time I picked it up, and I couldn't believe my ears: It was Gerry. He forgot to set his alarm, he said, and missed the flight. He knew I would be thinking the worst, so he called as soon as he turned on the TV. You know what he said?"

Max didn't answer. Barely breathing, he sat transfixed, his face drawn and sober.

"He said, 'Hello, Constance, this is St. Peter calling. I seem to have found something that belongs to you'. I started wailing like a crazy person. I cried and cried, and he could barely calm me down. It was the single happiest moment of my life. When he hung up, I was floating; life seemed so beautiful and kind." She looked at Max, her face beaming in the dark light of his car.

"My God," said Max, smiling now.

"About an hour later, the phone rang again. This time it was the Chicago police. I assumed they were calling about the crash, figuring that because Gerry's name was on the passenger list, he had been killed with all the others."

"Of course."

"But that wasn't it at all." Constance, her voice suddenly thin and wavering, wiped her eyes with Max's handkerchief. "Turns out that right after our conversation, Gerry left the hotel, probably to get breakfast. A bystander said he was right beside her on the curb waiting for the light to change, when he slipped, and trying to regain his balance, stepped into the street and was hit by a cab. He was killed instantly. The cop said, 'I don't think he even knew what happened'. I guess he thought that would comfort me."

It was dark now. Traffic lumbered along, horns blaring, tense drivers eager to start the weekend. Constance could hear Max's slow, heavy breathing, even though she could barely see his face. "I waited for another call from St. Peter, but it never came."

Max shifted his weight and cleared his throat; he placed one hand on the steering wheel and the other on the keys; then let both hands fall onto his lap. "I don't know what to say. Would you like to go home?"

Constance sat up straight in her seat, took a deep breath, shook her hair, and laughed. She opened her purse. Reaching for her

147

compact, she turned down the visor in front of her and clicked on the light, quickly reapplying her makeup and adding another layer of "Reliable Raspberry." "Now, Mr. Maxwell Ruth, I really think that what I need is a drink. Maybe two. And I don't want to drink them alone." She reached for Max's arm, squeezing it with her left hand.

Five minutes later, Max was standing on his tiptoes trying to get the attention of a hostess who was talking excitedly with some regulars. Constance looked around the crowded room, country music booming overhead, the smell of jeans and perfume in the air.

"Wow, things are really jumpin'. Wasn't like this when I stopped by with the girls," she said, looking at Max approvingly.

Max waved in the direction of the hostess.

"Wouldn't have thought this was your style, Max."

"Oh, a friend of mine and I have been coming here since long before it became Time Travelers. Back in those days, it was the Hideaway, and that's exactly what you got, a nice neighborhood bar where you weren't bothered by anyone or anything. Now, you've got all this to deal with." He waved his arm above his head and nodded at the twenty-somethings posturing at the bar.

"I love the energy!" Constance swayed to the sound of Lady Antebellum. "The place has a great vibe."

"I guess you could say that." Max scanned the room for a waitress, his face turning red, giving up. "I guess I'm invisible," he said to no one in particular. He smiled a moment later when his favorite waitress waved to him and crossed the floor to where they were standing.

"Hey, Max, right?"

Max smiled and straightened his shoulders, as if trying to add another inch to his modest frame.

"Mr. 'Guess-my-age'." she confirmed.

"That's me, all right," he said, awkwardly proud. "Constance, this is Cassie, who is much older than she looks." Cassie laughed at this. "And Cassie, this is Constance."

Constance squinted at Max, as if she was seeing him in a new light.

"Pleased to meet you, Constance," said Cassie.

"Likewise."

"Follow me; I'll squeeze you in."

"VIP, huh?" offered Constance.

Max beamed.

Cassie led them to a corner booth, wiped it briskly with her towel, laid down napkins and silverware, and looked at Max, a finger resting on her chin. "Let me see if I remember. Sam Adams, right?"

Max chuckled as Constance slid into the booth. "How do you do it?"

"Just one of my many talents," Cassie said breezily. "And for the lady?"

"Chardonnay?" Constance replied, studying Max's maroon visage closer.

"Chardonnay, it is. I'll bring you some chips and salsa, too."

Constance watched Cassie glide across the floor, her hair bobbing as she went. She was almost afraid to turn her attention back to Max, who was sitting quietly with his hands folded.

Constance pursed her lips, reached across the table, and placed a hand on his. "I can see the headline tomorrow: 'Man Runs Screaming From Bar After Crazy Lady Harangues Him With Tale of Woe'. Really, I am so sorry; I don't know what got into me. I haven't told that to anyone in such a long time, not even to the girls at work. It seems so pathetic in a way. I don't know why it came out."

Cassie leaned over the table, sliding their drinks onto coasters, setting chips and salsa in between them, leaving a few extra napkins on the side. "Anything else for now?" Max shook his head. "Enjoy!" she said and was gone. Constance withdrew her hand from Max's, curling her fingers around the stem of her wine glass. She looked at Max again, still unable to read his face.

He looked at his drink and then spoke, murmuring at first and then clearing his throat. "It's not pathetic at all, what you told me. It's awful. It's sad. And I'm sorry that someone as nice as you had to go through it." He drew a finger across his greying mustache, as if to halt the trickle of his words. "Life's like that, I guess. The very best moment of your life, followed by the very worst."

"Thank you, Max," said Constance reaching across the table again and patting his hand, Max twitching his thumb against her palm in response. "But, you know, time marches on, as they say; there have been other moments. I have a wonderful son and daughter-in-law and an absolutely precious granddaughter." Max raised his eyebrows in surprise. "I know what you're thinking. Oh, my God, I'm on a date with a grandmother! Not exactly what you were expecting, is it?"

"My grandmother wore thick stockings, practical laced shoes with squared heels, and calf-length house dresses. Trust me, you don't look like any grandmother I've ever known."

Constance leaned back, laughing. "That may be the sweetest thing anyone has ever said to me."

Max lifted his beer. "To grandmothers everywhere."

Constance clinked her glass to his. "To grandmothers." Max took a long draw from his glass and then another. He raised a napkin to his chin and then sipped again, smiling now and looking pleased with himself.

"So, Maxwell Ruth, now that I've told you the most awful thing that has ever happened to me, it's seems only fair that you tell me some dark something about yourself." Constance grinned playfully and tipped her glass to Max. Max had a mouthful of chips and was chomping as fast as he could. "Just kidding. Really, that was the wine talking," said Constance, suddenly self-conscious. "You don't have to tell me anything."

Max swallowed, cleared his throat, and said, "My mother was eaten by an alligator."

More More Time

Chapter 17

Max held his breath, wondering what Constance would say.

"I think we have a winner! Wow, that must have been something," said Constance, giggling. "What did your father have to say about that?"

"Not much. He was already dead by then." Max was surprised how easy it was to talk with her. "My mother ran over him with the family car."

"Don't you hate when that happens?" Constance took another sip of her wine. Max lifted his beer and took another pull, examining Constance's face over the rim of their glasses. He placed his glass on the table again and watched her expression.

"Max?" she asked, more soberly.

"How are you two doing?" interrupted Cassie, brightly. "Can I get you another?" Both Max and Constance raised their glasses. "All right. Be back in a jiffy." Max and Constance watched as Cassie walked away.

"You're kidding, right?" Constance asked, leaning forward, apologetically. "I mean. You've *got* to be kidding."

Max began with the Readers Digest version of his father's demise.

"Oh, my God, you weren't kidding! And you were just a boy! And your mother? What happened to her?"

"After Dad died, my mother fell apart. Not in a way that others noticed; in fact her friends thought she was doing quite well. But she lived with me, and I saw it every day: the mornings she couldn't get out of bed, the nights she cried herself to sleep, the times I found her talking to my dad as if he were still there. She clung to me like I was a life raft, even though I felt like I was sinking. She'd ask, 'Maxy, can you ever forgive me?' every day. When I'd walk into the house from school, she'd say, 'Please forgive me'. It just about drove me nuts. Then she decided I was going to die next, that every time I left the house I wouldn't return. After my dad, it was like the world was coming to an end in slow motion." Max paused and grimaced. "I don't have to bother you with all of this. We're supposed to be having a good time." Constance didn't respond, her eyes steady, inviting him to go on.

"I went away to college, which almost killed her, but I had to get away. To be honest, I never felt so free. I didn't write her; I didn't call. I left her letters unopened for weeks at a time. I'm not proud of how I handled things, but, what can I say, I felt like I was dying."

"Here you go," said Cassie, placing their drinks on the table. "Anything else for now? More chips and salsa?" She turned away before they had a chance to respond.

Max's chest felt tight. He didn't want to keep talking, but now that he'd started, he didn't know if he could stop. He looked at Constance, who was still leaning forward intently. She looked shocked, as if watching a train gradually derail.

"So, sparing you some of the gory details, I ended up moving back in with my mother shortly after I started teaching. I wanted to save some money, and I also thought my being there might calm her

154

down. Maybe she'd start acting normal again." Max dipped a chip into the salsa and slid it into his mouth. He pulled at his coat lapel, stretched his arms, and coughed into one fist, the chip having gotten briefly lodged.

"And?" said Constance. "And?"

"Next thing I know, I'm forty-seven. I'm forty-seven and I'm sitting across the kitchen table from my mother, a lopsided chocolate cake between us, three candles lit to honor the past, present and future, and I realize that there is no going back to 'normal', that normal had left town long ago. In a way, she'd been right."

"What do you mean?" Constance moved her glass onto the Corona coaster that Cassie had left behind.

"When Dad died, she acted like the world had come to an end. I tried to convince her that that was not the case at all. She would rebound; life would go on. But, you know what? Time may have passed, but life never really went on. The world as we had known it had ended. We were just waiting for the headline to appear in the paper." Max was hearing himself say this as if for the very first time. He sighed and leaned back in his booth. Cassie came and went again. Constance took a chip and dipped it in the salsa, but then laid it on her plate.

"Alligator?"

"Alligator. For my forty-seventh birthday, my mother arranged for us to take a trip to Florida. To Pompano Beach. This came as a complete surprise to me. It would not have been my choice of how to spend my spring break, but she was so excited that I couldn't say no. I could tell she was trying to make amends, trying to thank me for everything, I guess. I don't know."

There was shouting at the bar as two men chest bumped and a gaggle of young women howled. Constance picked up the chip she'd put down and placed it in her mouth, then brought her glass of wine to her lips.

Max frowned into his beer. "Anyway, she didn't feel well after the flight, and we laid low in the motel. But when I woke up the next day, she was dressed and ready to go. She had made plans for us to take a boat tour of Miami. Even I thought this would be fun. So while I jumped into the shower, Mom walked to a nearby Seven-Eleven to buy some snacks. It must have been two blocks at the most."

Max stopped, took another long drink, then leaned forward, and, with a low voice, continued. "So I'm getting dressed and there's a knock at my door; when I open it, two cops are standing there, one holding my mother's purse. Turns out that on the way to the store, she walked past a golf course where an alligator came out of a water hazard and attacked her. Passersby tried to help her, but there wasn't anything they could do; the alligator pulled her into the water, where it finally let go after a foursome of golfers beat the animal with their clubs. By then, though, it was too late. She bled to death before the ambulance could get there."

Constance reached across the table and took Max's hand. "Oh, my God, that's horrible!"

"It was on CNN. It made both Leno and Letterman. I guess one of the golfers complained that he had broken a new driver. Worse, despite the efforts of an alligator rescue team, the alligator ended up choking to death on my mother's leg."

"What?" Constance covered her mouth with her hands.

"When the local paper reported the story, the headline read, 'Big Al Meets His Match'. Turns out the alligator was a local celebrity. He lived on the fifteenth hole and golfers believed it was good luck to have a Big Al sighting. The clubhouse wall was full of framed pictures of golfers posing with Big Al." Max paused and dipped another chip into the salsa. Constance's face seemed frozen behind her hands. "A few members held a wake in his memory." Max looked at Constance who didn't appear to be breathing. Tears, however, were running down her cheeks. "Constance? Are you okay?"

She shook her head 'no', unable to speak.

"Constance?" Max reached for her hand, but before he could touch her, she erupted in gales of laughter. She took breath after breath trying to control herself, but to no avail. She laughed so hard her face turned red and her nose ran though her eyes puddled. "That's the saddest..." but she couldn't speak. She tried again. "That is so awful..." but she began to snort. "Oh, my God! I'm *so* sorry."

Max watched, expressionless while she wiped her eyes.

"Oh my!" Constance exclaimed as she rifled through her purse, searching again for her compact. "I mean, couldn't they at least have also had a wake for your mother?" she asked, trying to force a sympathetic expression onto her face.

"Yes, that would have made all the difference...even a double wake would have been nice." Max grumbled, the grumbling turning into a low chuckle.

Constance, relieved, reached for Max's hand, then began to laugh again. Max turned his hand over so that his palm met hers. "Oh, my God, Max, that is awful. I'm so sorry I laughed. I don't know what got into me."

"I'm impressed that you're not overburdened with sensitivity." Max was grinning widely now.

"What a way to end," said Constance, her voice velvety low. "I can't imagine…"

"Neither can I. Choking on an old lady's leg is an awful way for an alligator to die."

Constance tilted her head to one side, but didn't laugh this time. Instead, she squeezed his hand, then released it.

Max paused, basking in the warmth that was left behind.

"My God, Max, that must have been horrible, really, and it came at such a bad time. Not that there would have been a good time, but after so many years, it looked like maybe things were about to change for you and your mom, you know what I mean? And then this totally crazy, random thing happens. I mean, an alligator?"

"A taxi cab?" replied Max.

"Yeah, really."

"If you think about it too much, it makes you a little crazy. I mean, mostly life is pretty steady; it moves along in an orderly way, everything in its place, everything mostly okay. It's like you don't have to think about it much at all. It's just there. And then, out of the blue— Boom!—the whole thing blows up in your face; someone loses his balance and steps off a curb, or a goddam alligator attacks your mother. All of a sudden you see how fragile the whole damn thing is, and you think, 'Jesus! Wake up, for chrissakes! Pay attention! This is important!' But you don't, you know? Pretty soon the routine takes over again, and whadaya know, you're back where you were to begin with; nothing has changed; you're sleepwalking again. You're acting like you have all the time in the world. Then, the older you get, the more you understand that's not the case at all; you come to realize everything comes to an end and you panic a little, thinking, 'What have

I done with my life? I need more!'—more time, that is—like that's going to protect or save you somehow. I don't know."

Max's glasses had slid down to the end of his nose. His forehead was damp and his hands were clasped together on the table before him. He pushed his glasses back up the bridge of his nose and looked at Constance, whose face was hidden in a shadow outside of the dim light of the bar. He opened his mouth to speak again, but then stopped. He had spoken without thinking; he had said all that had needed to be said for so long. He was, after all, a simple history teacher whose time had passed.

Max's head buzzed with The Words, taunting him with their repetition. He could ignore them for short periods of time, supplant them with other sounds and distractions, endure them, but never completely eradicate them.

Constance's expression was strangely calm, her face full and warm back in the dim light surrounding them; she gazed steadily at him without judgment. Should he tell her? If he did, what would she think? What would she do? If he didn't tell her, what then? What was left? Max took a deep breath and straightened his back. He leaned forward, about to speak, only to be relieved of the responsibility by Constance.

"My granddaughter is five years old. Her name is Elena, and when she was about eighteen months old, she loved to play this made-up game with me whenever I came to visit. She would lie on the hardwood kitchen floor at my son and daughter-in-law's house and ask me to pull her around the floor by her arms. She'd laugh hysterically as she swished back and forth, around and around until my arms felt like lead. When I was completely out of breath and ready to drop, I would say, '*One* more time, Elena', but she thought I was saying '*more* more time'. Soon that's what she thought the name of the game was, so when she'd meet me at the door, she'd flop down on the floor and yell, 'More more time, Grandma, more more time!' She couldn't get enough of that game."

Max raised his eyes and spied at Constance's smile across the table. She took her glasses off and laid them in her lap, her blue eyes deep, the corners crinkled. She looked down at her glass and then up again at Max.

"We're like her; we never want the game to end. More, more time is what we all want. If only my husband had lived longer. If only your mother had lived longer. What? What would have been different? I don't know. Once I accepted Gerry's death, I swore that I would never again expect anything to last forever, that I would never again pretend that there would always be more, and, you know what, every once in a while, I can do that, and when I do, life's a little sweeter."

For a brief moment, Constance looked like a school girl, her eyes relaxed and wide, unassuming, genuine. In her presence, Max felt the molecules in his body separate just a little, as if he was becoming a vapor, a mist, ephemeral, floating, all lightness.

"Constance Young," he said, feeling himself coming together again, everything settling back into place, only differently. "Could I interest you in another glass of wine?"

"Yes, Maxwell Ruth, you could."

Chapter 18

It was almost 6:00 p.m. when Bob rolled the lawn mower out of the garage, removed the gas cap, and slowly tilted the nozzle of the gas can into the miniature tank. It was the one thing Beth had asked him to do, something he had forgotten during his long hours hunched over the computer looking for a job, filling out applications that he then sent into the void. Did he really want to be a fast food shift supervisor or a high school custodian or a used bookstore cashier? Or did he want to "pursue an exciting career" in customer service?

"I am trying," he said to Beth that very morning.

"Uh huh."

"I'm telling you there's nothing out there, Beth."

She looked right through him. "There's always something out there. If you want it enough."

"Maybe that's it, Beth. Maybe I haven't found what I want. I don't know anymore. I feel like I'm spinning my wheels doing things that don't matter. Maybe I'm tired of doing things that I don't want to do?"

Beth had chuckled at this, her hands on her hips. "My God, Bob, all you ever do is what you want to do."

Bob wanted to say, "The only thing I ever did that I wanted to do was marry you, and look what that got me," but he thought better of it.

"I need time, Beth. I need more time to figure this whole thing out."

"It's not rocket science, Bob. Get a job."

Bob looked up from the mower as a car rounded the bend. He was relieved it wasn't Beth. In recent months, he was often relieved it wasn't Beth. Especially since she had found out about Becky. He pulled the mower cord three more times. "Jesus Christ," he said, shaking his head in disgust.

Becky was about twelve years younger than him; she had long brunette hair, parted in the middle, with red highlights; her eyes were jet black; her smile was marked by a chipped tooth that made you look at her face just a second or so longer. She had a high-pitched laugh that some thought annoying, but Bob found enticing. When she walked by, nothing moved, everything was taut, everything was firm. And, yes, she was the boss's daughter. That should have been a large enough No Trespassing sign to keep him away, but it only made him want her more. He was attracted to her from the moment he saw her in the office, filing orders, making copies and answering the phone.

But he was attracted to lots of women. Nothing wrong with that. Even Jimmy Carter—a president, and a Christian to boot—admitted lusting after women in his heart. Surely Bob was not expected to exercise greater self-restraint than a former president of the United States of America. As long as he didn't act on anything, there was no harm, no foul. There were no such things as thought crimes, not as yet. Anyway, he knew for a fact that Beth looked at other men. She as much as admitted it after she saw their new doctor for the first time, Dr. Davenport. "If all doctors looked like him, waiting rooms would be overflowing with women needing checkups of a certain kind." They both had laughed when she said this, and Bob even found it a little titillating to think Beth might be having sexual fantasies about another man, something that benefited him the next time they made love.

He never worried about Beth being unfaithful. Before Becky, Bob would have said the same thing about himself. He was pleased with his marriage, though at times Beth's nagging was depleting. But he figured every rose came with thorns, and, to him, Beth was as sweet a rose as he had ever seen. When he got to work on the day of his first transgression with Becky, if asked, he would have said he was happily married. He would have said the same thing after he and Becky had had sex the first time, too. Nothing changed the way he felt about Beth.

Becky was just so…available. Bob closed his eyes, remembering in detail that day. It was 5:15 p.m. and everyone had gone home. Bob was finishing some paper work when he went into the main office to find a stapler. Becky was there, all alone, sitting on the desk, her legs dangling, spread slightly. He couldn't help but look. Their eyes met and she smiled. "You're welcome to take a closer peek, if you'd like, Bob." She had flirted with him before, as had he with her, but she had never been so explicit. Part of him kept saying, 'No, no, no', but the rest of him wasn't listening. The result was a new found, though ill-advised, boldness. He laid her back on the desk.

When the stupidity of what he had done jump-started his brain again—"I was out for two seconds and look what you've done! What the fuck!"—he felt so guilty that he fled the office without saying another word. "Bye," Becky had called as she fished her panties out of the wastebasket.

On the way home, he vowed that he would never do anything like this again. Never! And while he was thinking about it, maybe he would turn over a new leaf entirely. Maybe this was the time to start being a better person in general. Maybe he would start going to a local church, synagogue, or mosque. Maybe even go to confession (Did he have to be Catholic to do that? He'd have to look it up). Maybe some volunteer work, some community service. Maybe that would do it. Two hundred hours? No, too much; it wasn't like he was a drug dealer or something. Maybe ten hours. He would be a changed man. Maybe a couple of hours at a food kitchen. Or picking up trash along a country road. He liked the outdoors.

Two days later he and Becky were perched on the sink in the men's room. The following week they were in the backseat of his car. Then her car, which actually was her father's car. Then in a motel room in the city. Then again on the desk in the main office, which was where her father found them.

When he came home that day and told Beth that he had lost his job, he had explained that it was because of the boss's daughter; she didn't like him for some reason. Beth stared at him while his face turned a dozen shades of red. When she asked what really happened, and he stumbled like a child and began to cry, she knew.

He didn't tell her how many times he had had sex with Becky, because he was afraid she'd leave him. Maybe even kill him. His fling with Becky was never about wanting to leave Beth. He loved Beth. In a sense, he thought of himself as faithful. He hadn't been looking for someone else; he hadn't wanted a relationship. But it was something that had happened. Becky was so... Jesus, Becky was so wild, so uninhibited, so exciting; being with her was like being in suspended animation; everything else fell away, leaving only a scintillating sensation that he could not resist.

When he saw how much it hurt Beth, it was easy to promise her he'd never do it again. She was too important; their life together was all that really mattered. But in the aftermath he missed that feeling he had with Becky. He missed being able to escape from everything, being able to take, and take, and take some more, never having to worry about giving. With Beth, it always felt like he was auditioning, but never getting any word back about how he was doing.

His head down, the whir of the mower engine in his ears, Bob hardly noticed that the sun had set. He was almost finished with the front yard when Beth's car rounded the bend. He turned the mower off and pushed it under a tree. He waved into the headlights, smiling, pretending that she might be waving back. He took the mail from the box as Beth disappeared into the garage, the door closing behind her.

Once in the house, he called to her, but Beth had already gone upstairs to shower and change. He sat at the kitchen table and read the sports section of the paper. Then he rifled through the usual array of bills, stopping at an envelope that was addressed to him. He looked at it, turned it over, shook his head, not knowing who it might be from, and then tore it open. He read it slowly, still confused, but then began to smile.

"I ate a late lunch, so I won't be having dinner." Beth entered the kitchen wearing a robe, her hair still wet, her feet bare.

Bob looked at the note again, and then dropped it on the kitchen table, got up and walked slowly into the family room where Beth was wincing, stretching her neck from side to side.

"Is there anything wrong?" said Bob.

"The usual."

Bob joined Beth on the couch, sliding in beside her carefully.

"Hard day?"

"Yeah."

Bob could not remember the last time he had asked two consecutive questions without it leading to a fight. He plunged on confidently.

"Getting more patients?"

"Clients."

"Sorry, clients."

"Yes. Suddenly. And not sure why."

Bob stared at her face, more full than it had been in years past, and yet beautiful for the perfect turn of her nose, the gentle arc of her chin to her neck.

"Maybe because you're so good."

"Maybe." Beth leaned back and put her feet up on the coffee table. Bob leaned back, as well. For a few moments, they were any couple anywhere watching the evening news together, looking, to a casual observer, like a portrait of a healthy marriage.

"I'd be happy to give you a back massage if that would help." Bob spoke tentatively, almost apologetically.

She looked at him for several seconds, expressionless, before responding. "Okay."

He spread his legs out and she sat between them on the couch. Bob placed his hands on Beth's upper back, pressing and rubbing gently. He couldn't remember the last time he had given Beth a back massage. Bob pressed more firmly, and Beth leaned back against his hands. He curled them around the muscles in her neck and shoulders, kneeding the tension, the tightness, the tiny knots that had accumulated there. She exhaled and bent forward slightly, elbows on her knees.

"Here, let me do this; it will be easier to get at things." He lowered her robe so her back and arms were exposed. Beth's skin was milky white, firm, smooth. He focused more intently on the muscles around her shoulder blades.

"It's a bag of knuckles in there," he said, a smile in his voice.

Beth did not respond.

Bob ran his fingertips down her rib cage to her waist and then pressed his thumbs into the small of her back.

She exhaled heavily.

Bob eased his palms up the ridge of muscles along her spine until his hands were under her arms, his fingertips near the base of her breasts, feeling the silken bra. He slid his fingers further, massaging gently, until he held both breasts in his hands. He rotated his palms slowly, then undid the front clasp of her bra, her breasts relaxing into his hands, her nipples firm. Bob then reached between her legs with one hand. He kissed her back, then laid his head on her warm skin.

"I love you," he said.

Beth stood and turned to face him, letting her robe drop to the floor, slipped off her panties, and knelt before him. She unzipped his jeans and unbuckled his belt, then straddled him, settling onto his lap as he gasped, "Beth, I love you."

She looked at him, her eyes fierce and swallowed hard. "You do?"

"I always have. Nothing else matters."

"Really?"

"You know I do. You have to believe…"

Beth pressed down hard, moving her hips back and forth, side to side.

"I thought this was the only thing you really loved." Beth stood suddenly, wrapped her robe around her and headed toward the kitchen.

More More Time

Bob pulled his pants up and called, "Beth, come on!" When she didn't answer, he went into the kitchen where he found her reading the mail on the kitchen table.

Her hands shook as she raised Gwen Stinson's thank you note and peered at the handwriting.

Chapter 19

Gwen Stinson guided her Honda Civic carefully, slowly, through traffic, ignoring as best she could the honking of frustrated drivers sweeping by her whenever they had the chance; most glanced back menacingly, as though she had murdered someone. For several weeks, she had made it a daily ritual to take the car out and "give it a run" as she would say, much like the owner of a new dog. She was gradually pushing the limits of her world, adding new streets, neighborhoods, and suburbs, even parts of the city, enjoying the freedom afforded her by merely holding onto the steering wheel and following her nose. Hargrove didn't know the extent of these explorations. Since his outburst over the cemetery, she had decided that her outings were a private matter, best kept to herself, much as she believed Hargrove kept certain matters to himself, such as meetings that never occurred, concocted school commitments that were always "really nothing," and, more recently, regularly scheduled absences that were never explained.

She never had reason to suspect Hargrove of doing anything out of the ordinary. On the other hand, she had never looked closely. Until now. Those silly boxers, for example. His evasiveness about his own comings and goings. Small things to be sure, but each telling in its own way. He was always just beyond her fingertips, just far enough away to appear present, while being completely absent, unknown, unknowable.

Despite the stress, here she was out and about in her car on a regular basis, enjoying new adventures. And it was all because of that most innocent of things, her most innocuous of encounters with that young man, Bob Hazelwood: the momentary kindness of a stranger when she had least expected it, a kindness that, when juxtaposed with the chill of Hargrove's caring, seemed monumental. She tried to minimize it, to put it in its proper place as a mere nothing among the millions of brief encounters one might have in a lifetime, and yet it would not go away, it would not let her be. More to the point, she would not release it; instead she cultivated it and created from it a reason to come out of her shell into a world she barely knew. How could a moment of kindness counter what felt like a lifetime of grief and loneliness? The moment she stopped trying to answer the question, she began following the quickening of her heart.

Hargrove's white Chevy Impala sat in its usual spot in the faculty parking lot. Gwen parked in the adjoining student lot on the opposite side of a Camaro. It was nearing 4:30 p.m. He had told Gwen he was meeting at 4:45 p.m. with a community group that was interested in the Revolutionary War and whether Castlewood had played a role of any kind. Although it was unlikely Castlewood had been on the forefront of the revolution, beyond sending its boys and men into battle against the British or the Indians, he was, nevertheless, happy to meet with them, he said. Community outreach was an important function for district teachers; it might influence the local citizenry when they went to the polls each year to vote on the school budget. "Maybe this will get us a much needed raise," he joked.

He'd placed a sheaf of papers in his backpack when he left for school in the morning, notes, he said, he had made for this occasion. When she asked where the meeting would be held, Hargrove cleared his throat and fumbled with his papers. "At a church, I believe; I left the information on my desk; I'll have to check when I get to school."

Gwen watched as teacher after teacher trooped out of the building and the lot slowly emptied. Finally, Hargrove and Max came through the exit, engaged in conversation of "some import," as Hargrove was fond of saying. They stood together in the middle of the lot, gesticulating like two puppets on the end of invisible strings. Max appeared none the worse for wear, despite the tumble he had taken. Gwen had called him to convey her sympathies, but Max had not answered his phone. She settled on a well-worded phone message, letting Max know she was thinking of him and that if he needed anything, to let her know (she knew he wouldn't). Much to her surprise, Max had called some weeks later to thank her, and in his awkward, throat clearing way, ask how "life was treating" her. She had said, "fine," understanding that his having asked the question was not so much an invitation to reply at length, as it was an expression of thoughtfulness, something he had in full measure. Such was Max, misunderstood by students and others, even Hargrove, who often complained about Max's negativity, his narrow-mindedness, as if Hargrove were immune to such character flaws.

From a distance, Gwen measured Hargrove, an impressive figure even in later age. His straight back and square shoulders, always at attention, as if ready at a moment's notice to salute or march or do whatever might be expected. As a young woman, she had seen in him a pillar, someone who could not and would not falter, no matter life's currents and storms. Always attentive, but never one to show affection, he gave her a daughter, despite his reticence about having children. He confessed he never pictured himself a father, yet he clearly loved Sally more than he had ever loved anyone else, even if he did so in a watchful way, overseeing her as a shepherd might a sheep.

They never spoke of her first pregnancy, the one that had brought them together, the one that had preceded Hargrove's gravely sincere proposal of marriage, the pregnancy that had ended almost as soon as the words had left his mouth, the one she knew he had wondered about all their married life, as if it might have been a hoax, a ploy. Yet, having proposed, having spoken the words and taken the vow, Hargrove honored them, because that is what one was supposed to do. Gwen could see glimpses of that honorable man across the parking lot, standing in the fading light, his head wagging slightly as he listened to the shorter Max, who presented him a thin smile and stiffened sadness along his forehead.

She could not remember when exactly she and Hargrove had stopped loving each other. It was easy to think of Sally's death as their death, too, because in so many ways it was, and yet the death of their relationship had come sometime before then, not as an event, but as a slow viral process, almost invisible. They had done nothing to treat it, but had accepted it as the reasonable outcome of all that had happened. They had walked down the lonely years, both of them neglecting what life had given them: the chance for an intimate relationship with all the possibilities that come with it.

Max and Hargrove shook hands, then leaned into each other for a masculine half-hug. Both took to their respective cars, Hargrove blinking the right of way to Max, who pulled out, Hargrove following close behind, each turning in opposite directions after they left the lot. Gwen started her engine and eased onto the road behind Hargrove, staying at what she thought was an inconspicuous distance. He did not take the on-ramp which would have led him home, but instead continued on for a few miles before turning into a small plaza. He parked between a pizza parlor and a hair salon. Gwen drove past the plaza and entered a gas station where she pulled off to the side and watched. Hargrove sat in his car, headlights off, foot on the break, for five, then ten minutes. Discomfort stirred inside Gwen for doubting her husband, for suspecting him, for needing proof.

"My God, Gwen, there is nothing to explain," he had said emphatically. "There is *nothing*. Do you understand?"

When he said these things, Gwen watched him more than she listened to him. He had a habit of biting his lower lip and rubbing his thumbs against the inside of his forefingers when he was stretching the truth to make a point, or when he was giving an answer even when he had none. So there he stood, biting and rubbing, the falseness of what he was saying betrayed by the truth of what he was doing.

Yet she hoped she was wrong. Perhaps he was getting his hair cut. Perhaps he was waiting for a pizza to bring home as a surprise. He was known to do that, bring something home for dinner that she liked, something they could share together in front of the TV before he retreated to his room to work.

The brake lights finally went off and his car door opened. Hargrove stood in the dark for a moment and then walked to a storefront and entered.

Gwen was startled from her spying by a knock on her window. "Hey ma'am, anything wrong?" said a young man, wiping his hands with a greasy rag. He motioned with his arm, signaling her to open the window.

"I'm sorry. Am I in the way?"

"Oh, no," he said. "I thought you might be having a problem, since you've been sitting here for a while."

"No, no, everything is fine. I'm just waiting. Is that all right?"

"No problem, ma'am. Wait as long as you like."

Gwen smiled and looked across the street to make sure that Hargrove's car was still in the plaza lot.

"I'm sorry to bother you," said the young man, broad smile on his face, ball cap turned around on his head. "Are you waiting for someone over there? Is there some kind of trouble?"

"Oh no, no, nothing like that." Gwen turned to face the young man more squarely. "There is something you could do, though."

"Shoot."

"That place over there," she said, pointing.

"Antonio's?"

"No, the place three doors down. Do you know what that is?"

"I'm pretty sure it's one of those massage places. I think it's called Serenity or something like that. I see the woman coming and going a lot. She's even stopped here a few times. Blonde, very nice lady. My boss said she's a masseuse; I'm not exactly sure." He shrugged and rolled his eyes at the word masseuse.

Gwen squinted and her mouth crinkled. She looked at the young man and then across the street again.

"Is there anything else I can do, ma'am?"

"No. But thank you."

As the young man went back to the station, Gwen studied the scene across the street. Hargrove was not the sort of man who liked to be touched, at least not by her. He rarely undressed in front of Gwen. He bathed in private, the door always closed. From the beginning, even when they were dating, they always made love in the dark, the covers up. In those days, she half-joked that if she hadn't felt him inside her, she wouldn't have had any proof that he had a penis. Hargrove did not see the humor. Even when they embraced, it was as if he put his arms around her, but did not hold her. She had convinced herself over the years that this was normal, that his modesty was a virtue that she must learn to accept despite her own need to be touched, to be caressed.

She pulled her car slowly into traffic, through the intersection and into the plaza parking lot, and eased past Hargrove's car, parking in front of the door where he had entered. There was soft light in the window. Gwen sat for several minutes. What had seemed like a reasonable thing now felt foolish, small, even deceitful. Even as she thought this, she opened the car door and walked to the entrance.

Gwen leaned in the front door.

"Hello?" she called.

No one was in the tiny waiting room. She entered and closed the door quietly; the smell of incense and the tinkling of distant chimes filled the room.

"Hello?" she said again.

There were three straight-backed chairs and a wall rack full of magazines. She walked across the room and peeked into the adjacent office, but no one was there, either, so she went back to the waiting room and took a seat. That was when Gwen noticed a third door, and this one had light under it.

She walked to it and whispered, "Hargrove?"

She listened but could not hear a thing. She stepped back, unsure of what she was doing, and yet, more than anything, wanting to know what was going on. She stepped forward again, pressed her ear against the door and closed her eyes as she listened. She could hear the murmur of voices.

She held her breath and opened the door. A pretty blonde woman stood by a table full of lotions and creams. The man, sprawled out motionless on his back on the massage table, a towel over his lower body, an arm across his face, didn't even notice Gwen's entry.

"Hargrove?" asked Gwen.

The man on the table lifted his arm, a look of confusion crossing his face. "Gwen, my God, what in the…"

Gwen smiled at the blonde woman and reached out to shake her hand. "Hello, I'm Gwen Stinson, Hargrove's wife." She turned back to Hargrove who had covered himself with a sheet and was struggling to sit and put on his pants.

"Gwen Stinson?" the woman half-asked, half-acknowledged.

Gwen looked back at her, this time sizing her up from head to toe. "So, he has been coming to see you. For massages."

The woman stepped back, placing a hand over her mouth in surprise.

"Gwen, I can explain," said Hargrove, but Gwen didn't look at him. "It's not at all what you think."

"And what is it, Hargrove, that you think I think?"

Hargrove fell silent, the skin on his stomach and chest becoming mottled. Gwen waited for an answer, feeling a hint of disappointment at what she had discovered. "How long have you been coming here?"

"I don't know exactly. What does it matter?" Hargrove's jaw stiffened. "Let me get dressed so we can go home. This is ridiculous."

The blonde woman reached out to Gwen but didn't touch her. "I'm so sorry, Mrs. Stinson, if you thought…if you got the wrong idea.

I know when some people hear the word 'massage' they think something else…This is not that kind of place. I'm not…"

"Gwen, I come here to relax a little, to settle my nerves," said Hargrove.

"I'm sure it settles your nerves, and I'm happy for that. But don't kid yourself; you come here because you no longer want to come to me."

Hargrove's shoulders sagged.

"It's not the kind of thing you would admit to me. I understand. You don't have to. I know. I suppose I've known for quite some time. Even though neither of us wanted to admit it."

Gwen looked icily at the blonde woman. "And what is your name?"

"Beth."

"Beth, I don't know how long he's been seeing you, but I can assure you that this is the most intimate thing he has done in years. I suppose you meet a need. Something I can not," adding, "and perhaps no longer want to."

Gwen could feel her legs weaken, her knees buckle slightly.

Hargrove reached out to steady her. "Gwen, please. Look at you."

She pulled away from him. "Beth, I don't know if he has told you anything about me…"

"Not really."

"But he has taken care of me for a long time. So well that after a while I couldn't take care of myself. That should feel like love, shouldn't it? But it doesn't." Gwen glanced at Hargrove.

"Gwen, please stop. Let's go…" Hargrove took her arm.

"I don't need your 'help'," she she said quietly, but distinctly. "I need something else. I need your love." She laid her hand on his chest. "But both you and I know that is something you can't give me."

"Gwen, please, this is not the place or time…"

"Hargrove, surely you understand, there is no other place and there is no other time. This is it." Gwen's legs steadied. She took deep breaths, trying to relax the knot in her stomach.

Hargrove stood behind the table now, covering himself as best he could with his shirt and trousers, his face drawn and gray, his eyes hollow. Sadness gripped her as she searched his face for the person she once knew. How much of their marriage had been a performance, scene upon scene, the curtain never falling, stuck together on a stage they had built unwittingly, playing roles neither had wanted, but neither could reject. Until now.

"Gwen, let's go home. I can explain everything. This is a big misunderstanding. Really."

Beth tried to speak and then stopped and tried again, but nothing came.

Gwen's gaze at the two was unwavering. She had crossed over to a place from which there was no return, and having reached the other side, she felt unexpectedly strong. Her voice was matter-of-fact, her words precise. She smiled at Beth, seeing in her something familiar.

"Can I tell you something?"

Beth froze, not knowing how to respond, but nodded reflexively.

"I don't know if what I say will mean anything to you, but I want to say it anyway." Gwen's shoulders relaxed. She took another deep breath and let it slowly out. "Don't wait. For anything. I thought I should wait for so many things in my life. I thought I should wait for love. I should wait for Hargrove to want me. But waiting killed it."

Gwen swallowed and swept a tear from her eye. "And no matter how much you may want to, you can't go back to change it. To change anything, really. Once gone, it's gone. Go forward, if you can. It's the only direction left."

"Gwen?" begged Hargrove. "Gwen?"

"Mrs. Stinson, I'm so sorry. I never..."

"Good-bye," Gwen said and turned towards the door. Looking over her shoulder at Hargrove, whose body looked like a willow, hanging lifelessly, she commented, "And good-bye to you, as well, Hargrove."

More More Time

Chapter 20

Not only had Gwen Stinson taken all the air out of the room when she left, she had taken Beth's breath away as well.

Beth stood beside the table, unable to move, staring blankly at Hargrove.

Hargrove slumped back onto the table and lay there, equally immobile, while his color slowly returned, shade by shade. When he finally sat up, he smiled sadly, but did not speak. He stood slowly, not covering himself with the modesty he displayed in previous visits. His exhausted body appeared even more marked by age.

Beth looked away while Hargrove started to dress, then looked back at him, studying this man she had touched, but knew not at all, a stranger like most of the men in her life.

"Gwen is still my wife," he said pointlessly. "I am sorry that she came here, that she disrupted your workplace, that you had to hear all of that." Hargrove kept his back towards Beth.

"You needn't apologize. Your wife, she did whatever she felt was necessary, whatever was right for her."

The music hovering in the background, the sound of chimes once so soothing, felt like clutter, like noise. Hargrove looked cold, his skin goose-bumped and raw. He quickened the pace of getting dressed while Beth removed the sheets, tossing them into a large wicker basket in the corner. Hargrove Stinson was taller than she realized. She continued watching him out of the corner of her eye, seeing loss in his every movement.

"I'm sorry, Mr. Stinson. Hargrove. I'm sorry that you are going through this. I'm sure it's painful." Beth could see that Hargrove wasn't every-single-man-she-had-ever-met. He was a unique individual with a story she would never know, someone who had gone down a road that was as full of triumph and disappointment as she could imagine. She breathed deep, the smell of her father somehow dissipating.

"We had a daughter. I guess I told you," said Hargrove, looking at the wall. "Her name was Sally." Hargrove turned to Beth, leaning as if to take a step. "I suppose I should go now."

Hargrove reached for his coat, draping it over one arm. He smiled at Beth, reached for the door, opened it, then walked into the waiting area. He stopped and looked around, then went to the front door.

Beth followed.

Hargrove paused, turning to say goodbye.

"What happened here?" asked Beth.

"I don't know exactly." He looked askance at Beth and then put his coat on. Turning again to face her, his lips pursed. "Good bye… Beth," he said with finality.

"Good bye, Hargrove."

Beth put the magazines back in their rack. She straightened the chairs and picked up a gum wrapper from the floor. She went into her office and erased all of Hargrove's upcoming appointments from her calendar, then dropped the pencil on the desk and leaned back, breathing slowly, pulling the hair away from her face. She bent forward, placed her elbows on the blotter, and looked into a small mirror tilted against a coffee mug. The face staring back's eyes were filled with tears. She thought about what Gwen Stinson had said.

Picking up the mirror, she held it closer, examining every detail of her face, every line, every wrinkle. She looked at the worry in her eyes, the exhaustion, fear, and sadness. She looked at her skin, once so smooth, a child's skin turned old so early, so young. She looked at her mouth, the corners down, the lips dry. She looked for the little girl that she once was.

Beth laid the mirror on the table face down, and buried her face in her hands, then pulled them away and sat up in her chair, back straight, chin raised. She reached for the elastic in her hair and pulled it out. She shook her head, her hair loosening to her shoulders.

"No more," she whispered.

More More Time

Chapter 21

Gwen stood in front of Hargrove's closet, examining the old, tweedy sport jackets and button-down cotton shirts, short sleeve no matter the season, the handful of pullovers that she learned not to buy for him once she realized they never left their hangers, the plaid work shirts he liked to wear when he puttered in the garage or backyard, the Buffalo Bills sweatshirts, the long forgotten paisleys, the belts, all black or brown, the ties of varying width.

She laid five pairs of Dockers on the bed: black, navy, green, and two tan. He preferred tan above all because, in his words, they made him look "younger." He didn't wear wing-tipped shoes or knee-high black socks or white shirts or striped ties. He'd lengthened and shortened his hair and sideburns according to fashion, though never obviously so, not wanting to seem like he was paying attention to such things, though he always was.

Unlike his good friend Max, Hargrove never railed against aging and yet in every way he fought a guerrilla war against the passage of time. He took forgotten skin moisturizers and toners from Gwen's cabinet and kept them on his shelf behind the English Leather that he stopped using years ago. He was nice to look at, Gwen had to admit, like an oil painting that had never quite dried.

She pulled his Nikes and a pair of Timberland casuals from his shoe rack; she took several pairs of argyles, crew and V-necked tees, along with some underwear from his dresser. The whites were all gone now, replaced by colorful boxers and sleek, thigh-length silks. She folded them neatly and placed them with everything else on the bed, which looked like a display of assembled evidence from a crime scene.

She found the old Dopp kit Hargrove had bought years ago for a trip to a teacher's conference in Atlantic City. Inside there were Band-Aids, a pack of gum, a glasses kit, as well as an ID badge on a long, red lanyard. She added his shaving soap and mug, a razor, floss, toothbrush, and paste. He could buy whatever else he needed.

She got a zippered bag from the guest bedroom for Hargrove's sport jackets and packed the rest of his clothes neatly into a navy blue duffel bag. She remembered to add the biography of Jefferson that he had been reading. Another man of secrets. He wouldn't need the reading light that he used each night until Gwen was sound asleep.

She checked each bag one last time and then brought the duffel and the Dopp down the stairs, returning for the jacket bag. She placed them all on the kitchen table; then got the local white pages out and looked for the number.

"Hello, I'd like to make a reservation…one person…one night to start…uh huh…non-smoking, please…a queen will do…no, not for me, for someone else. Yes, his name is Hargrove Stinson…late arrival…credit card…Visa…" Gwen wrote down the confirmation number. "No, he won't need directions. Thank you."

Gwen stood for a moment in the kitchen, the house quiet except for the grandfather clock in the hall that they had bought on their fifth anniversary. In the drawer under the telephone, she found a pad of paper and wrote a brief note to Hargrove, then attached it with tape to the handle on his duffel bag. She put the pen and tablet back and leaned against the kitchen cabinet for a moment as if re-gaining her balance. *Was this really happening?* Her left foot found a loosened tile, one of a dozen they had talked about replacing in the years since Sally's death; one of the many things that had lost its importance, one of a litany of things that sat waiting, things that, left unattended, had slowly fallen into further decline. With her toe, she moved the loose tile back and forth, click-click, and then walked away.

Gwen carried Hargrove's bags to the garage, setting them side-by-side in the empty space that awaited his car. She hugged herself in the chill air and then turned back to the house, locking the door behind her.

Gwen sat on the love seat near the window of their bedroom, the lights out, watching the street for Hargrove's car. She glanced around the darkened room, taking in its silence, its calm. She had sat in her car for several minutes crying after leaving Hargrove and the woman, Beth. Then, almost as quickly as they had begun, the tears stopped; she wiped her eyes and took a deep breath. She sat for several more minutes trying to think of what to do next. Above all else, she didn't want to be sitting in the parking lot, a jumble of emotions, when Hargrove came out. It would be too easy for him, the stalwart comforter. She'd be the weakened bird with the clipped wings, and he the noble one. She had to leave before he emerged; she could not be found wanting.

Gwen stopped at the gas station to thank the young man who had been so considerate.

"You're very welcome, ma'am. I hope you found what you were looking for."

Through the lace curtains, Gwen watched Hargrove's car inch down the street like he was looking for an unfamiliar address. He stopped one house before theirs, parked briefly at the curb, and then pulled forward and into the Stinson driveway. In her darkened bedroom, she listened for the rumble and squeal of the garage door opening, something she waited for each day, initially hopeful, then disheartened. The car stopped halfway into the garage, the parking lights flicked on. Moments later, she heard him, luggage in hand, open the rear door and tossed the items into the back seat. She imagined him opening the driver's door and standing in the soft light, surveying the garage as if it were the last time, a persistent ding, ding, ding reminding him that the key was still in the ignition.

In the garage, Hargrove put his hand on the hood of the car and looked down at his distorted reflection. He then stepped back from the car and closed the door, walked out of the garage and started up the front sidewalk.

Gwen's heart skipped. She stood and began pacing the room. She came back to the window and looked down at Hargrove who now was standing below her at the front door. She walked to the hall balcony overlooking the entryway and listened for a key in the lock, or a knock on the door, or the Westminster chimes of the bell. When she heard nothing, she went back to her room and looked out the window in time to see Hargrove walk back to the garage, back his car down the drive, and pull slowly away.

Gwen collapsed onto the love seat, and began rocking back and forth, her arms gripping her stomach as if her insides might fall out. After a moment, she steadied herself. "Stop it, Gwen," she said in a gentle whisper. "Stop it right now."

Standing slowly, as if testing the strength of her legs, she let her arms relax to her sides. She walked into the bathroom and ran cold water into the sink. She held a washcloth under the spigot and raised it to her face, wiping slowly. Pulling the cloth down from her eyes, she studied her reflection in the mirror, gradually lowering the cloth until her whole face, clean and unmade, filled the glass, her eyes wide, her jaw firm.

More More Time

Chapter 22

Today was the day. Max's appointment with Dr. Davenport wasn't until 9:00 a.m., but he decided to leave a little early so he would have time in the waiting room to consider what he wanted to say. His awkwardness increased as he drew closer to the office. He thought about canceling at the last minute, but reminded himself he had to go through with it.

He and Constance had spent almost every evening together, going to movies or out for dinner, or just sitting in front of the TV leaning against each other, sometimes holding hands, sometimes more. They ate a lot of chips and dip, drank a lot of wine, kicked off their shoes, and behaved like an old married couple in every way except one.

Finally, one night after watching Casablanca, they found themselves in bed together for the first time, but despite considerable effort, they did little more than sleep, something they both blamed on the two bottles of Chianti they'd consumed. Max, however, remained unconvinced by this explanation, worried that years of coital neglect were the true culprit, he of the "use-it-or-lose-it" school. To address the dilemma, Max had decided he needed the magic blue pill. All he had to do was see his doctor.

He had put off thinking about this appointment, hoping that each succeeding rendezvous with Constance would make such a medical consultation irrelevant; but sadly, their efforts in bed had only underscored the necessity of a doctor's visit. Recently, to his horror, he found that being together "in that way" only made things worse, despite the fact that most of his daily thoughts about Constance were accompanied by an embarrassing quickening below his belt.

He arrived at Davenport's as the office opened. He nodded to Marcy who was sitting at Constance's station, and then he slinked to a far chair behind by a partition. He peeked around the corner to make sure that Constance wasn't there yet, then picked up a *Sport Illustrated*, leafed through it quickly, tossed it onto the seat beside him, and leaned his back against the wall, closing his eyes and listening to The Words.

When Max had come to see Davenport about the fall down the basement stairs, he had been worried he was losing his mind, and that if he had told his doctor about what he was hearing, he would be sent to the far end of the hospital that Gwen knew so well. A lot had happened since the fall, and Max still didn't know why he was hearing The Words or what, exactly, they meant. Rather than being an apocalyptic warning shot across the bow of his existence, however, he had come to wonder if perhaps they were merely sounds, meaningless syllables, the product of his dysfunctional inner ear. So why had he not told Constance?

"Mr. Ruth," came the call, startling Max out of his reverie. He stood, answering "Here!" like a student on the first day of school. He came around the partition only to find Constance sitting at the window. She smiled and cocked her head to one side, pinching her eyebrows together as if to say, "What's up?"

David B. Seaburn

"Hi," said Max sheepishly, struggling to come up with an acceptable lie. "I'm...er...it's just a follow-up visit, that's all. You know, have to make sure all the marbles are still in the right place."

"You didn't mention it," said Constance, concerned.

"I meant to, but it slipped my mind."

"You're sure it's nothing more?"

"Yes, yes, everything's okay." Satisfied that he had passed the test, he changed the subject adroitly. "I'm surprised to see you here. I thought you were going to the outlet mall today."

"Plans fell through," she said, her mouth turning mopey. "But at least I get to see you."

"Mr. Ruth!" came the call again; this time the nurse had a stern look on her face.

Inside the exam room, the nurse asked Max curtly to disrobe and put on the pale blue paper gown she placed on the examination table. She took his blood pressure and pulse in silence. "You're elevated today; sometimes seeing the doctor does that," she offered.

Max didn't respond.

"Okay, then." The nurse left the room.

Max rolled the gown into a ball, threw it into the wastebasket and sat dismally on the exam table.

Dr. Davenport knocked as he opened the door. "Haven't seen you for a while." He shook Max's hand and then pumped the Purell dispenser on the wall before taking his place in front of the computer screen. "How's it going? How's your head?"

"Fine, I'd say."

"Good," said Davenport, still studying the screen. Having completed his review, he turned back to Max. "So, how can I help you? The problem sheet says you wanted to 'talk privately with the doctor'." He tilted his head forward, looking over the top of his glasses. "You're not pregnant are you, Max?"

"How did you guess?" Max forced a chuckle.

"Years of training." Davenport listened like an obedient spaniel to an overhead page, then continued. "Okay, so really, what's on your mind?"

Max took a heaving sigh and rubbed his hands on his pant legs. He got off the table and sat in a chair opposite Dr. Davenport. He pressed his elbows into the armrests and leaned forward. "You know I'm not a young man…"

"You're plenty young, Max; don't kid yourself."

"Okay, but in some ways, I'm not so young anymore. I'm older or more mature, whatever you want to say, and consequently, I'm not exactly the same in some ways; I can't do exactly the same things that I used to do, at least not as easily, and sometimes not at all. I mean I don't have the same…I don't know. Some things are more difficult than they used to be, you know. I never had problems before. I mean when I was a young man, believe me, no problems at all. I could tell you stories; but now I'm finding that I do. Have problems, that is. Or one problem, anyway." Max's explanation was as clear as an impressionist finger painting. He looked at Davenport hopefully, who curled forward, placing his hand over his mouth. "Max…?"

"I mean, maybe I haven't, you know…it's like when you don't use a muscle for a long time…"

"Yes, I think I get the picture," said Davenport leaning back now in his chair. "Let me ask you something."

"Okay."

"Is there someone in your life?"

"I think so."

"You think so?"

"No. I mean, yes, there is. Recently."

"Okay. And are you having problems in the bedroom department?"

"You mean in bed with her?"

"That's the idea, yes."

Max breathed hard through his nose, his lips tight. "I guess you could say that."

"Difficulty getting or maintaining an erection, I would assume."

Max nodded his head barely an inch.

"I feel confident we can help you with this. It's not unusual for men your age."

Davenport then barraged Max with questions about his sexual functioning. When was the last time he had had intercourse? Max stopped talking about his affair when the details seemed to cross the invisible line between clinical relevance and exhibitionism. Did he masturbate? Did he awaken in the morning with an erection? Did he have erections at other times? Were they twelve o'clock erections or more nine o'clock in form? Eight o'clock? Or seven-thirtyish?

Just when Max feared bestiality might be the next area of inquiry, Dr. Davenport stopped questioning, crossed his hands in his lap and smiled knowingly. "So, I assume you would like some medication for this difficulty. Am I right?"

"Well, yes," said Max, feeling odd that he was basically telling his doctor that because he couldn't have sex the old fashioned way, he hoped for a prescription that would make his penis look like the Washington Monument instead of a weeping willow.

"Okay. Good. Well, I find that my patients have good success with sildenafil. You know it as Viagra. Your BP goes up and down a little, but nothing very worrisome; you have no history of heart problems, so you shouldn't face any significant additional risk."

Max wondered how sex, all by itself, might be a risk to his heart.

"Do you have any questions?"

"Are there side effects or anything?"

"Well, in a small percentage of cases there can be side effects, yes. Itching, hives, swelling in your mouth or throat, chest tightness, problems urinating..."

Max felt like he might be taking his life into his own hands just so he could...well, it was worth it.

"...fever, change in heart rate, burning in your hands, arms, legs..."

Or was it?

"...nosebleeds, fainting, changes in vision, ringing in your ears. Well, that one shouldn't be a problem." Dr. Davenport paused to catch his breath. "Let's see. There are less important things to watch for, as well. Tiredness, difficulty sleeping, skin rash, headache, that sort of thing."

Max stared at him blankly.

"I don't think any of these...are you okay?"

"Yes, I guess I didn't realize..."

"Well, there's always a chance of side effects with anything you take, but you should be okay." Dr. Davenport asked his nurse to do an EKG on Max, which she did. Moments later, Davenport returned, saying everything looked fine. He stood and patted Max on the shoulder. "I'm sure the benefits will greatly outweigh the risks. Take it about an hour before you think you'll need it."

"Okay," said Max, feeling like this conversation alone might eliminate any chance of him ever having another erection. Dr.

Davenport bent over his desk to write the prescription. "One other thing. As you probably know, if you have an erection lasting more than four hours, contact me or go to the Emergency Room immediately."

"Sure," said Max, thinking, *Are you kidding? If I have an erection that lasts four hours or more, I'll alert the media!*

Max stood by the aquarium longer than usual trying to see if Constance was at her station. When the coast was clear, he ducked out quickly, dropping his encounter form on Marcy's desk and hoping that Constance would not find out what was going on. Max then drove across the city to a Rite Aid where he perused the magazines while his prescription was filled in blessed anonymity. Then, home he went, a bottle tucked safely in his inside jacket pocket.

Max pulsed with youthful exuberance. He had taken the pill before leaving for Constance's apartment; looking at his watch he estimated that they might have to forego an early dinner for an early something else. He wasn't sure how long the chemically-induced virility might last.

Constance planned on making a casserole, but when things became amorous, she turned off the stove. "We can order a pizza later," she said. Never shy, she slid out of her jeans and cowl-necked maroon sweater and slipped into bed, patting the sheets beside her invitingly. Max made a quick trip to the bathroom, and upon his return, Constance said, "What in the world?" Max was intoxicated by the power of his resurrected member, feeling like Cyrano or Zorro or any number of o-suffixed swordsmen of myth and history, ready to take on the world, feeling ten feet tall and taller as he spooned with his fair maiden. He breathed deep her flaming hair and snuggled her back, warm as an oven mitt. He closed his eyes and imagined the headline, "Man Smashes Four Hour Mark as His Lady Swoons."

Constance rolled over and kissed Max, slow and long. "I guess you weren't seeing Dr. Davenport about the bump on your head." She kissed him again as he eased on top of her. "Oh!" she said, her eyes wide and then drifting shut.

Though unpracticed, Max was not a rank amateur when it came to women. He had had his women along the way. He had had his share of sex. But so few relationships that mattered. Two to be painfully exact. Two women in sixty-two years. He would have felt sad were it not for the fact that he was about to reach a summit he hadn't scaled in six years. Nothing else, not even the sparse history of his love life, mattered. He looked at Constance's reddened cheeks, the moisture in the curve above her chin, the flutter of one eyelid; he felt the tensing of her body, her belly rising, her feet pressed against his legs like fists. He moved slowly, following her responses, accenting her moves with his own, pressing slightly this way and that, to and fro, in and out. He kissed her gently, though nothing between them was completely gentle at that moment, for their bodies were in delicious battle. She clung to him, her fingers splayed, nails pressing flesh, her back arched, aching, gasping.

Max tried to breathe evenly as a tingling numbness announced itself, forcing his legs to clench. *Oh Jesus, don't get a cramp!* He tried to relax his legs and move with greater care, but no less insistently; he wanted to savor every second, every nano-second, fearing that he might not feel this again. Though his brain tried to control the pace, another organ was taking over quickly—fasten your seat belts! Again he tried to hold back, but he couldn't. He wasn't breathing at all now; he was holding everything, waiting, waiting, waiting until he was consumed by a single sensation of tortured ecstasy. *Omygod!*

As a young man, Max felt a kind of joy after reaching a climax, a feeling of grace and well-being, not only personally, but globally, as if the whole world were made better for his ejaculation. Every molecule smiled, though they felt nothing, cared nothing, and, with him, became one with everything. But at his age, it was more like he had survived a torturously wonderful ride that had ended just short of death itself. He lay exhausted, unable to move his limbs, unsure he had limbs to move. All in all, it was bliss.

He lifted his head and looked at Constance, who was lying on her stomach, looking sideways at him and smiling.

"My God, Max!"

"Yes, I agree." An old, old feeling of joy came back, not because of all he had just expended, but because of the one who looked back at him as he smiled.

He slid an arm around her shoulders, and caressed her back and neck.

She closed her eyes.

He smoothed her eyelid with the tip of his thumb and ran his finger along her brow. Her skin felt soft, moist still. It could never get any better than this, this moment, this collapse of time. While greatness had eluded him, it was clear that there was something else that mattered equally, perhaps even more: a caring person in a warm body, sharing space, breathing in unison, toes touching, words failing, eyes gazing, peaceful, satisfied.

Max had only ever told one woman that he loved her—Gail. Gail had cried, which only frightened him. She had told him she loved him unreservedly and that unreserved love was the only kind. He had said the words because at a certain point in a relationship, it's what one did if one wanted to continue calling it a relationship. Maybe he believed that what he'd said was true, or at least was intended to be true, one day, as if such things could grow into truth. But he secretly knew that he didn't *feel* that it was true. That is not to say he didn't have affection for Gail, and respect, but love? Since he had never felt love for a woman before, perhaps he couldn't be trusted to recognize it when it happened. Whatever the reasoning, he had said it, and, like an ill-fitting sweater he had only worn once, it wasn't something he could take back.

When he rehearsed his speech to Gail in front of the bathroom mirror, he had believed its reasoning was airtight. He could end this and not only would Gail be unscathed, she would, in all likelihood, think he was the most considerate and, yes, loving man she had ever known. Unfortunately for Max, her tears poured through every crack and crevice of his well-reasoned, though foolish, argument. She was devastated and he was a liar. Since that day, he had never again confessed his love to any woman, not even his mother.

Could that be the case? That he had never told his mother he loved her? Surely, somewhere along the way he must have uttered those words to her, leaning over to kiss her at night, tossing it out matter-of-factly when he left for work in the morning, but he could not remember a single instance. She told him she loved him so often that the words lost their meaning as they left her mouth. She could as easily have been saying, "Please, pass me the ketchup," or, more likely, "Don't you love me, Max?" Her love was like a summons he could not answer, a request for reassurance he could not give.

He'd never told his father he loved him, which didn't seem unusual since his father had never used the phrase with Max either. The only other man Max had ever loved was Hargrove, but it would have been the height of awkwardness to say such a thing to his good friend. They spoke it in other ways—jokes and stories and drinks together, shared complaints about this and that, sports talk, a pat on the back, an occasional hug—all the ways that bind men without them having to declare that they are bound.

I love you. Three words he would never need again, words he could retire from his internal lexicon, and thus from his interpersonal grammar as well. Still, though banished, these words, or more accurately their absence, still had power over Max, rendering him less and less happy over the years, more and more bitter, and, most notably, alone. Had he altered his emotional life so much through lack of use that he was no longer capable of love?

He thought of Lincoln in this regard, who as a young man, lost the only woman he ever loved; so affected was he by grief that his closest friends thought he might take his life for want of hers. His was a life potholed with lost loved ones. His life's work became the eradication of loss, be it of the nation itself or the freedom of its tethered people. Max often fantasized himself into The Great Man's struggles only to realize such noble escapism would never change the fact that he was an American history teacher, not an American history maker, a lesser man who had lost but had never loved.

How could he explain that the only words he could think of as he lay beside Constance were, "I love you"? They were the only words that could capture, even passingly, what he felt. But could he say them? Could he be so honest? So true?

Constance gazed at him, sleep-faced and satisfied. "What?"

"What do you mean, what?" asked Max.

"I don't know. Your face looks, different. Like something is about to happen."

"I think something already did happen."

She nudged his ribs. "Yes, it did."

"I guess there is something I wanted to tell you. Something I haven't told you before."

"And what is that?" she asked without moving, without looking.

Max breathed deep, the smile leaving his face, replaced by a look of anxious concern, even befuddlement. He shifted his weight slightly, raising his head from the pillow.

"Look, Constance, I've been hearing something."

"Hearing something?"

"Yes, ever since the fall."

Constance leaned on one elbow as Max spun his unusual tale. Mostly, he spoke to the pillow, explaining the events that had begun with his tumble down the basement steps. He paused occasionally during his narrative, trying to gauge the effect it was having on Constance, but her face was intent and focused, belying not a hint of what she thought or felt. As the story unfolded, Max became as much a co-listener as the storyteller, surprised by what had been building silently inside him over the weeks and months.

"At first I thought I was losing my mind, although I tried to convince myself otherwise. I was afraid that I'd turn into one of those doddering old fools sitting on a park bench, railing against God knows what, taken over by some crazy idea, convinced entirely of its truth and frightened by a world that looked at me only as an oddity, someone to be pitied or feared. But when nothing else changed, I mean, when I was able to go about my daily life without any evidence that I was a madman, I figured I must not be going insane, at least not yet."

Constance smiled sadly and placed her palm on his cheek.

David B. Seaburn

Max lay back on his pillow, staring at the intricate constellation formed by the cracks in the ceiling. "I thought I was doing much better until it dawned on me that I was still hearing The Words." Max shook his head and gulped. "I've tried to figure out why I'm hearing them; what they mean, or if they mean anything; why these words instead of others: Endingtimeendingtimeendingtime. What the hell do they mean? I don't know." His eyes were still glued to the ceiling.

Constance sat up and then leaned over Max, kissing him gently on the lips. "Thank you for telling me this, Max." She kissed him again and then settled beside him, her arm across his ample abdomen.

Max was puzzled. "So. What do you think? I mean, am I crazy or what?"

Constance pressed her thighs against his leg, her toes reaching for his. "Let me see. You told me your mother was eaten by an alligator. You like to dress up like Abraham Lincoln. And you are hearing words that suggest the world is coming to an end." She sighed. "Maybe it's just a virus."

It was quiet for a moment and then Max began to chuckle as Constance dug her fingers into his side.

"I actually look much better as Lincoln's wife, Mary Todd. Same height. Same body type."

"I've changed my mind. You are crazy," said Constance.

Max turned to her, kissing her cheek, startled that he was so close to someone so beautiful. How could this be? "I should also confess to you now, before it's too late, that I have been hearing other words, too."

"Oh, Jesus, no," said Constance.

"I love you. I love you, Constance. I'm sorry, but it's true."

203

More More Time

Max wanted to kiss her, but was unsure, hoping that his confession of love hadn't broken the spell that had inclined her toward him in the first place. He waited, wondering if she might be hearing the same words, if she might be crazy enough to feel the same thing.

"No need to be sorry, Max. I love you, too."

Chapter 23

When Max got the phone message that Hargrove was at the Extended Stay Facility of the university hospital, he assumed that Gwen had had another "spell" and that Hargrove, being the ever-faithful husband, had decided to stay close by so that he could provide support on a moment's notice. It never ceased to amaze Max how broad Hargrove's shoulders could be. "She's my wife," he would say, as if that answer alone were enough to explain his sacrifice. When Max returned the call, though, Hargrove did not mention Gwen at all; he only asked that Max come, then hung up before Max could ask what was going on.

Max turned onto Hospital Drive, looking for the small, motel-like building. The hospital complex, its massive, incongruous buildings stretching for blocks passed by him one by one on the right, a formidable brown brick one marked "Psychiatry" appearing near the tail end. He glanced at the the fourth floor windows where Gwen had stayed from time to time, and wondered if, yet again, she was there. What would it be this time?

He had been worried after seeing her in her car a while ago, wondering if it was wise for her to be out alone. He hadn't told Hargrove, though, not wanting to add more to his burden, and also feeling it inappropriate to rat on a sixty-year-old woman who had every right to do whatever she wanted to do, no matter the risk.

There were days that Max stopped by Hargrove's classroom on the way to the parking lot only to find his friend hunched over, supposedly correcting papers, even though there weren't any on his desk. "Too much to do," he'd say, when Max would urge him to lay down the day's labors and go home. It seemed this happened more and more in recent months.

Extended Stay parking was huddled in the middle of several competing medical center parking lots that backed up to the muddy Genesee River, the modest lot being defined by cracked yellow curbs and a few well-placed entrance signs.

The woman at the desk never looked up when Max stepped into the tiny lobby. A man in a T-shirt was pounding the cigarette machine with his fists while a woman watched. "I'm tellin' you, that ain't gonna do no good," the watcher said nonchalantly.

When Max reached room 316, the door was slightly ajar. He knocked lightly, and then called, "Hargrove?" When no one answered, he pushed the door open and leaned in, half-wondering if he had gotten the number wrong. But there sat Hargrove at the end of the bed, his coat rumpled on the night table, a small duffel bag beside him, his Dopp kit on the floor. "Hargrove?" he asked again.

His friend looked up in dazed bewilderment then down again at his hands.

Max went to his side, placed a hand on Hargrove's shoulder, and when Hargrove didn't speak, knelt beside him. "What's going on?"

Hargrove, his face pallid, his eyes red and mattered, looked at Max. "It's all over."

"What's all over?"

David B. Seaburn

"Everything."

"What are you talking about, Hargrove? Is Gwen okay? Did something happen?

"Yes."

"Yes, what?"

"Something happened."

"Where is she?"

"Home."

Max's face screwed into confusion. "Home?"

"Yes. Home."

"I thought she was…" Max stopped. He looked around the room, noting again the luggage, as well as Hargrove's shirts and trousers hanging in the closet. "Hargrove, tell me what's going on. Why are your clothes here?"

"I made a mistake, Max. A big mistake." Hargrove's voice was strangely calm though his face was drawn up to one side, as if someone were twisting his arm. He wiped tears from his eyes.

"What are you talking about?" Max could not remember the last time he had seen Hargrove cry. Never when Gwen had been in the hospital, which Hargrove always framed as "a step forward." When Sally died? He wanted to believe that Hargrove had wept during those bitter days. He remembered Gwen's wailing and tears, but he could not recall a single one from Hargrove.

Hargrove stood, turned and walked to the window, his back to Max. Slowly, he told Max his story.

"So? You were getting massages," said Max, still confused. It was true that in all the years since Gwen and Hargrove had been married, Max had never seen Hargrove even look at another woman with anything more than passing curiosity.

"I saw the ad. There was this pretty woman. I thought, a massage, where's the harm in that?"

"Right. Where's the harm?"

Max listened as Hargrove talked about how important this woman had become to him, how he felt cared about by her. "Sometimes, I didn't want to leave. Sometimes I wanted to stay and stay and never go home again. I wanted her to keep me, to love me, I suppose."

"Did anything ever…"

"No, no, nothing like that." Hargrove turned his head slightly, his profile a silhouette against the curtain. He turned towards Max, then slumped into the chair by the window. "She was always nice to me. She didn't want anything from me. I went there and she focused on my needs, no one else's."

Hargrove seemed like a child to Max. Someone he'd never known before.

"I would see her, and then I would leave, and by the time I got into my car, I wanted to see her again. It was all I thought about, day and night. And Gwen. Gwen knew from the beginning; she knew."

"She knew you were seeing this woman?"

"No. But she knew that something was up, that I was lying, even if she didn't know about what."

"What makes you think that?"

"I've been married to the woman for over thirty years, Max. I know."

"So, didn't that convince you to tell her?"

"No, it didn't."

Max stared at Hargrove, speechless.

"I didn't want her to know. I thought she would come apart." Hargrove finally looked at Max. "And I knew I would have to stop."

"Hargrove, I've known you...forever. You never take risks. I mean, you always cross at the corner; you stop when the light is yellow. So why go out of your way to do this? And keep it a secret? It doesn't make sense to me."

Hargrove, his eyes wide but empty, his mouth open slightly, looked at Max. "I can't remember the last time I felt good. It's been so long that I thought it wasn't in the cards, that it wasn't what life was about anymore, feeling good. Maybe I felt good with Gwen in the beginning, before everything, but I don't know for sure. Before we got married and I found out she wasn't really pregnant, I thought, *My God, what have I gotten myself into?* Everybody thinks the '60s were all about letting it all hang out; well, not for me. It was still 'do your duty' and I did. I did my duty." Hargrove swallowed hard. "I loved Sally more than life. I did. And for years I thought my love for her was also love for Gwen, and then Sally...well, I guess my love for Sally was just for her. Afterwards Gwen was so broken; I mean she was just in pieces. It was my job to help put the pieces back together, and when some were missing it was up to me to make up the difference. I was proud of what I did, if that's the right word. But I never felt good. I had felt good as a father for all those years, but I never felt good as a husband, as a man. After Sally, I didn't think I'd ever feel good again, certainly not with Gwen."

"Hargrove, that can't be the whole story. I've known you even longer than Gwen has known you. I've seen you with her when you looked like the happiest man alive. I wasn't blind, was I?"

Hargrove wasn't listening. "I saw the ad and went by the place several times, and one day between classes I called to make an appointment. She seemed so inviting on the phone. Her voice was, I don't know, like something I had never heard before. The phone almost slipped out of my hand, I was so nervous," said Hargrove, smiling briefly. "I went there with nothing more on mind than to get a massage, to have this woman touch me. She would never need to know how much it meant to me. I would know, and it would be my secret and it wouldn't matter. It shouldn't, should it?" He looked at Max as if the question contained its own answer. "I lay on my stomach with my face in this ring. It was exciting being with someone who didn't need me to do anything for her, someone who was there just for me."

Hargrove stood and looked out the window across the parking lots, now mostly empty, at the Psychiatric Hospital and pointed.

"The first time it happened to Gwen, I was terrified. I didn't know what to think or do. I could barely breathe when they shuttled her to a patient room. I waited and felt guilty, like I'd done something wrong, like I could have prevented it. I swore I would do better." He placed his palm on the window. "But after the second time, and certainly the third…" He shook his head and turned around. "You know what I did when we went to the hospital? I took a newspaper or schoolwork or a good book. Happy for the freedom that I got when Gwen was being taken care of by someone else. Hoping she might not come back at all." Hargrove turned again and looked out the window. "I hated myself. In the end, I always did the right thing; I'd bring her home; I'd look after her; I'd do whatever I could. Maybe it wasn't love and affection, but it was something, wasn't it?"

Max sat silent and still as a statue, watching his friend, listening, saddened that he never knew. He had always guessed at the struggles, the weight, the thanklessness of Hargrove's life, and when his friend refused to talk about it, Max marked him noble for his silence, never understanding the pain of the twists and turns that lay under the surface.

Max sighed. "What about Gwen?"

"What *about* Gwen?"

"I mean, what happened when she went there, when she found you? Was she angry? "

Hargrove's face was blank as a chalkboard, his voice low. "Angry? No. She didn't even get mad. I mean she didn't yell. She talked. It became clear that I had gotten it wrong all these years. She had only ever wanted one thing: Me. And I had kept her at arm's length. I hadn't let her in. When she was done talking, I knew it was over. There was no hint that the door might remain open, that I might be able to turn the clock back." Hargrove continued staring out the window at nothing.

"Come on, Hargrove, you've got to be kidding. I'm sure you're wrong. You've got to be. In a few days, maybe a week, the two of you will talk this out. All you did was get some massages. It's not like you had an affair, for Christ's sake; it's not like you fell in love with someone else. It was just this…this *thing*." Hargrove didn't seem to be listening. "You're still a more faithful husband than 90 percent of the guys out there."

"It's not that I fell in love with someone else, that's true. It's that I never allowed myself to fall in love with Gwen."

"C'mon, Hargrove. You just need to talk to Gwen. You've got to. You can't give up. You've been married for half your life. You don't just let that go."

Hargrove walked to the bed and sat, arms out, palms up, head tilted. Max could see his friend's hands trembling. "I don't know what I would be fighting for, Max. I really don't. You know, I asked her to give me a chance to explain and even as I was saying it, a voice inside me was saying, 'It's over'. And worse, though I felt ashamed, it was for feeling relieved that it was over. I could see it on her face, too. Maybe that's why she was so calm, why she didn't cry or scream or hit me."

"But Hargrove…"

Hargrove waved him off. "Our marriage was lost a long time ago. Even before Sally things had gone stale. I thought maybe that's what happens sometimes in a marriage. I didn't think there was a real problem. I always figured it would work itself out somehow. So we kept on going. You know what I mean. I got used to the daily routine, the habits of being together that carry most couples along; things got predictable, comfortable, I guess. Then one day it was like I woke up and didn't feel anything for Gwen. I looked at her and tried to remember the last time I loved her, and I couldn't. I mean, I loved her. As a person. But I didn't love her in any other way. When I couldn't even remember loving her, I knew it was over. Worse, at that point, I didn't care."

Max sat next to Hargrove and rested his elbows on his knees. He looked at his frayed shoelaces and then up and to the side at his friend. "So, it's over? Really?" asked Max.

An ambulance screamed in the distance. Hargrove looked at Max as if an answer wasn't necessary.

"You do know what this means?" Max asked.

Hargrove raised his eyebrows.

"It means you're going to be alone, that's what it means. Alone. By yourself. Every day and every night. Are you ready to eat alone and sleep alone, watch television because you want to hear someone's voice? Those are the consequences, my friend. And I'll tell you, it's no picnic."

"I've always been alone, Max. Alone with the person I was supposed to love." Hargrove stood and put his hand on Max's shoulder. Then he walked to the window again. A crescent moon rose above the hospital parking garage. "You want to hear something that will really make you laugh?"

"Sure," said Max.

"Every time I went there, every time I saw Beth—that was her name—it was like the sand stopped falling in the hour glass. For just a little while. No one knew where I was. There wasn't any place I needed to be. Nothing I needed to do. And when she opened the door and came in, it was like nothing mattered."

"Sounds like it mattered too much," replied Max.

Hargrove seemed transfixed. His arms hung limply at his side, his eyes looked dumbstruck, as if watching himself falling off a cliff. After a moment, Hargrove said, "Still hearing those words, Max?"

"Yes."

"Good."

"Good?"

"They're not so crazy after all."

More More Time

Chapter 24

When Bob first met Gwen Stinson at the grocery store, she had seemed like a mouse hiding in plain sight, so tentative that she could barely get up from her chair to help herself. Fragile was the best word to describe her, and Bob had treated her as such, bending, reaching, leaning, catching, wiping. She had hardly made eye contact and yet there was something beckoning about her, making him wonder whether it was possible to do enough for her. Her reassurance had felt like sweet charity, leaving him full of pride for having simply extended common courtesy.

Sitting with her again, this time at Jitter's Café, she was entirely different. She reviewed in humorous tones how they had met, her clumsiness, his chivalry, her gratitude, his humility. When their order came up, she walked to the counter, waving him off, and gathered up their coffees, placing them, without a spill, on their table.

Bob felt a growing discomfort, realizing that apart from a cup of spilled coffee, she was a complete stranger.

"So," he ventured.

"Yes, exactly!" she laughed.

"So...how have you been?"

"Well; I am doing well."

Bob chewed the inside of his cheek, his eyes inadvertently shifting from side to side. He grinned anxiously, raising the cup to his lips, to try and hide behind it as best he could.

"You know, Bob," said Gwen, reaching across the table with one hand, touching his wrist, and then just as quickly retracting it, "you are my butterfly wings."

Bob watched two coeds ordering vanilla chais and rolling their eyes about an English professor. Bob wished he were in school again, and that he could call out to these girls, joke and laugh, and then walk back with them to the dorm. He had no idea what Gwen meant. It made him nervous, her constant smile and leveling eyes. He looked down, wondering if he had spilled coffee on his shirt. He peeked at Gwen, his head still tilted. Her face was so earnest that he blushed into his coffee cup.

"I'm sure that must sound crazy," she stated.

"No, no," replied Bob. "I'm sure it's not crazy."

"Do you know what I mean?"

Bob took a deep breath, hoping that with his exhale a reasonable response might follow, but to his embarrassment only a long, nasal sigh filled the air.

"They say that a butterfly fluttering its wings on the other side of the world can cause a chain reaction that can unleash a storm thousands of miles away," Gwen said, still smiling. "From the smallest of things, big changes." She stretched her arms out in a gentle arc.

Bob shifted his weight, making the seat squeak. He curled and stretched his toes, and then looked up again just in time to see the coeds leaving the coffee shop. Bob watched them as they stood on the sidewalk gesticulating, then bending backwards in a fit of laughter.

Gwen's steady gaze never left Bob's face.

He smiled vacantly, like he couldn't remember how to spell the next word in a spelling bee. "Uh huh," he said, trying to add warmth to a grin that was sticking to his upper teeth.

Gwen laughed. "You really don't have the faintest idea what I'm talking about, do you?" she asked without disappointment.

"I'm sorry, I…"

She reached across the table again, placing her hand on his, squeezing it gently and then letting go. "Never mind, Bob. Really, I just wanted to thank you."

"For what?"

"For being kind. That's all." Mrs. Stinson's head was cocked to one side, her eyes deep as pools.

Bob watched as she got up from the table and walked away. He was completely unable to connect the dots between her coffee spill, his kindness, her butterflies, and whatever life changes she was alluding to.

The next day, Bob found out that Gwen Stinson was the one who was connecting dots. She had not only talked with him, she had also paid a visit to Serenity Massage.

Beth's story spilled out so quickly that Bob couldn't make sense of it.

"I know, I'm not being clear." Beth put her hand on her chin and paused, as if gathering her thoughts.

It was hard for Bob to imagine that the Mr. Stinson he had known in high school and the Mrs. Stinson he had recently met could be involved in any kind of controversy, especially one that included Beth.

"Beth?"

"You know, there was something about him that reminded me of my father."

"Your father? Did he try…"

"No. Nothing like that. I don't know exactly what it was. It always seemed like he had expectations, but never said what they were; like I was supposed to know everything he wanted."

"Then why did you keep seeing him?"

"What was I going to say to him?"

"Well…how about 'I'm sorry but I can't see you anymore. You make me feel uncomfortable'."

"I couldn't do that. He was just this polite, older guy," she said with a dismissive wave of her hand.

Bob felt uneasy. "Beth, I'm telling you, it's not a good idea to work on any guys. I mean you're all alone there…"

"I'm fine. Really." Beth paused, a jigsaw puzzle look on her face.

"What?"

Beth tried to explain that despite all the times she had met with Hargrove Stinson, it was his wife who left the greatest impression on her. Beth described "this woman" coming into her room unannounced, standing in front of them, calmly introducing herself, and then without hesitation or uncertainty, telling her husband that the clock had run out on their marriage. "Her voice was quiet, but strong. She didn't yell. She looked him directly in the eyes. She never blinked; she never flinched." Beth smiled at this and looked away. "She seemed so… sure."

"Sure of what?"

"Everything," replied Beth.

"What exactly did she say?"

"She talked to me as much as she talked to her husband."

"What?"

"Yes, she talked to me. She told me I shouldn't wait for anything; that I should never look back, that there was only one direction."

"Only one direction?"

Beth didn't seem to hear him. Her voice had become faint, as if she were talking to herself. "Forward."

Bob didn't ask another question. He watched while his wife tried to piece things together.

"You know, my mother never really looked at me, never really saw me for who I was. She wanted to *show* me but she never wanted to *see* me. And my father…" The corners of her mouth were pinned back and her eyes filled with tears. Bob came to her side and put a hand on her shoulder.

Beth had told Bob her story before, line by line, scene by scene, but always in the past tense, like it wasn't a part of her any longer, like the curtain had fallen and she had moved on. He had believed that the passage of time had worked its miracle, had erased the scars. Looking at her as she spoke, her forehead creased, her eyes hidden beneath folds of memory, he knew there had been no miracle. He knew that there was still a long road ahead.

Beth bowed her head, her hands on her knees, her hair in waves along her neck and face. "There was something about her, the wife, something that I can't get out of my mind. She looked like there was nothing holding her back. You know what I mean?"

"Well, I…"

"Remember the boats in Perkins Cove? How they were tethered before a big storm so they could barely move when the gale hit?"

"Uh huh."

"Kept them safe."

"Safe and sound."

"Yes. Safe and sound." Beth ran her fingers through her hair and sat up in her chair. "I've been tethered all my life. But it hasn't kept me safe or sound."

Bob stepped back so he could see Beth, so he could take her in.

"That was the thing about that woman, Gwen Stinson. She was untethered. Maybe for the first time."

It was a week or more before Bob reminded Beth that he also knew Gwen Stinson. She listened but said nothing. During this time, they talked more, not about anything in particular. Not about the Stinsons, not even about their own relationship. But the sound of their voices in the house was no longer jarring; the rooms were no longer battlegrounds. At night they lay face-to-face in bed, quiet, sometimes holding each other. Bob didn't know what to think of this.

Beth seemed different. She might not have been untethered, but she was plainly less encumbered than before. She was changing in ways that no one else would likely have noticed. There was something about her that seemed lighter; she breathed more deeply; she smiled more freely; she moved without pause or hesitation. It was as if the tectonic plates of her being had shifted infinitesimally and, as a result, she was different and yet the same, Beth and someone else all at once.

Bob doubted that these changes could all be related to Gwen Stinson, but there didn't seem to be any other explanation. One thing was clear to Bob: Gwen's willingness to take up her own life and chart a new course had shaken something loose in Beth. After they had met at the cafe, Bob had been dismissive of Gwen's silly notions. Yet now, he understood that he had been wrong about her.

Bob picked up his cell and searched through prior calls for a number. Finding it, he called Mrs. Stinson and listened as the phone rang time and again until it went to voicemail. "Hello, this is Gwen, and I'm so sorry I'm not here to speak with you. Please leave a message and I will call you back. In the meantime, look around you. It's all amazing. Thanks!"

"Hello, Mrs. Stinson, Gwen. This is Bob, Bob Hazelwood. So much has happened since we met for coffee. When you left me at the cafe, you said you wanted to thank me for being kind. I want to say you're welcome; and I want to thank you, too, for being, well, for being, I don't know what exactly, I guess for being you. That probably doesn't make any more sense to you than butterfly wings did to me, but it's what I needed to say. So, thank you. From me. And my wife. Good bye and good luck."

More More Time

Chapter 25

November 19 dawned like every other November day with dark, grumbling clouds spreading low across the sky, moving fast with the prevailing easterly wind, snow spitting and swirling in the gray morning light. As Max stood at his bedroom window, the curtain pulled slightly back so he could see the day's beginning, he thought of The Great Man who on this day so many long years before, had awakened in the village of Gettysburg. In the midst of many thousands dead, most of whom still awaited burial, twenty-five hundred living souls also woke and prepared to attend the ceremony that would consecrate a new cemetery.

Max had begun his annual recitation of the Gettysburg Address on its 120th anniversary. At that time, he did it as a lark, something to catch the attention of his students, something to make them laugh, if laughing would focus their attention and alert their minds to the importance of what had happened on that day in 1863. The first year, he had made his stovepipe hat out of construction paper, the brim stapled awkwardly into place. Max had bought a Santa Claus beard, trimming and dying it until he passed for the sixteenth president, if not exactly honoring him.

But when he stood on his desk for his first period class and began to recite those 272 words, barely three minutes in length, his students fell silent, and he felt for the first time what greatness, borrowed though it was, felt like. "Four score and seven years ago our fathers brought forth on this continent, a new nation, conceived in Liberty, and dedicated to the proposition that all men are created equal..."

The words, their cadence, their weight, a distillation of all that America meant, set Max back on his heels. It wasn't that he had never read or even recited the speech before. He had done so many times during the years preparing for his chosen career. There was something, though, in the pretense of being the president that stirred him as never before, and from that day on, he thought of Lincoln as The Great Man.

When he told Constance it was time for his annual re-enactment, she didn't laugh (the most common response); instead, she gasped with excitement and asked—demanded actually—that she be allowed to attend. "I wouldn't miss it for the world."

Slowed by an early morning headache, Max ambled to the hall closet, reached up to the highest shelf and pulled down a large round cardboard box. He took it to his room and laid it on his bed. He couldn't resist the smile of satisfaction that crossed his lips. Max carefully removed the silk stovepipe hat, as if it were fine crystal, and placed it on his knees. He ran his fingers across its surface admiringly.

Max placed the hat carefully on his head, the great silo elevating him to new heights, the shadow of its brim across his eyes, steeling his gaze. He stepped in front of the dresser mirror, his mouth firm at the corners as perhaps Lincoln's had been that morning at 10:00 a.m. when he had left for the cemetery. Endingtimeendingtimeendingtime. The Words, busy in the background, asserted themselves, like the beating drums of a distant, approaching infantry.

Max went back to the hall closet and, standing on his tiptoes, balanced another box on his fingertips. He carefully clutched it to his chest and returned it to his bed. He opened the box, finding each item of clothing neatly folded, the beard and pocket watch lying on top. He examined each article—black trousers, waistcoat, white shirt and collar, and silk frock coat. The boots were in his bedroom closet, too big for a shoebox, wrapped instead in a hefty bag cinched tight at the top. He put on each piece, attached the pocket watch to his vest, and then stood tall winding the watch then adjusting his waistcoat.

Each year when Max retrieved these boxes, he thought not only of The Great Man, but of his own father. When his mother had taken to her bed, it had fallen to Max to select the clothing for the funeral. He dutifully folded each item and placed them in an inconspicuous cardboard box for the undertaker. He had gone to the funeral parlor with what his mother had called "options," including several dress shirts, two suits, three ties, socks, and his best black shoes, which his mother insisted Max shine. When he pulled into the parking lot, Max realized he had forgotten underwear and a T-shirt. He sat crying in his father's car, at first because he felt he'd let his father down, and then because it dawned on him that, wherever his father had gone, underclothing was at best optional.

The funeral director was a kind man who smiled gently when he saw all the clothes. "We will only need one outfit," he said solemnly. "There won't be any costume changes." The man's eyes twinkled with sympathy when he said this.

He took the navy suit, white shirt, black socks, but no shoes. "Which tie do you think your father would like?" he had asked.

Max had studied the ties, trying to remember his father wearing any of them. He decided on a blue and gold striped tie because it would make his father look most alive. When Max asked, the funeral director confirmed that underwear was unnecessary.

Max grabbed the lapels of his frock coat and pulled them down. He turned to the bedroom mirror, studying every inch, every seam of his Lincoln-ness, satisfied with the replication, despite his comparatively diminutive stature. Perhaps his father would be proud.

Max did not affix the beard. He would wait until he got to school before adding the final touch. In fact, he would undress now and dress again when he got to work, not wanting anyone to see him in advance of his performance.

Max packed the clothes back into their boxes. As he bent to place them on the floor, he felt a sudden lightheadedness, as if his legs were no longer under him. He sat back on his bed, his head throbbing. He rubbed his temples until the pulsing subsided. He took several deep breaths. *Too much excitement?* he wondered, thinking not only of the address, but of his special guest who would be in attendance. He stood again, the dampness on his face and the tingling in his fingertips abating. His legs returned. "Four score and seven years ago, it is," he said.

Chapter 26

After her husband's death, Constance Young had promised herself to live as close to the moment as possible, and more importantly, never to form another serious attachment. Constance had looked at life's impermanence eye-to-eye and never since questioned its reality.

But then came this silly little man to her window, time and again, an Eeyore of the first order; so much so, that she had to smile at his struggle to find a dark cloud even on the sunniest of days. He was a curiosity at first. Her coworkers regaled her with stories of his eccentricity and downright oddness. She had joined in this perception without knowing the man at all. Over time, though, she found his respectfulness, even his kindness refreshingly old-fashioned, a horse-drawn carriage on the interstate. Constance didn't know how to describe what had happened next, so organic had been the process. All she knew was that they were two very different puzzle pieces that somehow seemed to fit. What did the future hold for such an unlikely coupling? She didn't know and, more importantly, didn't care.

The parking lot was almost full when she arrived. Students moseyed to the front door, dragging their feet as long as possible before going in. A gaggle of bundled kids stood across the street, outside the rules, smoking. In the car beside her, a boy and girl were making out. Or did they call it that anymore? Hooking up maybe. Or was hooking up the same as having sex? Whatever came before having sex was probably what they were doing. Who knew? The windows were steamed. Something was going on. Constance smiled.

At first Max had not been the most adept lover she'd ever met, almost virginal in his approach, like he had read a driving manual but had never been on the road before. Yet he was tender, sincere and attentive, always present in the most important ways. And he made her feel good. For all his befuddlement about his life, he was actually a simple person, someone she could love easily.

"Good morning. I'm Constance Young. Here for Mr. Ruth's third period class."

The office was full of pimply-faced, geeky boys and dark-eyed, cake-faced girls and a few punked-out hunks coming and going from the vice-principal's office. The air was hormonal.

"Excuse me?" asked the secretary, smiling.

"I think I'm supposed to check in. I'm looking for Mr. Ruth's office."

The woman looked away from Constance. "Natasha, please don't sit on that desk. How are you doing anyway, honey?" she asked, her eyebrows raised, at a slight, red-haired girl who slid off the adjoining desk.

"'Kay, I guess, Mrs. Almond. What can I say?"

"That's good, sweetie; you hang in there," said Mrs. Almond, watching the girl as she left the office. "Honestly, some of these kids come from the worst situations, you know?"

Constance, suddenly self-conscious, feeling like she didn't have a passport and might not make it through customs, nodded, took a breath and started again. "I'm here for Mr. Ruth's…"

"Here to see his performance, are you?" said Mrs. Almond, leaning back in her chair and shaking her head. "That man is really something."

Constance's frozen smile cracked a little at the corners. "Excuse me?"

Mrs. Almond searched through a metal box, as if looking for recipes. "You said your name was what?"

"Young, Constance Young."

The door opened and a teacher walked into the office.

"Good morning, Mr. Stinson," said Mrs. Almond.

Constance turned slowly.

"Morning, Glenda," said Hargrove. He put his coffee cup on the counter and retrieved the mail from his box.

Max's description made Hargrove seem familiar. Tall, slender, distinguished in a graying way, distant eyes. She wondered if he knew as much about her as she did about him. "Aren't you Hargrove Stinson?" she asked, leaning in, almost whispering.

Hargrove stared at her, blank-faced. "Yes, I am," he replied. "I have a class right now; if you want to make an appointment about your student, my hours are posted…"

"No, no, no. I'm sorry. I'm not a parent. At least not of someone who would be here," she said, laughing. Hargrove's jaw seemed to lock. "I'm here for Mr.…for Max's class. I'm Constance, Constance Young, maybe Max has…"

"Oh, my goodness, of course, I'm so sorry. I don't know what I was thinking. Yes, yes, Max speaks so fondly of you. Is it true that you hung the moon?" Hargrove's face softened enough to allow some warmth in.

"Well, I don't know about that. It's so nice to meet you. You've been friends for such a long time. He speaks highly of you, too."

Hargrove's ears turned maroon. "Highly…I don't know if… well…" he stammered.

"Here you go," interrupted Mrs. Almond, handing Constance a visitor's pass. "Wear this on the front of your coat. He's in room 309, second floor." She pointed across the hall to the staircase. "Good luck!"

"This is always a very important day for Max, made more so this year because you will be there," said Hargrove with a nod and a reassuring bow.

"Well, I'm happy I could come. Have you seen him this morning? Is he ready?"

"Yes, I spoke to him earlier. Unfortunately, his first period turned out to be a dress rehearsal in front of some very unforgiving critics. His beard slid off his face. I brought him some stronger adhesive." He tilted his head and raised his eyebrows. "I'm sure he'll bounce back."

"Oh no," she said, wincing. "I don't know why he does it."

"It is for Mr. Lincoln. Although, today it is most likely for *you* and only *secondarily* for Mr. Lincoln," said Hargrove, leaning near her conspiratorially, his eyes matching the color of his ears. He was so close now that Constance could smell toothpaste, a recent breath mint (spearmint, to be exact), and a hint of vodka. His smile bore no relationship to the rest of his face. He reeked of sadness and self-pity. She leaned away at the neck, almost imperceptibly. He straightened immediately. "Well, I should get to my class. How would they make it through World War II without me?" asked Hargrove, his smile more formal now.

"I am so glad I finally had the chance to meet you." Constance extended a hand.

"Oh. Yes." Hargrove took her hand in his, shaking it firmly once, then let it go. "Please give Max my best."

He turned to the door, bumping into a student who scowled at him. "I'm sorry," said Hargrove, as if apologizing for everything.

The stairs were packed with students changing classes. Constance clung to the wall as she made her way, hoping not to draw any attention. One boy whistled. Then another. She looked up. They were staring at her, cupping their hands in front of their chests. Constance stopped and students streamed around her. The boys waved and continued on.

"Can I help you, ma'am?" said a fresh-scrubbed, bright-eyed girl, her hair in a long French braid, her nose pierced. "Not everyone here is a dick. Although we have our share."

"Not much different than when I went to school," said Constance, testing a smile.

"As they say, boys will be pigs," said the girl brightly. "I hate it when they act like that. So what if you have giant boobs. I mean, you could be someone's mother and here they are acting like you're just a piece of ass or something. It's not right."

"Well, uh…."

"It pisses me off," the girl continued. "The really stupid looking one is my boyfriend."

"Oh."

"Don't even ask. Anyway, can I help you?"

"Well, yes, I'm looking for 309."

"Our Mr. Ruth. You're not his girlfriend or something?" she asked, her eyes bugging out. "No offense, but most of us took him for gay, you know. Nothing wrong with that. That other asshole who was whistling at you? He's bi. All types. Anyway, I guess we were wrong about Abe."

"Well…"

"Hang a right at the top of the steps. It's halfway down on the left. Had him last year. The Lincoln thing is way surreal." She receded into a mass of swarming students, waving as they swallowed her.

When Constance turned the corner, Max was standing outside his room trying to direct traffic. She felt like a mother spying on her son, suddenly realizing why all the other kids made fun of him. His stovepipe hat, a little on the large side, sat on his ears while his pants puddled around his boot heels. His coat and vest were a little tattered and a little small. And, of course, the beard.

She took a deep breath, put on her warmest smile and headed his way.

"There you are," said Max, his face damp with perspiration. He hugged her.

"This is so exciting," she said.

"That's one word for it," said Max, distractedly. He wiped his face with the palm of his hand and smiled. "Welcome to the asylum." He tried to laugh, but only exhaled.

"Yo, Mr. Ruth, break a leg today," called a boy several lockers down. Max didn't appear to notice. He leaned against the locker, his face gray.

"Are you okay?" she asked, her voice betraying more worry than she had intended.

"Hungry, that's all."

Constance pulled a granola bar from her purse. "Here."

"I can't eat it here in the hallway. It's against the…"

"Max, eat," she said, her voice clipped. They backed into his room where Max struggled briefly with the wrapper and then downed the bar in two bites.

"Max, you don't look good. Sure you're not coming down with something?" Constance placed her palm on his forehead.

Max pulled away, his lips pursed.

Constance stood straight up, her raised eyebrows betraying her alarm.

Max shook his head apologetically. "I'm sorry. I just want this to go well. I don't want you to see me fail."

"Max, what in the world are you talking about?" she asked, her face directly in front of his. "Look at me. Max! I love you! You know that. I don't care about all the other stuff. You can't fail for me. Relax, everything will be fine."

Max's mouth curled into a partial smile. "Thank you," he said. "Thank you for coming." He squeezed her hand and then sat down behind his desk. He removed his hat and took several deep breaths.

"Max, really; are you sure you're okay? Is there anything wrong?" Constance leaned forward, holding his face in her hands, searching his eyes.

The bell rang and kids began swarming into the room.

"Wooooooo, look at Mr. R," said the boy with the Syracuse t-shirt.

"My, my, my, Mr. Ruth, who's the pretty lady?" said a girl with purple bangs.

"No making out before the big talk, Mr. Lincoln."

"Presidential prerogative?" asked another.

"Thinks he's that other president—whatshisname?" said a boy in a muscle shirt to Constance.

233

Max looked at Constance, numb-faced. "Still excited?"

"Maybe we could each take a side of the room and start slapping them silly," offered Constance.

Max stood, put his hat back on, pulled at his lapels and walked slowly to the front of the room. He turned to the class, his face grave.

"We have a special guest today," said Max, his voice rising above the din. "I said we have a special guest today!" Max glared at his class until they settled. "Her name is Mrs. Young. And I say 'special' because, well, because she has come all the way from Washington D.C. to be with us today."

Constance squinted at Max and tilted her head slightly to one side.

"From the White House," Max added, eyebrows raised. "She is the Presidential Advisor for Educational Endeavors to Preserve the Memory of Abraham Lincoln. I expect you to treat her with the respect she so richly deserves." The class fell silent and seemed confused.

"Thank you for joining us, Madame Advisor."

"You are most welcome," said Constance, bowing her head and waving royally with the back of her hand. Constance winked at Max. Max nodded formally to her. She held her breath, avoiding a laugh, and settled back into the seat provided her, only then noticing something different about Max's face.

At first she couldn't tell exactly what it was. Perhaps the misalignment of his beard or the way his stovepipe hat shortened his forehead. Examining his face inch-by-inch, she could find nothing until she eased back and took in the whole. Then she saw a shadow at one corner of Max's mouth. It became clearer; one side of his mouth was drawn lower than the other, perhaps not noticeable to his class, but obvious to Constance. She looked away and then back at Max, to test her vision. Perhaps she was just seeing things, like Max was hearing things.

Her lower back and shoulders tightened as Max adjusted his notes on the music stand in front of him.

Standing stiffly before the class, he began: "I do this each year because there are some things that should not be forgotten. There are some people who should be remembered for the Greatness that defined them. Lincoln is one of those people. And the address he gave at Gettysburg is one of those things. Some lives erase the bonds of time and become eternal in their importance. They last and last while others come and go. They are the kind of lives that we often aspire to but rarely achieve. We are thankful for those lives because they provide us with a way to measure, to gauge, our own contribution to the betterment of the world, small though that contribution may be."

Max paused and surveyed his class. They were eerily silent and attentive. Constance leaned forward in her seat, her hands clasped on the desk, her knuckles white.

Max licked his lips.

Constance watched the corner of his mouth.

"So. On November 19, 1863, Abraham Lincoln stood before the people of Gettysburg and shaid these, *said* these worns, er, *words*."

Max paused again. He glanced at Constance. She could see bewilderment in his eyes. He looked down at his notes and cleared his throat.

What's going on? thought Constance, and she stood. "Max?"

"Foe shcoe an sev yeays ago, our fatha, our fa…" Max looked up from his notes again, this time with fear in his eyes.

"Max!"

He looked at her and tried to speak but nothing came. He clenched his head with both hands and grimaced, leaning precariously against the music stand.

Constance ran to the front of the class as Max fell, hitting his head on the side of the desk and crumpling to the floor.

"Max!"

Constance knelt beside him, cradling his head in her hands. "My God, Max," she said. The left side of his face was torn back viciously. "Max, can you hear me?" Max's eyes begged, but he could not speak. "I'm here, Max," she said as his eyes slowly closed. "Get someone! Quick!" she yelled.

The students scattered.

Chapter 27

When Gwen came down the street, she was surprised to see Hargrove's car in the driveway. She glanced at her watch, wondering why he wasn't at school. She pulled into the garage, turned off the ignition, and sat for a moment, wondering what he might want. He had come to the house before, but had always forewarned her. She felt strangely violated by this unannounced and uninvited visit. Of course, it was as much his house as hers, at least until the divorce was finalized. Nevertheless, she had made it her haven, a place where she felt safe, the place from which she had launched all her recent explorations. There was Zumba at the Y, yoga and her support group at the local Center for Personal Wellbeing, the book group at Lift Bridge, and possibly a job at the library.

For the first time in years, Gwen had a calendar. She studied it every day, amazed that there were events and commitments on its pages; that there was content to her days, and a future waiting with her name on its ledger. She had always felt smothered by the oppressive crawl of time, but now her hours had wings and her days held promise.

She had occasional pangs of guilt over this new found freedom; guilt that it was all because she had cashed-in the longest relationship of her life, the one she had thought would last forever, the one that had given her Sally. Yet, when she had walked out of that massage studio, she felt like a new person, even though her life, as she had known it, was all but gone. What quickly followed was an avalanche of fears, sleepless nights, and lost days. But that didn't deter her. Soon she realized that having, feeling, even being "nothing" was an asset. It was a block of marble out of which she could sculpt her new life. She had been chipping away ever since.

Her freedom had nothing to do with whether she loved Hargrove. She did. That hadn't changed. What had changed was her understanding of that love, what it had been, and what it had become. Her love, once a gift given freely, in time became an offering placed on the altar of a disapproving god. No matter how much she gave, it was never enough, or, more accurately, it was never what he wanted. She tried her best to solve the riddle of how to reach him, how to touch him. Sally was the most precious thing she could give, and for a time, Sally was enough. For a time, Sally fed them both; Sally held them together. Then she was gone. After Sally, a fog of despair became Gwen's most devoted friend, shrouding her in its cold comfort, making almost everything about her life invisible. She lived in it for years.

Hard to believe what a change of underwear could do. Had Hargrove not bought those vibrant, shrieking boxers, she would still be living in a fog. How silly. As if the underwear he wore mattered. Yet he was such a creature of habit, so predictable, that his brightly colored boxers seemed like the headline of a story she could not ignore. His glaring pastels and paisleys opened her eyes, forcing her to recognize the void that had been there for so long. She smiled to think of it. "Gwen," someone, seeing the smile, could have asked, "why did you leave your husband?"

"Because he bought some new underwear," she wanted to say.

She was relieved when he moved to an apartment. To her, his one-year lease seemed like a lifetime, or at least enough time for her to start anew, minus the worry that he might show up at her door, suitcase in hand, hoping to return, if only for the convenience of it. Had she become cold-hearted? She imagined the newlywed Gwen watching from afar, appalled at what the senior Gwen was doing. Mostly though, these thoughts, these doubts, had little adhesive; they attached but curled and fell away quickly.

Gwen removed the keys from the ignition, tossed them into her purse, glanced a final time into the mirror, and opened the car door. She entered the kitchen, expecting Hargrove to be there, but he wasn't. The house was strangely silent.

"Hargrove?" she called, but there was no answer.

She put her purse on the kitchen counter. "Hargrove, are you there?" Nothing again. Gwen felt a flash of anxiety streak through her, much as she had often felt awaiting Hargrove's arrival at the end of each day. What would he be like? What would he say? Some days the uncertainty left her pacing the floor for an hour or more before he came home.

Gwen reached the living room. There sat Hargrove in her rocker near the front window. He seemed unaware not only of her presence but of anything. "Hargrove?"

Hargrove, who was folded into the chair like worn fabric, was staring blankly at the floor. Loose hairs draped his forehead, giving him the countenance of an old man, uncaring of his appearance. He looked up at Gwen and then back at his feet.

"I didn't know you were coming." Gwen said, standing under the archway, unsure whether to enter the room.

"I didn't know I was coming either."

239

Gwen eased into the room. "What brings you here, Hargrove? Have you forgotten something? It has gotten much colder. Do you need your sweaters? I have them in the hall closet upstairs."

Hargrove leaned his head into his hands.

"Can I get them for you?" asked Gwen.

"I don't need the sweaters. Thank you."

"Is there anything…"

"I went to the cemetery."

Gwen stopped breathing.

"I never noticed how pretty it is there. The trees, the knoll, even a few remaining marigolds. And quiet. Peaceful, I suppose." Hargrove breathed deep and sighed long. "But so noisy in other ways. And ugly." Hargrove sighed again and looked out the window. "There was a rock on top of the headstone. Not a very big one. Small, actually. I reached down to knock it off. Then I wondered if you had put it there. So I left it."

Gwen stepped closer. "Hargrove," she said in a whisper.

Hargrove turned to her, a wan smile on his lips. "Sometimes I can't remember her face. I close my eyes tight and look, but it's gone. I panic. I sit up in bed and I think, *Did it ever happen? Was Sally real?*" He looked at Gwen, his eyes beckoning.

"Hargrove…"

"I don't go there as often as you do. But I go. Maybe it doesn't matter, but I wanted you to know."

"You loved her very much," said Gwen.

"Yes. I did. I do." Hargrove leaned to one side and pulled a handkerchief from his pocket. He wiped his nose and then refolded the cloth, stuffing it away. "I got back in the car. I wanted to leave, but instead, I sat there. That's when it came to me."

"What is that, Hargrove?"

"Why you don't want to be my wife." He paused. Gwen accepted his correction. "It's simple really. I think it's because I stopped seeing you. All those years I took you to the doctors, to the hospital, looked after you, tried to help; tried to pick you up when you fell down. But you could as easily have been a complete stranger as my wife, the mother of my only child." Hargrove leaned forward, elbows on his knees, hands folded, head down. "You were right there in front of me the whole time."

"Hargrove, really, there's no need for this." Gwen sat in the chair beside him.

"But I see now. I see you."

"Hargrove, please…"

"We could start over. It doesn't have to be like this. Maybe we could make it different." He looked at Gwen, but she did not look back at him. He waited, but she didn't speak.

"Well then, I suppose things end, don't they? Everything eventually goes away. You think things will always be there, but then they're gone. The clock ticks. It doesn't matter if you wind it or not. It doesn't need anything from you. It doesn't care."

A curtain of sadness fell across Hargrove's face.

Gwen knelt beside Hargrove, placing her hand on his. It was cold to the touch. She stroked its wrinkled surface, surprised at how dry, how old, it felt. She tilted her head, trying to make eye contact. "Hargrove, it's true. Things end. And it can be awful. I know. But things also begin. There's no end of beginnings. I know that this…"

Hargrove stood, his hand slipping from hers. He took a deep jagged breath. "Yes, beginnings, beginnings, beginnings. How wonderful it must be. You are the proof of that. Wouldn't it be nice if we could all just pick up and go on to the next thing?"

Silence, dry as chalk dust, filled the air between them.

Gwen stood, her jaw squared.

Hargrove shook his head from side to side; his shoulders went slack and his hands fell open at his side. He turned, though he did not look at Gwen. "I'm sorry. That was uncalled for."

"Hargrove, if you don't need anything from the house, then why did you come here today? What do you want? I know you are unhappy and I wish you weren't, but..." Gwen's arms went up in frustration, then down again, one hand on her hip. "But I can't do anything about that."

"No, you can't," said Hargrove, his eyes welling as he collapsed back into the rocking chair.

"Hargrove, what is wrong?" she said, startled.

"It's my friend." Hargrove began to weep.

"What do you mean, 'It's my friend'?"

"He's gone."

"Who's gone?" Gwen, shook her head, confused again.

"Max."

"What?"

"Max is gone now, too."

Chapter 28

Bob was rummaging through boxes in the far corner of the attic behind the Christmas decorations, when Beth came up the stairs.

"What are you doing?" she asked.

Bob was too engrossed in his search to answer.

Beth peered at him from atop the steps. "Bob?"

"I'm looking for something. I know I packed it when we moved, but I can't find it."

"That was years ago. What exactly are you looking for?"

"That old scroll," said Bob, his head in a box full of yellowed papers and books.

"From high school?"

"Yeah."

Beth walked to the middle of the attic. Bob looked over his shoulder at her tossing paper from one box, then another.

Bob stopped and sat back on his haunches. "I was thinking about Mr. Ruth. When we first moved here, we went over to his house, you know, to say hello. At first he didn't recognize me, but once I said my name, he actually smiled at me and shook my hand. He was so different than I remembered him in high school. Standing there in his doorway, he seemed like any guy. Just any guy shaking my hand; not the scary son-of-a-bitch who seemed to hate us in school; the teacher I could barely look at for fear of what question he might ask, or how he might humiliate me if I didn't know the answer. I don't know. Being able to stand there as his neighbor, shaking hands and exchanging pleasantries made me feel grown up."

Beth sat down on a box and nodded.

"Anyway, he asked what I had been doing since high school, which took all of two seconds for me to explain, and I asked how his teaching was going. Then he asked me if I still had the scroll he had given me at graduation." Bob frowned. "I was so taken aback that I lied and told him that I still had it. Then he asked me if I ever read it. I told him, yes, I read it from time to time. He looked at me, smiled and said, 'Good'. I didn't want to tell him that when I saw 'Gettysburg Address' across the top, I had rolled it back up and tossed it in my closet as soon as I got home after graduation."

Beth smiled. "And now you want to find it."

"Yes," said Bob turning back to the stack of boxes. "It just seems important. Especially now that he's gone. That he's dead. Hard to believe. He was always there. Year in and year out. Jesus. He's one of those people you didn't think would ever die. You know what I mean?"

"What makes you think you still have it?"

Bob spread his arms wide. "Look around you. Have I ever thrown anything away?"

Beth laughed. She stood up and then leaned over to kiss him on the forehead. "Good luck. Can I get you a cup of coffee?"

"That would be great."

As Beth walked across the grimy floor, Bob called, "Hey. Thanks."

Beth turned. "Sure."

The wheel of their relationship had moved forward slowly since Beth's encounter with Gwen Stinson. It was still difficult to tell, though, where exactly the relationship was going. Bob remained confused and uncertain about what to do. They still had sex, and they didn't talk much. Not about their future. Or their past, for that fact. They settled for being pleasant and civil and attentive in the most mundane ways, such as making sure the coffee was brewed in the morning and the bowl was filled with packets of Splenda. "Thank you," they would say to each other. That seemed like progress. Perhaps they still felt something for each other, though what was yet unclear.

"Do you love me?" Bob had asked one morning as he came out of the shower.

Beth was at the mirror putting on makeup. She had turned to him, her hair pulled back from her face with a hair band. "I want to," she replied. "And you?"

"Maybe, I think."

"Okay."

"Uh huh."

Bob was surprised that for now this was enough.

Bob continued to dig through boxes of personal memorabilia, old baseball gloves and report cards and attendance awards and presidential election pins ("Go Bush!") until he found a flattened roll of artificially aged parchment tied with a narrow red ribbon. He pulled it from the box and blew off the dust.

"Jesus," said Bob.

Beth reached the top of the stairs and crossed the attic, two cups of coffee in hand. "Here you go," she said.

"Thanks." Bob didn't look up. "Look at this."

"I can't believe you still have it." Beth leaned over his shoulder.

"I guess I can't either. It was a shock when he gave it to me. He wasn't that kind of teacher, you know what I mean?"

"Yet you kept it."

Bob raised his eyebrows, unable to answer why. He turned the scroll over in his hands, squeezing it gently back into shape. It still had the same crisp, crinkled firmness it had had on the day Mr. Ruth had given it to him over twenty years ago. His hands were no longer the hands of a teenager celebrating his first milestone. So much and so little had happened in the intervening years. He went to college that fall. He flunked out by December, relieved to be free of schooling. He moved away, believing that a geographic change would equal a fresh start. He met Beth. Married her. Eventually, moved back to his hometown, believing again that a geographic change would equal a fresh start. He had job after job and lost them all. He'd even cheated on his wife.

And now here he sat, prematurely gray at the temples, his muscles soft, his midriff wider than he could have imagined when he was eighteen. A cup of coffee in one hand, a parchment scroll in the other. Beth beside him, his one constant. Like that day when he was eighteen, his nose was pressed right up against another beginning. What to do with it?

"Aren't you going to open it?" Beth kneeled now beside him, sipping her coffee. Bob stared at the scroll, fingering the ribbon. "Is something wrong, Bob?"

"No. No. Everything's fine." Bob took a deep breath as he opened the scroll, holding it between his hands, top to bottom, the edges curled.

Beth leaned closer, her chin resting on his shoulder. "For score and seven years ago," she read, then fell silent. "What's that?" asked Beth, pointing to a note scrawled at the bottom of the page.

Bob's mouth moved slightly as he read the handwritten words to himself. Then he let the document fall in his lap. "My God." He held it up again, tilting it to the window so Beth could see. Beth squinted and read aloud:

Mr. Hazelwood:

I want to congratulate you on the occasion of your graduation from high school. I think you have a bright future. Remember, Mr. Lincoln once said, "Whatever you are, be a good one."

Respectfully,

Mr. Maxwell Ruth

"How thoughtful," said Beth.

"Jesus, I never even read it. All these years, I told him, 'Yes, Mr. Ruth, I read it from time to time.' Shit."

"I'm sure he didn't think anything of it. Maybe he didn't even remember what he wrote. Who knows?"

"I don't know of anyone else in my graduating class that got a scroll from him. People thought I was kidding when I told them." Bob looked at the document again. It was Mr. Ruth's handwriting all right, as jagged as a barbed wire fence. "I'm sure he remembered."

Bob was upset when he heard of Mr. Ruth's demise, saddened by how sudden it had been, but he had also smiled, picturing Mr. Ruth decked out in his Lincoln attire keeling over in front of his stunned students. *I bet that got their attention. "Mr. Ruth, will this be on the test?"* As ridiculous as it sounded, Bob felt that somehow he had contributed to Mr. Ruth's death by not having taken the man seriously enough. Bob never understood that what Mr. Ruth did day in and day out was actually his life. *Jesus Christ, I never even read the darn thing.*

Beth placed her hands on Bob's shoulders. "Are you okay?"

"'Whatever you are, be a good one'." Bob looked out the attic window at the treetops across the street. "What the hell am I supposed to do with that?"

"Exactly," agreed Beth.

Chapter 29

Constance Young sat at her desk, her palms on the blotter. She stared at the blank screen in front of her. The office was empty. She had come in early hoping to get some work done before the funeral. She glanced at the folder full of insurance forms yet to be processed, opened it, closed it, and set it aside. She leaned on her elbows, looking at the picture of her son and daughter-in-law and granddaughter smiling at her, all in swimsuits and sunglasses. She reached for the picture and with a finger swiped the dust from the frame.

As always, she had awakened to the 6:00 a.m. alarm, showered, dressed, and put on her face. Unable to sleep that night, she had sat in her darkened living room, cup of tea in her lap, watching the first sticky harbinger of winter collect on the sagging phone lines across the street. Rallying all her inner resources, she got into her car, drove onto the pavement, slushy from the heavy, wet snow that had come and gone during the night. and after a few minutes, pulled off at Dunkin' Donuts for coffee, this time ordering a jelly donut, which she left uneaten on the dashboard. Pulling back into traffic, she couldn't remember if she had said "Thank you" when the young woman with the bright smile had wished her a good day. She would be doubly friendly the next time. Constance sat through one light and missed a stop sign entirely. Upon arriving at the sleek glass medical arts building, she pulled into the parking space closest to the clinic door, the one that was never available. Coming into work, she tiptoed quickly through the mess through the office door, not wanting to ruin her navy pumps.

Max! The sound of her cry continued its rumbling, quaking passage through her heart. The students' heads had snapped, robot-like, in her direction, their teacher on the floor before them.

Max! They couldn't take their eyes off her as she raced to his side, drawn into the black hole that awaited her.

Max! When she reached him, she cried out for help, but the students had scattered in every direction. Max's stovepipe hat had toppled during the fall; it lay on its side nearby. His beard had slipped; she pulled it from his ashen face. The left side of his mouth and his left eye looked as if they were falling off a cliff. His body trembled. He strained, as if wanting to lift his arm to her. Nothing seemed to work. He fell motionless as a rag doll.

Buoyed briefly by denial—*This can't possibly be happening!*— she felt a wave of invincibility, believing that her touch alone, her steadying hand, her being there, her wanting this not to happen would somehow be enough. "Max, you've had another fall," she said as he stared. "We'll have to do something about that. We can't have you falling all the time, can we?" She smiled insistently, the corners of her mouth quivering.

Max's eyes calmed and seemed to focus on her face, her hair, her eyes. He tried again to speak, but his tongue wagged indifferently. He tried yet again, but stopped, his eyes filling now. She wiped his tears away with the tip of her fingers. "Max, just rest," she said softly, adding in a shout, "And someone call 911!"

Sitting at her desk, Constance didn't hear the office door open and was startled when Angela tapped her on the shoulder. "Are you okay, honey? What in the world are you doing here today? You didn't need to come in." Angela dropped her purse to the office floor, pulled up a chair, and sat beside Constance. "Connie, honey, I'm so sorry. We all are."

"Yes, yes, I know," said Constance, unable to smile, unable to look at her.

"There is no reason for you to be here. Really." Angela stopped, and then took Constance's hands in hers. "Look, I know what you're going through. When my Kenny died, I thought the world had come to an absolute end, you know what I mean? I did. I thought, *Oh, my Lord, what am I going to do?* I cried and I threw myself down and could barely walk at his wake. Afterwards, I sat on my porch for days. Little Kenny would come by the house and try to cheer me up, telling me his father wouldn't want me to go on like this, but it didn't matter." Angela kept talking, but Constance no longer listened.

Max! It made her wince, the sound of his name, that desperate cry.

"Max, don't worry. It will be okay. I love you," she had said.

She placed his head on her lap and caressed him, gently, slowly. She looked towards the door, wondering why it was taking so long for someone, anyone, to come. She leaned over Max, so that her face was all he could see. His gaze, unblinking, was steady, locked on her eyes. "Max," she said in a whisper and kissed his forehead. "My Max. You're going to be okay." But his eyes had already begun defocusing, staring now at an emptiness beyond her. She looked towards the door again. "Anyone! Is anyone there? Please!"

Hargrove rushed into the classroom, running headlong to Max. "What is it? Oh, my God! Max!" Max didn't appear to know he was there. "What happened?" Hargrove asked, kneeling beside his old friend, not looking at Constance.

"He fell. I don't know," said Constance, rocking Max slowly, then looking at Hargrove, her eyes distraught. She looked at Max again, searching his face, trying to find the Max she knew, the sardonic wit, the twinkle inside the cloud, the gentle Max, uncertain yet trying, always trying.

"This can't be," said Hargrove, bewildered, almost angry. "I mean, it just can't be. I was with him earlier. We talked. He was fine. He was himself. How could this..." He took Max's hand. "Max, it's me. It's Hargrove. Max? Can you hear me? Squeeze my hand to let me know you're okay." Max's hand remained limp and soft as putty. "Max!" Hargrove's face was nose-to-nose with Max. He yelled again. "Max!" He shook him. Max's face rolled unresponsively.

Constance felt someone patting her arm. "Constance? Honey?" Angela jerked at her, trying to get her attention. "Constance, please!" Constance looked into the deep creases around Angela's eyes and mouth. Her lips were dry and cracked, her eyes wide. "Constance!"

Constance pulled away, surprise and annoyance on her face.

"Constance, are you all right? Of course, you're not all right. You've gone deep into sorrow, you poor thing." Angela cradled Constance in her arms. "My goodness, you are as white as a ghost. Have you had any sleep at all? Of course you haven't. How could you with such a thing going on?"

Constance held Angela's arm and laid her head on her friend's shoulder. She closed her eyes, but all she could see was Hargrove's face straining to call his friend back.

"Max, please! Max!" he'd cried.

Constance had clutched Max to her again. His eyes were lifeless as a child's glass marbles. Hargrove felt for a pulse and fell back in tears. "Max?" called Constance quietly, hoping still. "Max?" She searched his eyes though she knew he was no longer there. "Oh no," she whispered. She threw her head back, her mouth contorted in a scream, but nothing came, only the silence that speaks to silence, the soundless cry; the wordless protest of the living for the dead.

More More Time

Chapter 30

Hargrove stood in Max's old classroom, quiet now in the days after his death. Scrawled across the white board in Max's hand was his final message: READ THIS: Lincoln profile papers are due no later than the end of eighth period on Friday!

Pens and pencils filled the holder on his desk; coffee stains dotted the well-worn blotter; the goose-necked lamp that Max brought with him on his first day of teaching bowed its head over notepads and workbooks and scraps of paper scattered across the desk top. Hargrove sat in Max's wooden swivel chair, its arms nicked, its cushioned seat permanently contoured to the room's long-time resident. Hargrove leaned back, hands folded in his lap, thinking of his friend's early enthusiasm for his chosen profession.

Always anxious about the opening day of school, one year Max had asked Hargrove to observe his first class because he was going to try "something a little different." Hargrove stood in the back of the room and watched.

Max drew a large circle on the black board and asked his students to imagine that the circle represented all of time. Then he drew a line across the middle of the circle, explaining that this was how we experienced time; like a straight line from the past on one side through the present in the middle and into the future on the other side. Then he drew a single hash mark on the line and asked them to imagine that this represented when the American Civil War had occurred, then turned to his class. "Now, the Civil War seems like ancient history to most of you, doesn't it?"

His students nodded their heads.

Max reminded them that in the 1860s there were no cars, no TVs, no airplanes, no movies, no internet, no cell phones or computers, no rockets blasting off for the moon, none of the things we take for granted; that Americans were fighting and killing each other; and that slavery was the norm. He reminded them that the president had had no formal education to speak of. Then he asked them, "How could a time like that, so far away, so different, have anything to say to us today?" He stopped and for a long moment said nothing. Then he asked, "Where would you put the present day on this timeline?" One student pointed to the other end of the line, far from the first hash mark. Max smiled and drew a second hash mark on top of the first one. "Actually, this is how close *long ago* is on a grand timeline; and this is also how close the *yet to come* is. It is all one. Connected like the cars of a train."

Hargrove smiled. *Max is right*, he thought. *The past, present, and future unfold simultaneously. Our time here seems long, but it isn't. We all assume that we will travel across the timeline endlessly, but we won't.* He and Max had walked that line together for all of their adult lives. And just like that, Max's toes had slipped off the timeline forever. No more beers, no more conversations, no more laughs. No more. Max had been folded into the circle of time, the Great "foreverness." *Max is gone from this world*, Hargrove lamented. *I hope he is somewhere.*

Later that morning, when Hargrove reached the funeral home parking lot, he hesitated for a moment beside his car and looked east where faint shafts of light, pink against the purple clouds, shown softly and then faded as gray clouds skulked in from the southeast. He watched as a blue heron, pterodactyl-like, drifted lazily, mournfully across the treetops, searching for a place to land. Golden leaves browned on the lawn, while each blade of grass, silver-gray from the frost, stood at attention. The earth was leaning over on its axis bringing shorter days and longer shadows as late November pulled up its collar. The world readying for winter. Hargrove felt the decomposition of nature so necessary for its rebirth. He took a deep breath and let it out, his head briefly engulfed in mist.

He watched appreciatively as car after car entered the lot, something that would have shocked Max. Colleagues, friends, school administrators, a few parents of former students, a handful of current students.

"They've come for you, Max...Yes, you're right—God only knows why." Hargrove whispered, smiling.

He headed toward the entrance, only to find himself side-by-side with Bob and Beth Hazelwood as they reached the door at the top of the pillared front steps. Without raising his head, Bob offered a warm, "Thank you," to Hargrove, who held open the door. Beads of perspiration rose on Hargrove's forehead as he nodded to Beth. "Hello," he murmured towards her.

Beth paused and searched his face. "Hello, Hargrove." She then linked her arm with Bob's and went with him into the parlor. After they were safely inside, Hargrove followed.

Hargrove spied Gwen standing beside the casket, holding a handkerchief to her eyes. He waited until she sat before he approached the mahogany box. He knelt in silence, then stood and patted the lid gently. He stepped back and bowed his head again. "Good bye, old friend," he whispered.

When he turned, Gwen was beside him. She put her arms around him. He clenched at first, but then began to weep. "Come, join us," she said and guided him to where she was sitting with Constance.

"I'm so glad to see you," said Constance, as he sat between the two women. Constance wiped her reddened eyes with a tissue and placed a hand on his arm. Hargrove looked up at her but could not speak. He reached for her hand, patting it lightly.

"Come to me, all who labor and are heavy laden, and I will give you rest," intoned the minister. He then spoke abstractly about the life of "Maxwell Anthony Ruth," as if anyone had ever called him that. When it was quiet again, Hargrove looked up; the minister was nodding to him, a sign that it was his turn.

Hargrove went to the lectern. He reached into his suit pocket for his notes but then decided against them. He cleared his throat. He looked at the people assembled before him, and for a brief moment thought he could see Max sitting in the back pew wearing his Lincoln attire, a sardonic grin on his face, perhaps enjoying his friend's struggle to find words. And who was that beside him? A young woman, a girl really, with dirty blonde hair and round cheeks, smooth, soft. She wore blue jeans and a loose-fitting peasant top. Blue green eyes, so bright, so sharp. Sally. He closed his eyes, hoping to conjure her smile. When he opened his eyes again, both of them were gone.

Hargrove cleared his throat again.

"You know, when someone dies, everything should stop. At least for a moment. The earth. The moon. The stars. Everything. Just to say, 'It was good that you were here. It was important. And we thank you.'

And for everyone who dies, there should be someone who is willing to stand up for them, to call attention to their life, call attention to that bright light that briefly crossed our sky, for someone to say, 'Look at that; wasn't it amazing?'

"I am Hargrove Stinson. Max was my best friend in this world. He always wanted to be a great man, like his beloved Abraham Lincoln, and it tortured him that he never quite achieved it. It tortures me that I never told him that he was my great man. Being a friend, being *my* friend, was not an easy job; and yet he did it with curmudgeonly grace and wit. With love. I think that is the stuff of true greatness.

"I guess I'm here to tell you, in case you hadn't noticed at the time, that the earth did stop when Max died. And so did the moon and the stars. I know this is true because I felt it. In my heart. And I am here to call attention to his light, a light that shown brightly, far too briefly. I am here to point to it and say, 'Thank you, Max. My amazing friend. I will never forget you'."

Hargrove held onto the lectern a minute longer, imagining that his words, his aching heart, had reached across to the other side, had found the one who now was beyond all words, beyond all feeling. He let go and steadied himself before returning to his chair where he sat, hands folded, his head held a little higher, his back a little straighter than it had been a few minutes before.

More More Time

Epilogue

Two months after the funeral, Constance found herself standing at the airline check-in, travelers bustling all around her. "Will you be checking these bags?" asked the woman at the Delta counter.

"Yes, these two, but not the box," said Constance, the faint roar of runway traffic in the background. Constance pulled the pocket watch from her jeans to check the time.

"That's an oldie," said the woman behind the counter. "I haven't seen one of those since I was a young girl."

"Yes, I love it. It was…a gift."

"And it even runs."

Constance smiled at this. "Well, not without a great deal of help from a watchmaker. But, yes, it tells time quite well."

"I see you have two tickets. Is there someone else we should be waiting for?"

"No," said Constance, a little embarrassed. "It's a long flight to California. I want to stretch out, be as comfortable as I can."

"Okay, then. Here are your boarding passes. You're at gate B-5. Have a great trip! I hope to see you again."

"Not likely," said Constance. "I'll be staying there. I have family."

"Well, then, enjoy!"

Purse over her shoulder and box in her arms, Constance made her way down the long corridor to her gate. When they called area two for boarding, she got in line with everyone else, holding her carry-on tightly.

"Welcome!" said the flight attendant, a young man with delicately moussed hair. "Can I help you with that?"

"No, thank you. I think I can handle it."

"Looks a little awkward. Are you sure?"

"Yes, I'll be fine," said Constance, a feeling of breathlessness overtaking her as she crossed the threshold onto the plane.

When she reached row twenty-two, seats D and E, she dropped her purse on the floor and pushed it with her foot under the seat in front of her. She laid the box in seat E and slumped into D. She caught her breath, redirected the air nozzle above her, reapplied her lipstick, took a bottle of water from her purse, and slipped it into the seat pocket in front of her. She then turned to the box and carefully removed the stovepipe hat, placing it gently on top of the box, her hand floating across the felt brim. She swept it with her fingertips, the surface lint drifting away as if caught in a mist.

The woman sitting in row twenty-two, seat F watched intently. "There must be quite a story behind that hat."

"Yes, there is."

If you enjoyed *More More Time*, consider these other fine works by the author:

When eleven-year-old Jackie goes to live with a distant relative and meets disfigured hermit and infamous local legend Charlie No Face, Jackie's life changes forever. Jackie and Charlie develop an unlikely friendship that explores the surprising truth about Jackie's mother, who died, as well as what it means to look at others with one's heart..

More More Time

and:

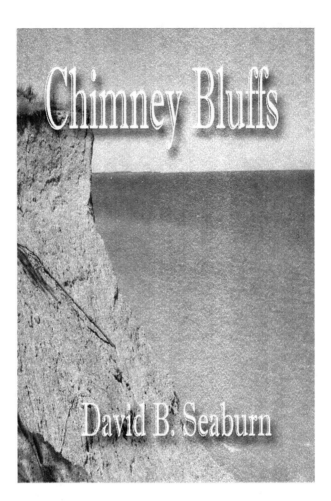

When their four-year-old son, Danny, dies suddenly, Mitch and Kate's grief overwhelms them. Conflicted about going on with their lives, Mitch and Kate decide to leap from a cliff at Chimney Bluffs. When the couple is found by park rangers, Clancy and Bobby, Kate is still very much alive. What follows is a poignant and powerful story of three strangers, each facing a tragic loss, who together find friendship and healing.

About the Author

David B. Seaburn is the author of four previous novels, *Chimney Bluffs* (Savant, 2012), *Charlie No Face* (Savant, 2011), a finalist in the National Indie Excellence Awards in Fiction, *Pumpkin Hill* (2007), and *Darkness is Light* (2005). Seaburn is a retired marriage and family therapist, as well as an ordained minister. He lives near Rochester, N. Y. with his wife, Bonnie. They have two wonderful adult daughters and two fabulous granddaughters.

Visit David at http://www.davidbseaburn.com/

More More Time

If you enjoyed *MORE MORE TIME*, consider these other fine books from Savant Books and Publications:

Essay, Essay, Essay by Yasuo Kobachi
Aloha from Coffee Island by Walter Miyanari
Footprints, Smiles and Little White Lies by Daniel S. Janik
The Illustrated Middle Earth by Daniel S. Janik
Last and Final Harvest by Daniel S. Janik
A Whale's Tale by Daniel S. Janik
Tropic of California by R. Page Kaufman
Tropic of California (the companion music CD) by R. Page Kaufman
The Village Curtain by Tony Tame
Dare to Love in Oz by William Maltese
The Interzone by Tatsuyuki Kobayashi
Today I Am a Man by Larry Rodness
The Bahrain Conspiracy by Bentley Gates
Called Home by Gloria Schumann
Kanaka Blues by Mike Farris
First Breath edited by Z. M. Oliver
Poor Rich by Jean Blasiar
Ammon's Horn by Guerrino Amati
The Jumper Chronicles by W. C. Peever
William Maltese's Flicker by William Maltese
My Unborn Child by Orest Stocco
Last Song of the Whales by Four Arrows
Perilous Panacea by Ronald Klueh
Falling but Fulfilled by Zachary M. Oliver
Mythical Voyage by Robin Ymer
Hello, Norma Jean by Sue Dolleris
Richer by Jean Blasiar
Manifest Intent by Mike Farris
Charlie No Face by David B. Seaburn
Number One Bestseller by Brian Morley
My Two Wives and Three Husbands by S. Stanley Gordon
In Dire Straits by Jim Currie
Wretched Land by Mila Komarnisky
Chan Kim by Ilan Herman
Who's Killing All the Lawyers? by A. G. Hayes
Ammon's Horn by G. Amati
Wavelengths edited by Zachary M. Oliver
Almost Paradise by Laurie Hanan
Communion by Jean Blasiar and Jonathan Marcantoni

266

The Oil Man by Leon Puissegur
Random Views of Asia from the Mid-Pacific by William E. Sharp
The Isla Vista Crucible by Reilly Ridgell
Blood Money by Scott Mastro
In the Himalayan Nights by Anoop Chandola
On My Behalf by Helen Doan
Traveler's Rest by Jonathan Marcantoni
Keys in the River by Tendai Mwanaka
Chimney Bluffs by David B. Seaburn
The Loons by Sue Dolleris
Light Surfer by David Allan Williams
The Judas List by A. G. Hayes
Path of the Templar - Book 2 of The Jumper Chronicles by W. C. Peever
The Desperate Cycle by Tony Tame
Shutterbug by Buz Sawyer
Blessed are the Peacekeepers by Tom Donnelly/Mike Munger
Purple Haze by George B. Hudson
The Turtle Dances by Daniel S. Janik
The Lazarus Conspiracies by Richard Rose
Imminent Danger by A. G. Hayes
Lullaby Moon by Malia Elliott of Leon & Malia
Volutions edited by Suzanne Langford
In the Eyes of the Son by Hans Brinckmann
The Hanging of Dr. Hanson by Bentley Gates
Written in the Stars - An Anthology edited by Sabrina Favors
Flight of Destiny by Francis H. Powell
Elaine of Corbenic by Tima Z. Newman
Ballerina Birdies by Marina Yamamoto

Coming Works

Crazy Like Me by Erin Lee
All Things Await by Seth Clabough
Valedictory by Daniel Scott
Big Heaven by Charlotte Hebert
Captain Riddle's Treasure by GV Rama Rau

http://www.savantbooksandpublications.com

CPSIA information can be obtained at www.ICGtesting.com
Printed in the USA
LVOW07s2304250915

455761LV00012B/170/P

9 780991 562237